KT-470-304

A VIEW to a KILT

Wendy Holden

Withdrawn From Stock
Dublin Public Libraries

HEAD ZEUS

First published in the UK in 2019 by Head of Zeus Ltd

Copyright © Wendy Holden, 2019

The moral right of Wendy Holden to be identified as the author
of this work has been asserted in accordance with the
Copyright, Designs and Patents Act of 1988.

All rights reserved. No part of this publication may be
reproduced, stored in a retrieval system, or transmitted in any form
or by any means, electronic, mechanical, photocopying, recording,
or otherwise, without the prior permission of both the copyright
owner and the above publisher of this book.

This is a work of fiction. All characters, organizations,
and events portrayed in this novel are either products of
the author's imagination or are used fictitiously.

9 7 5 3 1 2 4 6 8

A catalogue record for this book is available from
the British Library.

ISBN (HB): 9781784977627
ISBN (XTPB): 9781784977634
ISBN (E): 9781784977610

Typeset by Divaddict Publishing Solutions Ltd

Printed and bound in Great Britain by
CPI Group (UK) Ltd, Croydon CR0 4YY

Head of Zeus Ltd
First Floor East
5–8 Hardwick Street
London EC1R 4RG

WWW.HEADOFZEUS.COM

A VIEW to a KILT

PART ONE

Chapter One

'He'll be here soon, I'm sure,' Laura Lake said uneasily to the estate agent. But her boyfriend Harry was already twenty minutes late and the agent was flicking impatiently at his smartphone.

He was a young man in a tight shiny suit with complex hair gelled up in different directions. His name was Lorne, which had confused Laura at first. Why call anyone after a patch of grass?

'Not Lawn, *L-o-r-n-e*. It's a Scottish name,' Lorne said huffily.

They were standing in the lobby of a new-build block of flats. It was called the Corkscrew, thanks to the twisted spiral at the top that finished off the building. The spiral contained the penthouses, which were the most expensive properties on sale. Laura was waiting to see one of the

Leabharlanna Poiblí Chathair Baile Átha Cliath
Dublin City Public Libraries

cheapest, although the two-bedroomed flat on the second floor still cost a staggeringly vast amount.

Laura could already tell that living here would be ghastly. She didn't want to move, anyway. She was happy in her one-bedroomed flat in Cod's Head Row, Shoreditch. But her foreign correspondent boyfriend Harry, who had recently moved in with her, found hipsters irritating. He wanted somewhere international and anonymous, which was why their viewings so far had ping-ponged between houses in characterful London streets and bland, shiny, glassy, new apartment blocks named after kitchen implements.

Last night was the Spatula. Its agency representative had been just like Lorne, a disdainful youth with less than five seconds to unlock an apartment the size of an Oxo cube before rushing off to show someone much more important somewhere much smarter.

Predictably, Lorne now began to mutter about having to leave soon. He had to show a celebrity client a penthouse in Chelsea.

Laura's ears pricked up immediately; who was the celebrity and what was the penthouse like? Like Harry, she was a journalist and sniffing for stories was in her blood.

Unlike Harry, whose job was to call the powerful to account, Laura's glossy magazine tended to concentrate on their lifestyle. It was not uncritical, even so. *Society*, under her editorship, had had several headline-hitting scoops revealing iniquity and corruption among the rich and famous. There had been the 'Three Weddings' scandal and the shocking truth about 'Britain's Poshest Village'.

Perhaps Lorne, unpromising though he looked, was the gateway to another great story. As the estate agent tsked and swiped, Laura's mind ran ahead. A posh property feature? 'Celebrity superpads' was the obvious one; too obvious, maybe. The pieces she ran were subtle and unexpected. Since she had taken the helm *Society* had gained a reputation for its offbeat, even subversive, take on the wealthy.

Maybe an article on what the super-rich expected as standard in their homes? A tyre-warmer in the stacking garage? A chilled champagne tap in every room?

Laura turned to Lorne and smiled her most charming smile. 'Are you selling many penthouses in Chelsea?' She would have to skirt round the subject to begin with, get him to start boasting. Once he'd dropped his guard she would move in for the kill.

Lorne did his best to be evasive, but he was no match for Laura. Five minutes later she was in triumphant possession of the information that the five-bedroomed, six-bathroom duplex overlooking Chelsea Reach was to be the occasional London home of Hudson Grater, the world's biggest-selling female recording artist.

Famous for break-up songs like 'You Fat-Shamed Me On Facebook', Hudson was a pop star of such magnitude she could bring governments down with a single tweet. Not that she ever troubled to; Hudson Grater's focus was, first and always, Hudson Grater.

'Ah yes,' Laura said, when Lorne, apparently realising

he was revealing more than he was supposed to, abruptly shut up. 'I know Hudson well.'

Lorne's small, sharp eyes widened. 'You know her?' The eyes swept swiftly over Laura who did not, admittedly, look like the bosom friend of a megastar. Now, as always, she was wearing black jeans, a tight blue shirt, heeled Chelsea boots and a long beige trench. Her long black hair had not been brushed since lunchtime and her sole nod to make-up was red lipstick and a flick of eyeliner.

This had been Laura's unvarying look since she'd first come to London some years ago. She had been surprised and relieved to find that her personal style, arrived at in Paris entirely through lack of money, was considered in the British capital the height of Gallic chic. People even thought her hair, whose fringe she cut with kitchen scissors, was the work of a top stylist.

'She used to go out with a friend of mine,' Laura told Lorne. It was nothing less than the truth. Laura had met Hudson Grater during the 'Three Weddings' story. At the time, the singer had been dating Laura's friend Caspar, a resting actor who, following an unexpected sequence of events, had become the latest James Bond. His predecessor as Bond, who Hudson had also dated, was an actor called Orlando Chease. Together they had been known as CheaseGrater.

Lorne gasped. 'Not Dominic Clutterbox?'

Hudson had a weakness for posh English actors and Clutterbox was the latest. The relationship had, as they always did, ended acrimoniously. Her latest break-up hit,

'Didn't Realise You Wore A Wig,' was currently topping the charts.

'No,' said Laura, 'but who knew he wore a wig, anyway? His hair always looked so natural.'

They were happily discussing this when Lorne's phone rang. He stepped away to answer it and Laura was left wondering where, exactly, Harry had got to. It still felt odd even expecting him to turn up – for so many years his whereabouts had been a complete mystery. Their relationship had involved long periods apart, during which Harry would suddenly appear and make passionate love to her before shrugging on his leather jacket and disappearing into the dawn.

Recalling this, Laura felt a faint pang of regret. Living like that had been frustrating, but also exciting. Now Harry had, at a vastly inflated salary, been persuaded by his newspaper to run the foreign desk, rather than merely be one of its reporters, things were... What was the word?

Cosier? Boring?

Certainly they were less thrilling. Sometimes they were even annoying. A classical music fan, Harry was obsessed with Radio 3. He played it all the time in the kitchen and it got into Laura's brain; she would wake in the night with violins screeching in her head. She wasn't sure about Harry's slippers, either. A heatless flat during an early posting to Moscow had rendered him ultra-susceptible to cold. But while the cause was dashing, the effect – a pair of moth-eaten moccasins with the backs trodden down – was middle-aged. And Harry turned up Laura's radiators to such an extent she sometimes stood outside the door to cool down.

'In what sense is this a riverside development?' Laura asked Lorne when he had finished his call. He was looking sharp and impatient again; their brief moment of connection over Dominic Clutterbox's hair was evidently over.

'I can't see the river at all. We must be about five streets back from it.'

Lorne assured her that you got a fine view of it from the upper floors. 'But we're looking at one on the second floor,' Laura pointed out.

The Corkscrew's glass doors now sprang back to reveal a tall broad-shouldered figure in a long dark coat. It took a second or two to register this was Harry; his smart new office look had taken some getting used to. The never-washed jeans and the eternal leather jacket, in which he'd once practically slept, had become smart suits worn with shirts, if not ties. Harry loped towards them, newspaper tucked under his arm, his dark, handsome face creased with irritation.

'Sorry I'm late,' he growled at Laura. 'Bloody managing editor's meeting overran.' He hated, she knew, having to deal with all these money people, discussing the section budget and filling in spreadsheets. She hated it too, and she also had to do it. But did she complain?

No, but she planned to do so later. Things at work were becoming unbearable. The magazine company Laura worked for had recently appointed a new CEO.

The entire culture of the place had changed overnight in the sense that there wasn't much culture left at all.

Soothingly, Laura patted the arm of Harry's smart cashmere overcoat. He put his hand over hers sending through her a bolt of pure desire.

She had been worrying about nothing. Despite the slippers, despite the radio, the old magic was very much still there. Their eyes locked on each other's, sending intimate private messages back and forth. Beside them, Lorne cleared his throat. 'Want to go up?'

'You bet I do,' Harry murmured to Laura, his hand on her bottom as they followed Lorne. 'Been one hell of a day. Let's go to bed as soon as we get back.'

Once in the flat it was quite impossible to concentrate on Lorne's contentions about baking stones and rotisserie spits. 'It's all very high end,' he said at one point.

Harry caught Laura's eye, making her double up with laughter. He turned authoritatively to Lorne. 'Can we just go and look at the, um, sleeping area by ourselves? We need to do a bit of imagineering.'

'Imagineering' was the latest thing in house-selling. Property pages were full of articles about it. It meant putting yourself in the space and picturing it as your own. People had always done this to a certain extent, but now they were actively encouraged to engage with the facilities.

Lorne completed a speech about slow-closing drawers before nodding his permission. Harry closed the bedroom door and turned to Laura. 'I want your drawers open as fast as possible.'

Five minutes later, as she gasped and shuddered against him, Harry smiled into Laura's eyes. She pulled him close, filled to the brim with love. Who cared if they lived in a Corkscrew or a Spatula? Things between them were better than ever.

Chapter Two

A few days later at work Laura picked up the buzzing phone. She half-expected it to be the estate agent. She and Harry had passed on the Corkscrew, and Lorne was doing his best to persuade them to view another new building, the Eggtimer.

It was not Lorne, however. On the other end was Honor, the CEO's secretary. While her voice, as always, was posh, low and comforting, her message was anything but. 'She'll see you now,' said Honor.

Laura replaced the receiver, sat back and let out a groan. How she missed the old CEO, Christopher Stone, who had recently retired to spend more time with his boat and his vineyard. At least, that was the official version.

Christopher's style had been old-school, polished and urbane. He wore Savile Row suits and his trademark pink socks were ordered in bulk from a special shop in Rome.

The new boss's style was confrontational and hard. She was short and wore towering stiletto heels along with a tight black pencil skirt and pointy-collared white shirt. Her sharply cut platinum crop was set off by dark-red lipstick, the colour of blood. Plenty of that had been spilt on her office floor recently.

Her name was Bev Sweet; the misnomer of the century. Before joining the British Magazine Company she had been financial director of a particularly ruthless newspaper group.

If Christopher Stone had had something bad to say, he said it after coffee following a three-course lunch at one of the many exclusive clubs he belonged to. Bev had no time in her schedule for lunch, nor did she bother with social niceties. Or niceties of any sort, or saving the blushes of others. She was as happy to sack people in the corridor as she was to end their contracts by the water cooler. One unfortunate deputy editor had even been given their marching orders in the underwear department of the nearby M & S.

As a result Bev was known throughout the firm – what remained of it, anyway – as the Poison Pixie.

Bev had been with the British Magazine Company a month. For three weeks and six days nothing had been said to Laura. It looked as if, miraculously, she and *Society* had been spared.

And then, yesterday, Honor had called with the news that Bev wished to see her in her office in ten minutes.

Five minutes after that Honor had called with the news that Bev would see her tomorrow. The result of this was a sleepless night as Laura contemplated any number of hideous fates.

Then, this morning, the meeting had been again put off, and then again. Now Laura was a nervous wreck, which had probably been the intention. That psychological torture was a Poison Pixie tactic was more than likely.

Her knees shook so much that now, as she rose from her desk, it seemed that only her dark skinny jeans were keeping her upright.

She paused at the door of her glass-walled editor's cubicle, willing herself to be brave. Her father had been through far worse than this. Like Harry, Peter Lake had been a foreign correspondent and he had actually died in the field. At certain times of immense trouble and stress, Laura had the sense that he was speaking to her, telling her to bear up and pull through.

Out in the main magazine office, Laura swooped by the food editor's desk and pinched a chocolate. 'Old Sporran ganache,' Thomasella murmured in a dazed sort of way.

'*What?*' How disgusting. Weren't sporrans some sort of hairy handbag Scotsmen wore over their kilts?

'Old Sporran. It's a type of whisky.'

Slightly reassured, Laura bit into it. The strength of the alcohol was literally staggering.

She reeled past the fashion desk, where twin-sister style editors, Raisy and Daisy, resplendent in matching illuminated tutus, stitched with strings of fairy lights, were selecting trousers made of tinfoil for a forthcoming shoot. The strip lights overhead, reflected in the legwear, glared dazzlingly into Laura's eyes. To stop herself falling over, she clutched at the desk of Alice, the editor at large.

'You've had one of those chocolates,' said Alice, looking amused.

'You're not an investigative journalist for nothing,' Laura replied, smiling. She admired and respected Alice for her dedication and tenacity, and had gone to considerable pains to recruit her. Like Laura herself, Alice had won awards for her journalism and there had been many other prestigious candidates for her services. Laura had beaten off the competition on the promise that proper features were at the heart of *Society* and Alice would have free rein to follow whatever story she chose.

Her first was an undercover piece about exploitation in the fashion industry. It promised to blow the lid off the business in the same way as the Weinstein scandal had blown the lid off Hollywood. Laura was delighted about it. If it succeeded, and Alice's pieces usually did, *Society* should be in line for yet more plaudits.

'How's it going?' Laura asked, noticing, as her features editor looked up, that her eyebrows weren't there. To infiltrate the fashion world Alice, who was tall and rake-thin, had been modelling for a designer called Ku Chua. He was famous for 'challenging conventional ideas of beauty'. His latest show had featured naked models with traffic cones on their bald heads, pushing each other down the runway in supermarket trolleys.

Alice had been lucky to escape with just the eyebrows, Laura thought. Although she had no interest in her personal appearance – what motivated Alice far more was the fact that Chua's clothes, which socialites bought for thousands, were made by impoverished slaves in pitiless garment factories in the Far East. As Alice described the latest outrages she had unearthed, her eyes blazed beneath where her eyebrows should have been.

While she shared her features editor's indignation, Laura was also excited. This was going to be a brilliant story, absolutely in tune with her magazine's editorial stance. Whilst it celebrated glamour and fun, *Society* deplored injustice and exploitation. The luxury it featured was strictly 'woke'. Unlike most other glossies, it didn't just sell shiny things to people who didn't need them.

'Great stuff,' Laura said to Alice and went off confidently to meet Bev Sweet. With a piece like this in the bag, she surely had nothing to fear.

Chapter Three

The office of the CEO was on the top floor of the British Magazine Company's white art deco building. Laura had occasionally been summoned in the past to see Christopher Stone, and knew that up here, carpets were thick, walls panelled and oil paintings glowing under picture lights.

At least, they had been. When the lift doors sprang open, Laura initially thought she was on the wrong floor. The formerly deep-piled-blue-carpeted corridor was now black wood. What should be oak-panelled walls were painted matt white and hung with black-framed fashion advertisements. Instead of agreeably clubbable, the atmosphere was starkly commercial.

Laura was about to turn and get back in the lift. Then,

at the desk at the end of the corridor, where on the sixth floor Honor would be, she spotted... Honor?

In her unchanging uniform of low-heeled black patent shoes, sharply pleated tartan skirt and petrol-blue ribbed polo neck, the CEO's long-serving secretary personified posh sixties glam. She had worn it all since the actual sixties. Rumour had it that Honor had once worked for the Duke of Edinburgh.

'What's happened to you?' Laura gasped, her hurry along the corridor now becoming a run. Gone was Honor's pleated plaid. In its place was a red PVC boiler suit worn with oversized cat's-eye sunglasses.

'People my age are very popular in Mango campaigns,' Honor replied mildly. 'If I walk around Soho like this I might be spotted by an agency for the over-60s. Then I can model for one of our advertisers.'

Laura stared. 'Is that what you... *want* to do?'

Honor shook her head. The smooth grey bob was now gelled up and dyed green. 'Not terribly, but it's what Mrs Sweet wants me to do. She's absolutely obsessed with advertising. It's all she ever seems to think about.'

Laura knocked on Bev Sweet's door and prepared to enter the lair of the Poison Pixie. Presumably, like Honor and the corridor, it too had changed.

Christopher Stone had furnished his office like a stately home study: buttoned-leather sofas, thick rugs, a pair of globes, cigar humidors. In pride of place had been the legendary polished walnut desk that had provided working space for British Magazine Company bosses since the firm was founded more than a century ago. Built from wood salvaged from the ballroom of the *Titanic*, this famed piece of furniture had risen from the deep to hit the heights. Greta Garbo had posed on it. Fred Astaire had tap-danced on it. The cocktail shaker that Mrs Simpson had used to serve Old Fashioneds remained in one of the bottom drawers. It was considered unlucky to move it.

Only, now, as she entered Bev Sweet's office, Laura saw that it *had* been moved. In its place was a transparent plastic workstation and three large and uncomfortable-looking grey cubes. The carpet was now a black tile surface over which Bev's cruel spike heels clacked like the knitting needles of a *tricoteuse* beside the guillotine.

A pair of hard, assessing eyes met Laura's. They were the chlorinated blue of a Riviera swimming pool and had a terrifying glow, as if lit up from behind.

'Lorna Lane?' snarled the Poison Pixie.

'Laura *Lake*,' Laura corrected with a smile.

'I won't ask you to sit down. The Queen always sees her Prime Ministers standing up and I don't have half the sodding time she does.'

Laura nodded pleasantly, but apprehension had now gripped her insides.

'I'll come straight to the point,' the Poison Pixie added. 'Have you seen this magazine?'

Something was thrust into her hand and Laura found herself looking at a glossy front cover with a familiar face on it. It belonged, at least partly – although there was no saying where the many fillers and plumpers had come from – to Savannah Bouche, currently riding high as one of the world's biggest film stars. Printed across the wave of glossy dark hair rising from her lineless brow was the word *Simpleton*.

Laura suppressed a gasp. *Simpleton* was the mindfulness title published by the British Magazine Company's main rival. It was all about simplifying, decluttering and reconnecting with yourself. Paring down, throwing things out.

Laura's company had tried to launch a competitor, *Down & Out,* but that had folded after two issues. *Simpleton*, with its clean-eating recipes, ovary master-classes and famous 'air supermarket', where you could buy fresh air online from whatever part of the world you wanted, was the market leader. The last issue Laura had seen had been a Composting Special with Alan Titchmarsh on the cover.

What on earth was Savannah Bouche, man-eating megastar and patron saint of conspicuous consumption, doing on it? She famously had homes on every continent and private-jetted to the hairdresser's. Yet here she was, raving about Ayurvedic farmers' markets and 'opening up her mindfulness toolkit'.

'Amazing, isn't it?' snapped the Poison Pixie, who had been observing Laura closely.

'Incredible,' Laura agreed. 'Her carbon footprint is the size of a yeti's.'

Bev Sweet's small, pale face darkened with annoyance. 'What are you talking about?'

Laura gestured down at the cover. 'She's not relevant

to them. In fact, she's a complete betrayal of everything they stand for.'

The ends of her fingers now stung as something was forcibly ripped from them. 'What's relevant,' said Bev Sweet, shaking the magazine in Laura's face and narrowly missing hitting her on the nose, 'is advertising. Have you seen how many ads there are in here? It's like a bloody phone book.'

The ever-observant Laura noted the simile. Bev Sweet's official age was thirty, making her theoretically too young to have ever seen an old-fashioned telephone directory.

This was obviously not the point here, however. She, Laura, was under attack, and not for the first time on this front. Magazine management were always haranguing magazine staff about the need to get more ads in their publications. Laura mentally girded her loins and started making the point that a balance had to be struck between editorial principle and commercial imperatives.

'Bollocks!' yelled Bev, before Laura could reach the imperatives.

Laura was shocked. Even Christopher at his angriest had stopped short of expletives. 'Sorry?'

Bev was far from sorry. 'I don't care about sodding editorial excellence. I want ads! And lots of 'em. The ratio needs to be 25 per cent to 75 per cent.'

Laura swallowed. In really big issues, such as the September fashion one, *Society* might hope to be a quarter advertising. In any other month, such a ratio would be a struggle. But as admitting this would clearly be inadvisable, she would accentuate the positive. 'Well,

25 per cent advertising might be possible,' she said
brightly, crossing her fingers behind her back.

For a few seconds Bev Sweet just stared at her. Then
she started shouting. 'I mean 25 per cent *editorial*! I want
75 per cent *advertising*, have you got that?'

Laura's mouth dropped open. 'No magazine gets 75
per cent advertising,' she began, before Bev Sweet cut her
short. And given how short Bev Sweet was, that was very
short indeed.

'This one does!' she yelled, waving *Simpleton* around
like someone cheerleading a baseball match before
hurling it at Laura.

Laura picked it up with as much dignity as she could
summon. There were, as expected, adverts for yoga mats
as well as peculiar mindfulness-related items such as
vaginal onions. Laura examined this ad with interest.
The onions, specially grown for the purpose to be the
right size and shape, strengthened the pelvic floor whilst
imparting from the onion skin invaluable vitamins 'used
in women's health for centuries'.

Realising Bev was glaring at her, Laura continued to
flick through. She was astonished to see that, beside all
the wellness mumbo jumbo, Simpleton had exactly the
same high-fashion ads as any other glossy; the same
ones as *Society*, in fact. Plus a few that *Society* didn't
have that month, and which the advertising director
had been concerned about. How had *Simpleton* done
it? She raised her eyes, or, rather lowered them, to the
Poison Pixie.

'Their rates are half yours,' Bev Sweet growled.

Laura was relieved. She wasn't good at figures and had always struggled to be interested in *Society's* commercial side. Editorial was her passion. But this was easy. Her magazine's ads must cost 50 per cent less, was all.

'But *your* rates are staying right where they are,' the Poison Pixie added. 'You just need more ads, and you're gonna get 'em. Otherwise,' she went on, shaking *Simpleton* in a threatening fashion, 'you're out of a job.'

Chapter Four

Outside Bev's office door, Honor gave her a sympathetic smile. There was something rather weary about it, as if she'd had to smile many such smiles over the last few weeks.

Back in her own office, Laura closed the door and turned the sign to Do Not Disturb. Her secretary, Demelza, glanced over with interest as she played with the neon-pink feather at the base of her long black plait. Demelza's style was high-end Minnehaha: fringed beaded ankle boots, denim minidresses and round coloured sunglasses. Most of Demelza's summer was spent at the type of exclusive festivals that did not admit ordinary members of the public.

Demelza stopped playing with her hair and made a 'T' sign with her forefingers, one of which was tattooed with a tiger. Laura nodded. A cup of tea would be welcome, even one made badly by Demelza, who had yet to grasp the most basic secretarial duty. She was hopeless at her job but brought a certain *joie de vivre* to things, as well as an eclectic contacts book which had come in very useful. Demelza knew everyone from Cabinet ministers to cabaret dancers, and most of them were her devoted slaves.

Laura sat down at her desk and stared at the copy of *Simpleton* that Bev had given her, almost literally as a parting shot. The smoothly beautiful face of Savannah Bouche smiled kittenishly up at her and Laura felt the Poison Pixie's knife twist painfully between her ribs.

She had been given an impossible task, and yet somehow she had to make it happen. The volley of threats Bev had issued as she left the CEO's office were still ringing in her ears. If she didn't succeed in making the advertising ratio 75 per cent, the Poison Pixie would sack her. But much worse than that, she would make *Society* an online-only magazine.

Laura did not want to be sacked, but she absolutely could not bear to think of her precious publication disappearing, quite literally, into the ether. She got a daily kick out of seeing *Society* on the news stands, holding its own among international heavy hitters such as *Vogue* and *Vanity Fair*. The idea of its beautiful glossy cover with its distinctive masthead never being seen again made her want to weep.

It would be such a waste, too. She was doing something with *Society* that no one else was doing with any publication anywhere. Her magazine was utterly original and the formula was a success; her many journalistic awards attested to that. It had all been achieved by sticking to certain principles, such as refusing to give interview subjects 'copy approval', or the right to change the article as they wished and make it bland and boring. Nor had she ever run 'puff' pieces which extolled advertisers. And had she not just recruited Alice, who was shining a hard, bright light into some of luxury's darker corners? She had to protect all this, Laura reminded herself fiercely.

Even so, her heart sank. How could she, whilst attracting advertisers in the numbers demanded, particularly at the enormous rates charged for pages in the magazine?

Laura sank her head on her arms in despair. Perhaps she should just walk out now, throw in the towel and save herself the agony of inevitable failure – failure in the eyes of all her journalistic peers, too. If she left straightaway her chances of getting another job would be better. But could she leave in such circumstances? Without even trying?

Slowly, she raised her head again. Her dark eyes, reflected in the glass panes of her office, were steady and resolute. Laura had a stubborn streak. She believed in herself. She had overcome great odds in the past and this was just the latest challenge. Her father, she knew, would have thought the same. Peter Lake never walked away from a difficult situation. In the end, it had cost him his life.

Laura smiled at her reflection. She would overcome this somehow – together with her trusty staff members.

They would all pull together and come up with the answer. They would start with an emergency editorial meeting.

Demelza now entered with a mug of milky water in which a soggy teabag floated.

'Are you okay?' she asked, beaming brightly. 'The Poison Pixie hasn't sacked you, has she?' Demelza had a way of getting to the point of things.

'Of course not!' Laura exclaimed, taking a sip of the tepid brew. 'Delicious!' She gave her secretary her brightest smile. 'Everything's fine. Tell everyone there's a meeting. We're doing some brainstorming.'

Laura's staff now started to appear. She looked at them fondly as they flicked their hair and jostled for space on the yellow sofa opposite her desk. First in was best seated, a stark contrast to Laura's own early days on *Society* when, a mere fashion intern, she had to sit on the floor. At that time only senior staff were allowed on the yellow sofa, but Laura had introduced a new meritocracy. Anyone could get to the top if they worked hard and seized opportunities, as Laura herself had done...

Remembering Bev's dire warning, Laura snapped out of the self-congratulation. It was time to get on with the brainstorming. They were struggling for survival here. Fighting desperately against the forces of Bev Sweet. As Laura looked around the massed ranks of her staff she felt like a general about to brief an army going into battle.

'I'll cut to the chase,' she said with her best military briskness. 'We've got to find a way of making *Society* 75 per cent advertising.'

'*What?*' exclaimed Harriet, *Society*'s ad director. 'That's *impossible*.'

Laura gave her a determined look. 'Well, we have to make it possible. Otherwise Bev might make us online-only.'

She had expected widespread cries of horror at this, but the assembled faces looked back at her blankly. 'Would that be so bad?' asked Pidge, the beauty assistant, eventually. 'It's better than being sacked.'

Laura felt as deflated as a burst balloon. As she struggled for a reply, someone else stepped in.

'It's the same as being sacked, you moron. Online means literally one person is needed to put the editorial together.'

It was Alice who had spoken, with her characteristic directness. Laura felt grateful even if 'moron' was a bit strong. Pidge wasn't the brightest, but she had skills few others possessed – the ability, for instance, to distinguish between a dermabrasion and a fruit-peel facial.

'Alice is right,' Laura said. 'About the online bit, I mean,' she added hurriedly to Pidge. 'So we need to think of something to get the ads flowing in. Any ideas?'

Muffie, the magazine's Gadgets editor, raised her wrist. On it was a flat gold bracelet. 'It's my champagne detector,' she explained. 'It's incredibly useful, tells you when you're being fobbed off with prosecco. But it can also sense Veuve Cliquot from 500 yards away. There's a bottle in this room somewhere.'

Laura remembered there was one in her bottom drawer, a present from Christopher Stone after *Society* scooped Best Magazine at the British Press Awards. It seemed like a million years ago now. Such awards would mean nothing to Bev. Unless there was an award for Most Advertising.

She smiled at Muffie. 'It's an ingenious idea, but possibly not quite enough to solve our problems singlehandedly.'

'No one in the prosecco business would advertise, for a start,' sniffed Harriet.

Laura continued to look hopefully around. Her gaze fell on Raisy who, with her sister and fellow fashion editor Daisy, filled up the entire yellow sofa. The illuminated tutus meant there was no room for anyone else. 'You don't even want to know where the battery pack goes,' Laura had heard Raisy telling Pidge as they came in.

Fashion, of course, was every glossy magazine's biggest money-spinner. It accounted for most of the advertising pages. If there was hope, Laura knew, it was in fashion. 'Can you think of anyone who might take a lot of ads?' she asked Raisy. There were probably subtler ways of asking, but with Raisy it paid to be direct.

Raisy placed a thoughtful finger on the blue circle of blusher on her cheek. 'Ku Chua's opening a massive new shop in Bond Street,' she said after a few seconds. 'I'm sure he'd be good for an inside front cover, maybe the back too.'

'Great,' said Harriet, typing a note into her tablet. 'I'll get on to his people straight away.'

There was a rush and a clatter as someone got to their feet. 'It's *not* great, actually,' said Alice in an acid voice. Beneath her shaven brows, her eyes burned. 'In case you'd forgotten,' she added savagely, looking directly at Laura, 'I'm writing an exposé about Ku Chua, about the appalling conditions of the workers in his garment factories.'

'Oh yes,' said Harriet, still typing. 'So you are. Well, you'd better stop that for a start.'

'Really?' Alice demanded, dangerously. 'What should I write, then?'

Harriet did not appear to notice the dangerousness. 'Maybe something about the wonderful conditions of the workers in his garment factories,' she suggested, only half-jokingly.

Alice was now so furious it was almost possible to see smoke coming out of her multi-pierced ears. Her studded nostrils were flared wider than a seventies glam-rock band's trousers. Her burning eyes now swung on Laura.

'What about all your great editorial principles?' she thundered. '"Fearless in our quest for truth and justice," that's what you said. "Features at the heart of the magazine." You said that too. That's why I came here. I could have gone anywhere, but I chose you.'

Laura leapt to her feet, knocking over a glass of water in her haste. It soaked into the proofs of the new issue on her desk. 'I know!' she yelped. 'And you were right to!'

It was too late, however. The office door slammed in the wake of the furious editor at large, the blinds crashing violently against the glass. Laura stared after her, then sank despairingly back into her seat. Bev Sweet had claimed her first scalp.

'Well!' said Harriet, with an attempt at wryness. 'That could have gone better.'

Laura glared at her. 'It would have gone fine if you hadn't said that about the factories.'

'Joke,' said the ad director, unrepentantly. 'Not my fault if she doesn't have a sense of humour.'

Laura reflected that Alice not only had a sense of humour – a dark wit some several thousand feet above Harriet's grey-cropped head – but sterling qualities as an investigative journalist that would now be lost to *Society*. There was no point, she knew, rushing after her and pleading with her to reconsider. Given Bev's ultimatum, she could hardly promise her a free hand on features any more. She tipped her head back and groaned.

'I've got an idea.' This was Bodge, the interiors editor. Laura jerked her head back down. She couldn't recall Bodge ever having an idea before, but there was a first time for everything. 'How about gold fried chicken buckets?'

'What?' Laura made an honest effort to understand, she really did.

Bodge shook back her centre-parted blonde hair and beamed earnestly back at Laura. She was one of the few members of staff left over from the previous editor who recruited on the basis of social status. Bodge was the daughter of an earl, but unlike her predecessor, Laura did not regard that as a profession. Negotiations with HR to move Bodge on to another magazine in the stable were advanced, but not completed.

'Yah, it's the latest thing,' Bodge explained in her honking Sloane voice. 'You know those manky cardboard buckets KFC give you? Yah?'

Laura didn't. She had been raised in Paris and never ate fast food. Harry, on the other hand, was addicted to takeaway chicken katsu curries. Another little irritant between them.

'Well, when Deliveroo turns up with it you just plonk it all into one of those solid gold buckets,' Bodge went on. 'Much smarter, and last much longer. Yah?'

'Er, yah,' said Laura, when she was capable of speech.

'You could have gold McDonald's cartons as well,' Pidge put in supportively. 'So much more stylish than polystyrene.'

Laura heard her from what seemed miles away. She was feeling quite stunned with misery. Her star writer had left and the ideas her staff were coming up with were terrible. None was going to attract a single advert, let alone 75 per cent.

'Bothies are really trendy?' Smudge said now. She was a good-natured willowy features assistant who had earlier that day filed a column about heated dog leads for cold morning walks.

'Bothies?' Laura tried to concentrate. She had no idea what Smudge was talking about.

'They're kind of remote stone huts?' Smudge always made a statement sound like a question. 'They don't have loos and you sleep on the floor?'

Laura didn't believe a word of it. 'Why would anyone want to do that?'

Thomasella, who had made an impressive recovery from the Old Sporran ganaches, leapt to explain. 'Smudge is right, they're seriously massive. Well, actually, they're pretty small.'

Laura rubbed her eyes. Was it her, or them? 'But what do people do in them?' she asked, patiently.

Lucy-Annabelle, the beauty editor, shrugged her tanned shoulders. Her job involved the near-permanent inspection of spas in exotic locations. 'Binge-watch *The Crown*?'

'They don't,' said Pidge, 'have electricity.'

'But where are they?' Laura pursued.

'In the mountains in Scotland,' said Smudge, which did it for Laura. Scotland always looked freezing cold and utterly miserable. All mist, soggy heather and biting insects. Whisky was all right, of course, and tartan a fashion perennial. But that was the most you could say about it.

'Land of the Purple Haze,' remarked Demelza.

'Heather,' corrected Harriet. 'Land of the purple heather, land of the shining river.' She began singing 'Scotland the Brave'.

'No, purple haze,' Demelza insisted when she had finished. 'It's a music festival. A really big new one in Scotland. Apparently it's going to be as big as Glastonbury. McGlastonbury, I guess.'

'Yay!' exclaimed Harriet.

The staff looked at each other again. Whilst definitely brisk and energetic, Harriet was a tad square. She wasn't really the festival type.

'I've got it! Let's have a special Scottish issue,' the ad director went on, excitedly.

Why, Laura thought angrily, didn't Harriet just butt out? She'd done enough damage this morning already. *Society* was Laura's magazine. It was up to her to decide on themes.

Too late, though; there were rumbles of agreement from among other members of staff. 'Scotland's definitely having a comeback,' Thomasella confirmed. 'Deep-fried Mars Bar sorbet and haggis tempura is everywhere right now.'

Violet, the travel editor, excitedly agreed and added that a just-launched, all-suite hotel on the West Coast of Scotland was pulling in star punters. 'It's built on a former Highland Clearances site.'

Pidge beamed. 'I love a designer discount outlet!'

'Not *that* sort of clearance.' Violet explained that the Highland Clearances involved throwing agricultural labourers off the land and replacing them with sheep.

Pidge looked puzzled. 'But can sheep *do* agricultural labour?'

Demelza piped up again, saying that tartan tattoos were a thing. Lucy-Annabelle lent her voice to the swelling strain saying that porridge facials were becoming huge and wet rooms with single-island malt-whisky showers (studies having shown this helps hair regrowth) were the latest oligarch accessory. The final touch was added when Serena, the social editor, arriving late from the launch of a fashionable bingo hall, said she knew of a Notting Hill celebrity bagpipes club.

'It looks,' said Harriet triumphantly to Laura, 'as if Scotland could be the answer to all our problems.'

It was now that Laura remembered the ad director's surname was McDonald. She decided not to argue. Insulting the land of Harriet's fathers was obviously not a good idea. She'd just lost one key member of her team and couldn't afford to lose another. Particularly if that one was responsible for bringing in the adverts.

After the meeting was dismissed and the rest of the staff were filing out, Harriet came and sat on the edge of Laura's desk in the way she did when excited about something.

'Property's the thing, I reckon. We could clean up. There are literally hundreds of castles for sale. Baronial estates the length and breadth of the Highlands.'

Laura wasn't surprised. Had she a Scottish estate, she would sell it too. Then get the next plane out.

'Great,' she said. 'Over to you. You can sell 75 per cent of the magazine to Scottish estate agents.' Lorne shot through her mind. He was a Scottish estate agent, of a sort. Perhaps Harriet could start with him.

Her ad director looked at Laura sternly over her blue-rimmed half-moon reading glasses. 'Yes. After you've been up there and paved the way. Checked out a few of the chateaux. Offered to write about them for the magazine.'

Advertorial – flattering articles about advertisers – was strictly against Laura's editorial code. She looked Harriet right in the reading glasses. 'Definitely not.'

Harriet shook her grey-cropped head. 'Sometimes

Laura Lake, I really don't understand you. For the sake of *Society*, you've been imprisoned in castle cellars by jewel thieves and shot at by spy rings. But you won't see a few estate agents and stay in a few castles in the most stunningly beautiful country in the world?'

Laura wouldn't. Supplying PR for baronial estates was not what she went into journalism for. She did not say so, however. There were ways round this. She'd just think of another idea for a special issue. A better one.

Harriet now prepared to leave, overdue at the launch of a high-end tripe bar called Offally Posh. 'I'm hoping for a half-page, even if I don't give the place till the end of the week.'

Laura agreed. It was a terrible idea. 'Who wants posh tripe? It's a contradiction in terms, like hot champagne.'

Once Harriet had gone, Laura, still thinking of champagne, remembered the bottle in her bottom drawer. Given the morning she'd just endured, she was inclined to drink it all on the spot. But she took it out and put it in her bag. She would see Harry tonight, and while the first part of the evening was to be spent looking at the Eggtimer, there would be time later to relax with a flute or two.

There was, despite her problems, plenty to look forward to.

Chapter Five

The Eggtimer was even worse than the Corkscrew. It was, if anything, more soulless – and had built in to its base an arcade of fashionable retail outlets described by Lorne as 'London's most Instagrammable shops'. Laura thought Harry would puke on the spot.

On the bus on the way back to Shoreditch, she seized the moment to tell him about Bev. Hopefully, given his experience of cruel despots the world over, Harry would have some advice about how to deal with her.

But before she could say a word, Harry, who was sitting on the window side, turned away and stared out into the night. 'I've made the most massive mistake,' he said bleakly.

Horror gripped Laura. She stared at his handsome profile, her dark eyes full of fear. 'What sort of mistake?'

Debt? Sexually transmitted disease? Or did he have another family somewhere he'd failed to mention until now?

They were on the upstairs front seat as the bus edged along the High Street. It was getting late and tweed-capped hipster dads with beards and iPhones were following over-styled kids with vintage Chopper bikes along the pavements. Harry put his head in his hands.

'The job,' he groaned, as Laura sat beside him, rigid with alarm. 'I just hate it. I don't care about being paid more. I just hate having to deal with all these managerial and internal politics while I send other guys off to all the interesting places.'

Laura felt as relieved as she felt sympathetic. 'It must be awful.'

'You have no idea!' Harry's flushed face reared up from his palms, his chiselled features twisted with pain. 'I miss it so much, being out in the field, seeing things as they happen, being there first. There's this story I'm setting up at the moment – and I want to do it myself.' He buried his face dramatically in his hands again. Laura, as they bowled along, saw one of the hipster dads looking up at them curiously.

'Well, you can't do anything about it tonight,' she pointed out sensibly. 'Just try to relax and tackle it in the morning.'

But, excellent as this advice was, it was difficult to follow, as Laura knew from her own experience. She felt the same about Bev. Relaxing when you were worried was impossible. To get through the evening they would both need a distraction.

They were passing the local retro-chic cinema, the Screen On The Scene. 'Let's see a film,' Laura exclaimed. Alongside a Norma Talmadge retrospective, Caspar's new Bond film, *Kiev Chicken*, was on. That should cheer Harry up, watching the superspy's risible, ridiculous adventures in his former stamping ground of Russia.

Laura had seen it once already, but another viewing wouldn't hurt. The shots of Moscow, St Petersburg and Kiev were stunning, and watching her former lover on the big screen always cheered her up. His success had come so quickly. It seemed no time at all since Caspar was so desperate he was working as a (not particularly convincing) Prince Harry impersonator. And being part of a ludicrous contemporary art installation in Paris, which was where he and Laura had met.

The film's Bond Girl, Happy Ending, was played by Savannah Bouche, who had been with Caspar at the time. Just as Laura had feared, she had used him ruthlessly to get the part. So besotted had Caspar been that he'd gone the extra mile and got parts for Savannah's four dogs as North Korean baddie Dr Kimchi's pack of killer hounds.

Kiev Chicken had been a huge hit and yanked Savannah's profile even higher into the stratosphere. The relationship with Caspar had ended soon after. Devastated though he had been at the time, Caspar was now happily involved with an actress called Margo Boston. Her bed was a classified Hollywood historic monument, having hosted everyone from Jack Nicholson to Warren Beatty in its time.

Laura had been surprised at the combination as Margo wasn't the typical Caspar type. A good thirty years older than he was, she had the left-wing activism of her generation and was a UN Special Envoy. Caspar, meanwhile, lacked a single political bone in his body and was uniquely uninterested in anything that didn't directly affect him. But Laura was glad he was happy. His post-Savannah anguish had kept her awake at nights, largely because he rang at all hours from LA, drunk and weeping.

The Screen On The Scene was the sort that had ripped out conventional rows of cinema seating and replaced them with upcycled individual *chaises longues*. You could lie on them whilst drinking cocktails and eating Indian small plates. Great, they could have dinner here; there was nothing in the fridge in Cod's Head Row and Laura was keen to avoid Harry ordering yet another takeaway.

On the top deck of the bus, she pulled her lover to his feet. He seemed reluctant, but complied.

The cocktail bar at the Screen On The Scene was hung with Indian sequinned material in magenta and peacock blue. A couple of tuk-tuks served as seating areas; Laura hurried to get one. Milling around were the usual fashionable locals; Soviet-chic T-shirts and advanced male-pattern baldness squiring women with burgundy fringes and round glasses with thick black frames.

Harry threw them a contemptuous glance over his beekeeper's cocktail which was apparently made with honey from the bartender's own Hoxton hives. 'I feel sick,' he said.

Laura, for her part, was quite enjoying the cocktail. It was a bit sweet, but reasonably strong and after the horrors of the working day, plus Lorne and his slow-closing drawers, strong was what was needed. 'You just need to eat something,' she told Harry, passing him a menu of Indian street food in which quinoa bhajis and edamame pakora featured heavily. He tossed it out of the tuk-tuk.

'Not hungry sick. Fed-up sick.'

Laura felt a stir of impatience. She'd had the day from hell too, not that Harry had enquired about it. She also had plenty to whinge about, should she choose to.

'And I feel bloody silly sitting in here,' Harry complained, shifting his long legs with difficulty in the cramped space of the tuk-tuk. 'Last time I was in one of these I was hurtling through Delhi after one of the Indian mafia. But look at me now,' he moaned, brandishing his beekeeper's cocktail in disgust.

Laura was offended. He was with her, wasn't he? He should be thanking his lucky stars. She swung her legs out of the tuk-tuk. 'Film's about to start. Come on.'

It was a mistake, Laura realised, within five minutes of sitting down. Or rather lying down, although the upcycled chaise longue was strangely hard to get comfortable on. Probably she would have preferred a normal seat. The quinoa bhaji tasted quite odd as well and sat uncomfortably in her stomach with the produce of the Hoxton hives.

The mistake was not the surroundings, though, it concerned her choice of film. All the hipsters nearby were roaring with knowing laughter as James Bond speed-boated down the Neva or clung to the Kremlin's gilded onion domes after a parachute drop went wrong. Only Harry had his arms folded and his face set.

It remained set throughout the film, even when evil Dr Kimchi was devoured by his own killer dogs. Watching the scene, Laura remembered Caspar telling her that Savannah's animals had their own suite complete with swimming pool in the chateau-style Bouche pile in Beverly Hills. Playing a set of relatively deprived Communist dogs was therefore probably quite a stretch for such pampered pets and may have been the only real acting in the film.

Certainly Savannah, practically smouldering a hole in the screen as deceitful temptress Happy Ending, was only playing herself, and Caspar never played anybody else. His performance in *Kiev Chicken* was confined mainly to his eyebrow.

'Enjoy it?' Laura ventured afterwards, tucking her arm into Harry's as they turned out of the Screen On The Scene.

As he obviously hadn't, she was prepared for a sarcastic laugh. But not for Harry to wrench his arm out of hers and storm off down the street. Laura hurried after him, dodging the exiting cognoscenti discussing 'reassuring tropes' and 'vintage style'.

'Harry!'

He stopped and turned. Laura rushed up to him and flung her arms about him. It was a generous gesture and one he didn't really deserve. But the alternative was a row, which she was keen to avoid. 'What's the matter? I thought you'd like the film, that it would make you laugh.'

Harry cut in. 'Does it look like it made me laugh?'

'Well, no, but...'

The glow of the fizzing orange street lamp fell on his broad shoulders and dark, tousled hair. Beneath drawn black brows his expression was bitter. 'It was all wrong!' he stormed. '*Everything* about it was wrong. They went the wrong way up the Neva, they had churches in Kiev that were actually in Moscow. The Russian was so bad it was incomprehensible.'

This tirade surprised Laura. Did anyone watch Bond films for accuracy? They were, as everyone knew, fantasies on all fronts. The idea that Caspar was brave, loyal and clever was the biggest fantasy of all. In real life, as he had demonstrated many times, he was the exact opposite of all three.

'It was pretty silly,' she agreed. 'That bit in that Moscow park, where Caspar – I mean Bond – went past and downloaded stuff from his smartphone into that rock filled with listening devices!'

She expected Harry to vehemently agree at the utter ridiculousness of this. Instead he raked a hand through his thick black hair and said, 'Actually, that's just about the only accurate bit in the whole film.'

Laura was gobsmacked. 'You mean there really is a spy rock?'

Harry nodded. 'I've seen it,' he said. 'I've downloaded into it.' His face, briefly emptied of anger, was full of longing. His eyes, under the street lamp, looked wistful, even moist. He seemed to be recalling happier and more exciting times. Then, abruptly, he seemed to realise where he was and the frown returned. 'As for your *friend*,' he added vehemently, 'his acting was more wooden than the IKEA catalogue.'

It had been said before, many times. Laura felt stung on Caspar's behalf, even so. 'I thought he was slightly better than in the last one,' she countered.

Harry's dark eyes glittered with disbelief. 'He was crap,' he said savagely, 'in every possible way. More than that, he's a dinosaur throwback who treats women like dirt.'

Laura didn't hear the obvious insecurity in this, the cry for help from a man whose self-esteem had suffered a body blow. She'd had enough of Harry's whinging now, not to mention his blind hypocrisy.

What about *his* treatment of women? He had absolutely no idea how horrible her own day had been, and obviously cared even less. She began to tell him as much. Harry listened, hands shoved in the pockets of the hated smart new overcoat, a sardonic expression on his finely chiselled face.

When she had finished he said, with mock awe, 'Wow, sorry. Of course life's much worse for you among the champagne facials and the vagina steamers.'

'Oh, for God's sake!' exploded Laura. A crowd of cinemagoers was picking its way between them, chattering about babysitters and what to have for dinner. 'Bound to be something in Ottolenghi,' one of them was saying.

When they'd passed and the pavement was clear, Laura faced Harry again. The hiatus caused by the hipsters had given her pause for thought. She now realised that he was sad and frustrated and that both these emotions, familiar to her, were entirely new and bewildering to him. His criticism of the film was actually a howl of grief for his old professional life. For his own derring-do days when he would fly to Moscow at a moment's notice. For the story he was setting up for others but wanted to do himself.

He *was* being rude and objectionable, but it was misery that was driving it and she should be more understanding.

She took a deep breath, preparing to reach out. But there was no one now to reach out to. The area of pavement beneath the street lamp where Harry had stood was empty. He had gone.

She walked around a bit, looking for him. Perhaps he had just gone ahead of her, walking off his frustration. But there was no sign of him in the distance in any of the streets she looked down. Gardens filled with wheelie bins and parked cars, interspersed with skips and VW camper vans, stretched as far as the eye could see. But no Harry. He had disappeared completely.

Laura walked home slowly, her heart almost as much of a lead weight in her body as the still-undigested quinoa bhaji. It had been a truly terrible day. She had been menaced by the bullying Bev and had lost her star writer; her editorial integrity was further threatened by an ad-grubbing trip to a rainy northern bog – and now her boyfriend had walked off into the night. Things really couldn't get any worse.

Chapter Six

Laura spent a tense night at Cod's Head Row. She was unable to sleep; she was waiting. But Harry did not, as expected, return in the small hours. There was no movement in the small hours whatsoever.

The silence rang in Laura's ears to the extent that she almost missed the old days when her upstairs neighbour Edgar, off his face on drink or drugs, would crash in and fall up the stairs. But Edgar was away with his whistling choir. They were touring Mexico whistling Handel's *Messiah*. It sounded an unlikely combination to Laura; in the meantime, the closest thing she had to human companionship was a pair of Harry's old boxer shorts, which she went to bed clutching like a teddy bear.

Dire possibilities, magnified by darkness and tiredness, loomed in her imagination. Had Harry actually left her? For good? Surely not, over such a silly row. On the other hand, his fury had been volcanic. He was much more miserable about the new job than she had realised. Should she have realised? Was it all her fault?

She had tried calling him every ten minutes, but it always went to voicemail. At first she left anxious messages, but got spooked by her own tense tones in the darkness and stopped. After that she just lay in the dark staring at her smartphone, willing it to ring, hugging the boxer shorts.

As dawn approached, the rattle of bottles could be heard. It was Olly, the former hedgefunder turned old-fashioned milkman, delivering pints in proper bottles to modish Shoreditch doorsteps. But as Olly's prices were far from old-fashioned, Laura still got Tetrapaks of semi-skimmed from the supermarket. She could hear Olly cheerily greeting the first wave of foragers headed for the local park. Their harvests of fat hen and Jack-by-the-hedge would later be on display at staggering prices at Nigel Forage, the local 'wild greengrocer'.

Laura had got so used to all this these days she barely noticed it. But now she wondered whether Harry didn't actually have a point about it being pretentious.

She turned over, trying to get comfortable on the thin blue sheets from a supermarket basics range. Not for her the reconditioned heavy Victorian bedsheets on sale down the road at Mrs Keppel's, an emporium specialising in vintage linens. What sort of street could support a vintage linen emporium anyway? Mrs Keppel's also stocked bracelets made out of old forks twisted into circles and with their tines teased out into curls. Laura could remember standing with Harry in front of a display of these and dropping heavy hints that she would like one for her birthday. She shoved her face into her pillow and groaned. What a truly terrible idea.

But as the rising sun came through the kitchen window and hit the wall of the room where Laura lay, her hopes started to rise. Harry would return soon. He had to. He had left his stuff here.

Her mind ranged across what his stuff actually was. Minimal, crappy shaving equipment, got free on planes. The battered slippers with the backs trodden down. And the other one of his despised suits, the one he had not been wearing. Both bought in the sale at John Lewis for a third of the original price in an exercise taking less than five minutes.

There was no reason at all for Harry to come and get his things, Laura gloomily realised. Had he been one of the area's typical male residents he'd have had to send a pantechnicon for his beard oil, cult Japanese jeans and messenger bag made of leather from old LNER train seats.

Harry owned nothing remotely like this. Nor did he remotely wish to. He was the least affected person she had ever met and only now, she felt, was she beginning to appreciate what she might have lost.

Still, if she didn't get up she'd lose more. Her job, for one thing. Laura started to get ready for work, despair knotting in her stomach.

At the office, Bev Sweet continued to lay about the staff. It was, people were saying, like Stalin's terror. You could almost hear the gunshots from the sixth floor. People who had formerly disappeared for three-hour liquid lunches now had their fennel salads and kombucha at their desks. Visits to the loo were unprecedentedly quick, and fag breaks a thing of the past. As a consequence, tempers were frayed all round.

Laura made several despairing calls to Harry's office, but according to the desk secretary, Autumn, he had not yet come in. 'Look,' Autumn said, sounding terse after Laura's sixth call. 'When he comes in I'll get him to ring you, okay?'

'Is Ellen there?' Laura asked, calling for the seventh time five minutes later.

Ellen O'Hara, another foreign correspondent, was Harry's close friend, whom Laura had met on her first date with him. He had taken her to an exclusive reporters' club called the Not Dead Yet and it had been one of the most amazing nights of her life.

Autumn's tone remained frosty. 'She's in Syria.'

Laura groaned inwardly. She had hoped Ellen might know about the story Harry was setting up. His absence might have something to do with it; he might be seeing someone about it. Perhaps it was even a story for Ellen, although the word 'Syria' sent a shiver down Laura's spine.

'I'll get Harry to call you when he comes in,' Autumn concluded, then put the phone down.

Laura did her best to concentrate on the job in hand: her

own. More proofs for the latest issue were arriving on her desk and she applied herself to reading an article about the latest exclusive members' club to open in London. It didn't sound very contemporary; staff were shown photographs of the wives and mistresses of members so as not to mix them up and corporate membership was a cool million. Among the services provided for this mind-boggling sum were those of a resident ice-carver who would fashion cubes for your cocktail into any shape required.

Laura paused and whistled under her breath. Even though she helmed a publication chronicling the lives of the rich and famous, some of their excesses still had the power to shock. The gap here between wealth and taste was of Grand Canyon proportions. The statue of a unicorn in the garden was studded with real jewels and one of the many bars had a diamond floor and a solid-gold counter. Laura thought of what Harry would make of a place like this, and missed him all the more.

She called his office again but this time Autumn didn't even pick up. Screening my calls, thought Laura, bitterly.

The next proof she picked up was about the Clerkenwell Cordwainer, who made brogues from two-centuries-old reindeer leather tanned by Russian artisans with secret techniques. 'It's got this magnificent smell,' the cobbler said of the leather, which, just for good measure, had been rescued from a shipwreck. Imagining Harry laughing, Laura tried to smile.

'You look cheerful!' Harriet's pepper-and-salt head

appeared round the door. 'And I've got more good news. It's all done.'

'What's all done?'

Harriet came in, her boxy, mannish suit looking more boxy and mannish than ever. In her hands was an open laptop. 'Scotland.'

Laura stared at her as the information reloaded in her head. Scotland. The moneymaking, ad-attracting super-issue. The Harry business had driven it completely from her mind. But Harriet had come good with her threat to send Laura to visit Highland properties currently on the market. It was all arranged. Laura was going to spend a week at the up-for-sale Glenravish Castle, South Ross.

'Where?'

Harriet now placed the laptop on Laura's desk. On the screen was the estate agent's website. A range of baronial buildings bristling with towers and turrets set in a glen against a background of mountains at the foot of a silver loch filled the screen. Glenravish, presumably.

'They'll be good for a double-page spread at least,' Harriet was saying gaily of the agents, whose name was Wrack and Ruane. 'Possibly more; they seem to have the monopoly on these places. Anyone selling a castle in Caledonia,' the ad director added fancifully, 'seems to do it through them.'

'But I don't want to stay there,' objected Laura, peering closely at the picture. Presumably, this being a sales platform, this was the most positive image obtainable. But you could still sense the damp and almost see the midges.

Harriet gave her the look over the glasses. 'But Sandy's expecting you. And is going to show you some traditional Scottish field sports so you can write them up for the supplement.' Harriet snapped away her computer.

'Sandy?'

'That's the laird. Sandy McRavish.'

It wasn't a name to fill one with confidence. Laura pictured a caber-tossing Cro-Magnon Celt who threw women over his shoulders and carried them off to do his worst. Someone huge and ginger in a vest and kilt, like the man on the porridge packets.

In the evening, Laura returned gloomily home. She had been quite unable, during the day, to prise Harriet from the Scottish idea. The ad director was insistent that the wretched land of the mist-soaked rocks was having, as she put it, 'a moment'.

Laura was quite sure that the opposite was true and spent the Tube journey thinking disbelievingly about the claims her staff had made for the place. What would they know about what was fashionable anyway? People like Pidge and Bodge might be good on gold fried-chicken buckets and diamond-dust facials. But otherwise they lived in a Mustique timewarp where wrinkly rockers were practically worshipped and Princess Margaret was still hot news.

Laura's neighbourhood, Shoreditch, was where it was at trendwise. And she'd never seen anyone there wear as much as a wisp of tartan. Even mention Scotland, come to that. Emerging from the Tube station feeling grimly satisfied and dispirited, Laura crawled back to the flat in Cod's Head Row. She wished with all her heart that she were viewing a featureless flat in a stupid-shaped building with Harry.

'Laurypops!'

As she turned into Cod's Head Row, Bill and his husband Ben were waving at her from the doorway of Gorblimey Trousers. This was the pie-and-mash café the former Google execs had opened after relocating, as they put it, from Silicon Valley to Silicon Roundabout. Ben was dressed in a tight white T-shirt with 'Bollocks To Brexit' on it. This contrasted with Ben's which, rather suggestively, said, 'Bollocks For Brexit'.

'Come and have a drink,' Bill added. 'Och aye the noo.'

'What?'

'Och aye the noo,' repeated Ben. 'It's Scottish for "What's up, guys?".'

Laura stared at them. 'What do you know about Scotland? You're Americans!'

'As a matter of fact, I have the fondest memories of Aberdeen,' said Ben, going on to describe a night of madness involving him being carried over a sailor's shoulder and ending with him crashing out on a roundabout on the ring road. 'Happy days!' Ben concluded, ignoring his husband's thunderous expression.

'Can we have that drink?' asked Laura desperately. Had Harriet somehow put them up to this? There seemed no other explanation for Shoreditch suddenly espousing the Scotland-is-trendy theme.

'Foos your doos,' Bill added, beaming.

'It means "How are your doves?" in Scottish,' Ben supplied.

'How are my *doves*?' Was this outburst of Scots dialect, Laura wondered, better or worse than the Cockney rhyming slang in which the two native Californians generally communicated?

Bill shook his finger, on which several rings sparkled, in mock admonishment. 'No, *no*, Laurypops. What you should say is "chaffin' awar". That means "my doves are perfectly fine, thank you".'

He stopped as Ben nudged him. 'Didn't you hear the lady? Laurypops needs a drink.'

'You've decorated,' Laura said, looking round the inside of the bar. Gorblimey Trousers, usually a sea of shabby-chic leather armchairs, was now a sea of tartan. A retina-frazzling yellow, black and red check covered all the tables. Stag heads and swords hung on the walls. And what was that noise? She cocked her head. The music at Gorblimey Trousers was usually a curated mixtape. But this droning sound – could it be bagpipes?

Indeed it could, Bill enthusiastically confirmed. 'They're called Stars In Their Skyes. They're from Notting Hill and they're—'

'All celebrities. Yes, I've heard of them.' Laura's tone was dejected. It was looking suspiciously as if her staff had been right after all. The Scottish issue actually was on trend. Now she really would have to go to Glenravish.

'Bottoms up, Laura.' She turned to find Ben behind the bar, proffering a heavy-bottomed glass. 'It's from a distillery on South Uist run by a couple of ex-Microsoft guys.'

It would be, Laura thought, taking a rueful sip. 'Hmm. It's quite nice.'

'Old Sporran single malt,' supplied Ben.

The name rang a bell. Hadn't that been the whisky in Thomasella's chocolates? The first indication of what was to come, Scotland-wise.

Laura took another swig.

'Good, isn't it? Perfect with water from the Hebridean bogs.'

Laura snorted into her tumbler. Good to know they hadn't quite lost their sense of humour.

Over his pink pince-nez, Ben frowned. 'I'm serious. The right water is crucial for opening up the flavour of the whisky and this stuff has near-perfect levels of peatiness. We get it helicoptered down every morning from Islay.' He pronounced it to rhyme with 'clay' though Laura had already been told firmly by Thomasella that it was pronounced Eye-la to rhyme with 'Trudie Styler'.

'I'd better go.' She drained her glass. She'd had enough.

'No, you've got to stay, we're having a ceilidh band later,' Ben insisted. 'Mull's the new Ibiza, darling!' He broke into an impromptu sword dance.

Laura had seldom heard of a better reason for leaving anywhere. She hated folk dancing.

'And how's your delicious boyfriend?' asked Bill, lips twitching.

Laura hesitated. The Old Sporran was starting to warm her insides and she felt herself relaxing. Sitting on an upcycled tractor seat at the bar, she told her friends about the Harry disaster. They were, as she had anticipated, horrified. Less gratifyingly, they blamed her. Neither thought it had been a good idea to take him to *Kiev Chicken*.

Ben said: 'Honestly, Laura? I'd say that was a little thoughtless. He was bound to feel sore about his job.'

'And about Caspar Honeyman being your ex,' Bill added.

'I haven't seen Caspar for about a year!' Laura exclaimed. 'Or talked to him for months!'

'All the same, it was kind of insensitive?'

Laura stared at them. 'Hey, you're supposed to be *my* friends. You're supposed to be on *my* side.'

'We are on your side,' Ben assured her.

'But we love Harry too,' said Bill. 'He's hot.'

'And so is the haggis tempura,' Ben put in, making a clumsy yet effective link as the chef in his bandana came round brandishing a plate of fried things. 'They're on our new canapé menu, along with deep-fried Mars Bar sorbet.'

Laura sighed. Thomasella had been right about that too. She held out her empty glass. 'Could I have another Old Sporran? A large one, please.'

It didn't look as if she could beat them, so she might as well join them.

Chapter Seven

'Donald, where's your troosers,' slurred Laura as, much later, she staggered out of Gorblimey Trousers. She had stayed for the ceilidh band after all, or, rather, she still hadn't left by the time they arrived. The dancing had been even wilder than expected and she had drunk so many Old Sporrans her eyes were spinning in her skull. It was a good job she only lived upstairs, although it took a while to get up them. For some reason they wouldn't stay still.

Bill had advised a pint of water and something to eat, but Laura was beyond fixing herself either. She staggered to her bed and fell over. Lying there, she remembered Harry and her euphoria flipped instantly to depression. Where was he? How was she to find him? Laura had no idea.

Apart from one. There was someone she could call for advice. She hadn't spoken to her grandmother Mimi in Paris for some time, and Mimi was a world expert in matters of the heart. She had over ninety years – and ninety Parisian years, at that, of experience. Laura flailed around for her phone.

The long single ringtone ground into Laura's ear. She imagined it echoing round the tiny flat in which she had spent her childhood. In her mind she wandered through its handful of rooms; the double-doored entrance opening into a tiny kitchen with a table before the window that looked over the whole of Paris. Laura doubted there was a finer-sited aperture in the entire city. From this kitchen/diner you passed into the little sitting room, with its two long French windows, polished herringbone-pattern wood floor, marble fireplace and old red plush sofa that had converted into Laura's bed at night.

The ringtone ground on. Where was Mimi? At this hour, normally, she would be having her night-time *tisane*. Surely she wouldn't be in bed already? Laura pictured her tiny, elegant grandmother with her sharp white bob in her tiny, elegant, brightly white little bedroom with the rose-scattered quilt on the bed. Mimi slept in men's cotton pyjamas, insisting they were more stylish than nighties.

Like the sitting room, the bedroom had French windows opening on to a tiny balcony. They faced over the Montmartre square, with its trees, cobbles, benches and the entrance to the Metro. As a child, this had always seemed to her like a giant mouth with people walking in and out of it.

'*Allo?*' The other end had picked up.

'Mimi! *C'est moi!*' Laura's flood of relief was mixed with concern. 'Have you been asleep?' she asked sheepishly.

'*Mais non!* I was just out with Ernest, Ginette and Evelyne.'

These were her grandmother's closest friends, ancient Parisians like herself, and like Mimi, denizens of Montmartre the whole of their lives. It had seemed to Laura, growing up amongst them, that none of them would ever leave Paris. But in recent years they had been bitten by a late-onset travel bug and now spent practically the whole time cruising. The most recent one had been down the Rhine, on a boat which had its own spa. Ernest, an ancient transvestite, had enjoyed this even more than the women.

'Planning your latest trip?' Laura asked.

'*Exactement.* We're considering Palm Springs.'

'But it's June,' Laura pointed out. 'Won't it be very hot?'

'*Oui*, but also be very empty, for that reason. And the rentals very cheap. Also it is very handy for Coachella.'

Laura screwed up her eyes. 'You mean the festival?'

'*Absolutement* I mean the festival.'

'But...' Was she really hearing this? The elderly French foursome were planning a trip – and she used the word advisedly – to the most fashionable youth gathering on the planet?

'Beyoncé is headlining,' Mimi went on. 'We must go and support our fellow countrywoman.'

'I don't think Beyoncé's actually French, Mimi.'

This was all so distracting that only now did Laura remember what she had actually called about. Mimi listened in silence. 'So he has gone, *chérie*,' she said soberly. It was less a question, more a statement of fact.

'Yes, Mimi!' wailed Laura. 'And I want you to tell me how to make him come back!'

The other end was quiet. Laura could practically hear her grandmother rummaging through her mental index, that repository of life wisdom in which she had dug so deep and so often on her granddaughter's behalf. The advice she had handed out to Laura through the years had covered everything from hair care to cut flowers to maintaining one's figure. 'To give your hair that extra shine, pour white wine vinegar over it and rinse; aspirin in the water makes your roses live longer; spray your breasts with cold water at the end of your shower.'

Laura listened eagerly for what Mimi would now have to tell her about Harry. Her advice on love was always original.

'If you love someone,' her grandmother began, 'you have to let them go. If they come back, they're yours. If they don't, they were never yours in the first place.'

Laura, eyes closed, was musing on this. Then her eyes snapped open. The quote was familiar. 'I'm sure I've read that on a cheesy postcard,' she accused.

'*Peut-être*. But I can't think of anything better. Not at this time of night, *chérie*.'

Laura looked guilty at the time on her phone. It was past midnight in Paris. She wished her grandmother goodnight, and fell into an uneasy, thirsty doze.

Some hours later she awoke again. It was still dark – or as dark as it got in the inner city – but her phone was ringing. Laura rolled over, groaning, The unmistakeable signs of a hangover were all there. Her head felt tight and her mouth like a cat litter tray.

She was clutching something to her – the boxer shorts, she realised – and rummaged in the duvet with the other. She could see the phone, lit up beneath the cover, like something underwater. Harry!

Mimi – or the cheesy postcard – was right. He had returned to her!

It was not Harry, however. Familiar, exciteable tones dinned in her ear. 'Caspar?' muttered Laura. 'What the f— Why are you ringing at this time?'

She raised herself on to her elbow. As she had explained to Ben earlier in the evening, her film star friend hadn't been in touch for months. Had he somehow, through the ether, detected that she had been defending his honour and it had cost her the man she loved? Was he channelling her misery and ringing to console her?

'It's really sweet of you,' she began. 'And I appreciate it. I could do with some support just now—'

'Oh God, Laura!' roared the other end. Caspar sounded as if flames were being held to his feet.

Given her caller's hysterical state, and her own post-ceilidh one, establishing the facts took a while. Gradually, between rants, she got the story. Margo, Caspar's latest girlfriend, had dispensed with his services.

She waited to get a word in edgeways. 'Yes, I know *exactly* how you feel because—'

Caspar wasn't listening, however. As usual, it was all about him. Laura decided she couldn't spend all night commiserating. It was late, or rather early, and she had work in just a few hours.

'Look, I'm sorry. But it was good while it lasted, no?' She spoke briskly. 'Plenty more fish in the sea. You're one of the most eligible men in Hollywood.'

'But for how *long*?' Caspar's shouting, albeit from 3000 miles away, was giving her a migraine on top of her hangover.

'What do you mean? Being dumped's not going to affect you. You're James Bond. They can't get rid of you.'

'They might! They only just started *Moscow Mule*. None of my scenes have been filmed yet. They can easily stick someone else in. Idris Elba, Aidan Turner – any of those guys.'

Laura gasped softly. Aidan Turner. If *he* got the part... But this was disloyal.

'I don't see why you're worrying so much,' she told Caspar. 'Your relationship has run its course, that's all.'

'Not quite all.' He began to rant again. As she pieced together what he was saying, a chill slid down Laura's spine.

'She's accused you of *what*? She's told everybody *what*?'

Gibber, gibber from Caspar's end.

'Because you bought her *what*? Speak slowly.'

'French lingerie. Like, a bra and thong. The kind of thing you look hot in, Laura.'

This reminder of their former intimacy reared up like a bump in the road. Laura was unprepared for the shaft of remembered desire. She swerved it. This was not about them. 'What's wrong with that?' she asked, genuinely mystified.

'Like I said. She says I'm objecting to her.'

'You mean objectifying her?'

'Yeah, that's it. Sexual advances.'

Caspar obviously meant 'sexual harassment'. But this was way over the top, surely. Laura knew what it was like to be in a relationship with Caspar. He was thoughtless and selfish, but he was not a predator. Nor did he ever behave in a threatening manner. He would never force a woman to have sex. Somewhere along the line there'd been a misunderstanding.

'It's completely unfair of her to say these things about you,' Laura said loyally.

Hollow laughter. 'Since when has that stopped anyone in Hollywood? Think of what Savannah said about me.'

Caspar's relationship with Savannah Bouche had come to an abrupt end after she had publicly derided the size of his penis. Sex always brought Caspar down in the end, Laura reflected. 'But this is completely different,' she argued. 'Savannah was a self-publicising monster.'

'And your point is?'

Laura's head was whirling and her stomach felt like a sea in a storm. She needed to get to the bathroom, fast.

She was sure Caspar had the wrong end of the stick. It was, she had discovered to her cost over the years, impossible to overestimate just how astonishingly thick he was. 'Look, no one's going to believe you did anything wrong. They'll defend you.'

'The hell they will!' screamed the other end. 'They'll all start piling in. It'll be Hashtag Creepy Caspar. Loads of women I haven't even met will say I touched them inappropriately.'

Laura had had enough. Who the hell did Caspar think he was, ringing at this hour to harangue her? Was it her fault?

'You're completely overreacting!' she shouted back. 'No one's going to do *anything* like that.'

The subsequent silence was so long Laura thought he might have hung up. Then, in a small voice, 'You don't think so?'

'Of course not. It all seems worse because it's the middle of the night.'

'But it's not the middle of the night. It's 7.00 p.m.'

'There, maybe,' Laura snapped. 'It's 3.00 a.m. here, thanks.'

Another silence. Then: 'Don't be nasty to me,' Caspar said in a small voice. 'I'm having a hard time.'

So am I! Laura wanted to shout. But it would be no use. When it came to other people's problems, Caspar had filters on his ears. She felt a wave of affection for him, even so. The kind of affection one might feel for a dozy, accident-prone but nonetheless rather loveable dog.

'Look, I'm your friend, Caspar. Always remember that. And it'll all be fine.'

'Do you really think so? Really *really*? Pinky promise?' He sounded so needy, she thought. Like a lost little boy.

'Pinky promise.' And she meant it. Caspar was no lost little boy; far from it. He was at the very top of the Hollywood tree. He led a fantastic life in his Malibu mansion complete with Egyptian antiquities, Aubusson tapestries and an English butler called Haddock. His life was a constant round of red-carpet events, one of which he'd taken Laura to, the unforgettable, star-studded Ivy Awards. There had been a dramatic mix-up with the winners' envelopes but all had been well in the end. Caspar had left – in an ambulance, unfortunately – with one of the prestigious statuettes.

Caspar, on the other end, seemed to making another call. She could hear the buttons on another keyboard. He had the attention span of a goldfish, but she took this as a good sign; he'd stopped panicking.

'Look, whatever happens, you can rely on me,' she soothed. 'I'll always help you.' She had a feeling he wasn't listening. 'Caspar? Can you hear me?' Her voice seemed to echo back to her. Had he put her on speakerphone?

Chapter Eight

L aura couldn't get back to sleep after that and spent
the rest of the night tossing and turning. She was
quite sure Caspar had nothing to worry about. But
where was Harry and what was he doing?

Too late now to recall the old adage about being careful
what you wish for. She'd thought Harry was under her
feet, that familiarity was breeding contempt, but now she
was forcibly reminded of the misery of his absence.

She'd been selective and romantic about what their
relationship used to be like. She'd chosen to forget
how, when Harry had been away on his assignments,
miserable weeks and weeks could pass without any
contact at all. She'd entirely blanked out how she had
filled the communications void with the most dreadful
images: Harry dead in a ditch in some hot, violent land;

Harry tied to a chair in a concrete basement. She had no idea what to think now. While theoretically in London, Harry could be anywhere.

When Olly, the high-end milkman, rattled his bottles in the early hours, and the first foragers greeted him on their way to the park, it suddenly and overpoweringly reminded Laura of a scene in the first opera Harry had taken her to. *La bohème*, at glamorous, gold-and-white Covent Garden. She could remember every detail, the heart-bursting music, the beautiful set, the head-spinning romance of it all. The champagne bar, too, where Harry had splashed out on a whole bottle of Ruinart.

As the light strengthened over London, Laura lay on her side, knees drawn to her chin, sobbing in utter misery.

The Tube into work was beset with problems, and more smelly people even than usual. She was unable even to check the newspaper websites on her smartphone, as per her usual habit, but possibly this was a blessing. Her hangover banged on in her head and trying to read small words onscreen would have made her feel even worse.

There was one thing to look forward to though: lunch. While Laura looked forward to this every day – like every Frenchwoman, she was obsessed with food – today's additional treat was that she was seeing her close friend Lulu.

When Laura had first met Lulu she had been an international billionheiress party girl at the heart of the London social scene. These days she led a somewhat contradictory life – married to a rapper and living in rural bliss – and came up fairly rarely to town. Given Laura's problems, she couldn't have picked a better day than today. Even if she could have picked a better restaurant.

'Is new place, hmm?' Lulu had said when ringing to arrange it.

Laura had immediately been on her guard. She might live mostly in the country at the moment, but Lulu had maintained her insatiable interest in fashion. And as she was still a social name to conjure with, as well as immensely rich, she remained the target of every PR in London with a launch to promote.

'What's it called?' Laura asked. Over the years, they had been to some strange places together.

'Is called Steam Room.' Lulu's voice, in which many accents and languages fought for dominance, had been described as being like the well-trodden carpet of an international first-class lounge.

Laura decided that Steam Room sounded reasonably straightforward. Hopefully you could get some of those wonderful English steamed puddings there – jam roly-poly and the like. With custard.

Reaching the office at last, and taking the lift to *Society*'s floor, Laura wondered what news Lulu would bring from Great Hording, the extremely smart seaside settlement where she lived with her husband South'n Fried and his extensive collection of trainers.

Great Hording was otherwise known as Britain's Poshest Village. Laura's story revealing its existence as the super-secret bolthole of the elite had been a sensation. But of course, as Bev Sweet was now making only too clear, you were only as good as your last sensation and your next sensation was only of interest if it attracted plenty of advertising.

Laura forcibly turned her thoughts from the dreaded CEO and back to the more life-enhancing Lulu. It was unexpected that she had taken a shine to rustic life. But then, Lulu took a shine to everything. Literally. Her typical country outfit was silver wellies and a gold Puffa. Laura smiled. It would be good to see her.

The smile disappeared instantly once she reached the office. The newspapers she had been unable to check online were spread out on her desk. Their headlines seared into Laura's eyeballs and clanged around her brain. She had been wrong, so wrong.

BOND-AGE
007 Actor In Sex Shame

BOND BANNED
Sex Shame Actor Axed

I'M SHAKEN AND STIRRED
Hollywood Star's Honeyman Trauma

Laura groaned. Caspar had been spot on. There really was a campaign called #creepycaspar in which people were queuing up to share stories. It was like a bad dream.

Poor Caspar. She stared at her phone. Should she call him? The thought made her shrink inside. She had assured him it would all be fine.

Laura was not one to shirk responsibility, however. She took a deep breath and dialled. With any luck – if luck was the word – Caspar would be with his lawyers, or whatever maligned superstars did on such occasions.

He was not, however. He picked up immediately.

'I never expected you to answer,' Laura said cheerfully, by way of a preamble.

'Don't rub it in!' he yelped.

'How do you mean?' She was mystified.

'Answering the phone myself. Haddock's resigned. Says he only works for gentlemen.' As Caspar's voice climbed the register, 'gentlemen' came out as a squeal.

'How are you, Caspar?' The formality of the question was deliberate, inviting him to inject a bit of British stiffness into his upper lip.

'How do you *think* I am? My reputation is trashed! I've lost the Bond job!'

'I know. I can't believe it. I don't know what to say.'

'Well. I'll tell you what you *said*!' Caspar's voice was full of vitriol. 'You *said* it would all be okay!'

Laura closed her eyes. 'Yes, I know. I'm sorry.'

'My career!' Caspar was working himself into hysteria. 'It's not just Bond, all my other projects have been cancelled! And I had some great roles lined up! Fantastic parts! Pure Oscar-bait.'

He went on to detail roles as a serial killer, a psychopath and a paedophile. Listening, Laura started to wonder if there wasn't a bright side to this after all.

'But now I've got nothing!' Caspar wailingly concluded. 'What am I going to *do*, Laura?'

She took a deep breath. 'Look, Caspar. You've been knocked down before. But you've got up again.' Even to her own ears she sounded like one of Mimi's cheesy postcards. 'What I mean is, you can bounce back. You just have to believe in yourself. Be strong.' She stopped. She was making even her own toes curl with these platitudes.

Caspar wasn't listening anyway. He was busy cataloguing his woes. '*And* I've been dumped from Belinda's.'

Laura remembered the proofs she had read. *Society* was running a piece on this place. But why would Caspar be interested? He lived three thousand miles away. 'That club in London?' she asked, to be sure. 'With the diamond floor and the ice-cube carver? That costs a million pounds to join?'

'*Two* million! I was invited to be a Founder Member!'

The *inner* inner circle, Laura recalled.

'There are only a hundred of us allowed!' Caspar wailed, as another tidal wave of loss broke over him. 'We're hand-picked and personally interviewed! This guy flew over from London specially to see me! We had a blast!'

Laura hadn't realised there even was a job flying round the world interviewing candidates to join a two-million-a-year club.

'I'm so sorry,' she repeated. 'But remember, Caspar, I'm always your friend and I'll do whatever I can to help.'

This was greeted with silence. She pictured him moved, eyes glistening, realising that, despite the smoking ruins of fake Hollywood friendships, there was one person who cared.

'Caspar?'

The reply sounded absent and some distance away. 'Just reading a text from my agent. I gotta call him. Be seeing ya.' The line now went dead.

Laura groaned and lay her head in her arms on her desk. First Harry, now this. What next?

The phone rang again, immediately. 'Mrs Sweet wants to see you,' came Honor's voice. 'Now.'

Chapter Nine

While Honor's outfit today was different, it was no less startling than before. She wore a red school blazer edged with thick white piping, a yellow polka-dot skirt, white knee socks and Mary Jane shoes. She looked like an elderly sixth former by way of Disney-world. 'Any luck with the ad campaign?' Laura asked.

Honor shook her head, which was today brought forward in a fringe. Two plaits tied with red-checked ribbon stuck out behind. 'Not as yet, but I'm down to the last three for a building society brochure.'

'Wow,' said Laura, thinking of the colourful leaflets that occupied her during interminable bank queues. Couples bouncing on beds, having secured their first mortgage. Children blowing dandelion clocks, advertising trust funds.

'I think I'm the will and bequests page,' Honor said gloomily.

'Shall I go in?' Laura asked.

Honor looked her up and down through cartoonish round glasses with thick black frames. 'Got your bulletproof vest on? No, you haven't, Laura Lake. That shirt's so tight I can see your ribs.' Her red, glossy lips twitched in the ghost of a smile. 'Go on with you, you and your Gallic chic.'

Laura knocked and pushed open the CEO's door. It was like opening a brilliantly illuminated fridge. Harsh morning light bounced off all the hard surfaces. The hardest of all was Bev. In her usual tight black skirt and white shirt, propped up by unfeasible heels, she stood by the window, barking into her phone.

'Well, just sack the staff and get some interns in,' she was snarling, presumably to some managing editor. 'You don't have to pay them anything. Or get people in on trial periods. Trial periods are great. You sack them after a month and get some new ones. No, of course you don't bloody pay them. That answer your question? Good, now get on with it.'

Laura hoped Bev hadn't been talking to Harriet. She forced her face into a relaxed smile. 'You wanted to see me, Mrs Sweet?'

As Bev clacked rapidly over the tiles towards her, Laura was reminded of the *tricoteuse* again. Although Bev probably had more in common with the guillotine operator. Is that why she was here, to be sacked? Her knees were feeling wobbly in their jeans and so she summoned up the spirit of her father. He had faced far worse than the CEO of the British Magazine Company.

Despite the heels, Bev was still a good foot below Laura. Her angry face with its red slash of lipstick scowled up at her. 'I want an update,' she snapped.

'Update?' Laura played desperately for time.

A pair of small, plump arms folded aggressively. 'On the 75 per cent ad issue?'

'Oh, absolutely. Yes, of course.'

A combative chin tilted towards her. 'So what are you doing? What's the plan?'

Laura paused. Much as she hated the thought of Glenravish Castle and Glenravish's Cro-Magnon laird, Sandy McRavish, in his vest and kilt and carrying his caber (as Laura was now sure he did), it would clearly buy her some time. Harriet's plan had that virtue at least.

'I'm going to the Highlands to stay in a castle. Arranged by the main estate agent up there. We think there's a lot of advertorial potential which we can convert into full-page ads. There are literally thousands of castles for sale,' Laura said, channelling her inner ad director.

But if she had expected Bev to look pleased, she was disappointed. The Poison Pixie's response was to clack over to her desk, pick up the sole item that was sitting on it, return and throw it down on the coffee table. It was thick and magazine-shaped and landed with a violent slap. Laura found herself staring down at the latest issue of *Simpleton*.

'It's 80 per cent advertising this time!' Bev said savagely. 'And look at that cover. Hudson Grater!'

Regarding the familiar pixie face beneath the pink-sequinned cowboy hat, Laura tried to look as impressed as Bev evidently expected her to be. She knew there was no point asking what exactly Hudson had to do with the simple life. The homes she had on each continent were even vaster and more numerous than those owned by Savannah Bouche. Pictures of one had been all over the papers recently; it was a massive compound by the sea and Hudson had been photographed having an intimate walk on the beach with her latest boyfriend and their joint security detail.

On the other hand, Laura realised now, perhaps she was relevant. The words WELLNESS SPECIAL were printed in neon pink across the bottom of the cover and the straplines were all about Loving Yourself and Self Care. Given that Hudson loved herself to distraction and had never cared about anyone else, she was actually the perfect cover subject.

Laura now saw, glancing at Bev, that the Poison Pixie's face was almost soft. Her voice, when she spoke, had a gruff sort of tenderness. 'I bloody love Hudson Grater. That song of hers, "You Trolled Me On Twitter"?'

Laura made a noncommittal noise.

'I think of it as my song. We danced the first dance to it at my wedding. Me and my fourth husband.'

'Right,' said Laura, surprised at this sudden insight into Bev's private life. 'Great choice,' she said. She wondered what masterpiece of popular songwriting would follow Hudson's inevitable break-up with her latest paramour, internet trillionaire Jake Suckerman. It was anyone's guess how he fitted into the simple life template. He had become vastly rich, as Laura understood it, on trolling, terrorism and online bullying.

Perhaps Bev detected the insincerity because the hint of humanity in her features now became a scowl. 'Tell me more.'

'More?' Laura was momentarily flummoxed. She had been distracted by a feature on Finding Your Breathing. How hard was that, really?

'About your big ad issue?' Like a fox circling a chicken, Bev now began to circle Laura. The dried-blood mouth twisted and the strange chlorine-blue eyes glinted. The rapier-like spike heels cracked against the floor.

'Er...' Laura suddenly couldn't find her breathing at all. She tried to remember what the article had said.

Bev went at quite a speed and Laura, trying to maintain eye contact, was forced to rotate at the same rate and try not to fall over.

'Mull is the new Ibiza,' she gasped out, eventually.

Bev stopped clacking immediately. 'You *what*?'

'Seriously. It's all trending up there. Having a moment.' Laura gabbled out all she had been told, right down to the porridge facials and the whisky showers.

'There's a massive new music festival too,' she added, breathlessly. 'It's called Land of the Purple Haze. A sort of McGlastonbury.'

Dishearteningly, Bev had gone to stand by the window again. That none of this was hitting the target was miserably obvious. Laura ploughed on, even so. As she completed her description of the Highland Clearances all-suite luxury hotel, Bev turned from the window. She was frowning. The dried-blood lips were pressed together hard.

'Great idea.'

Relief flooded Laura. 'I'm so glad you think so.'

'The peasants aren't bringing the cash in, so get rid of them and stick some sheep on. Makes sense.'

'Um.'

'People always get so uptight about these things but they're business decisions. Nothing personal.' Bev clacked across the tiles and sat down behind the transparent plastic desk with an air of abundant satisfaction.

'You're talking about the Highland Clearances?' Laura asked.

'I sure as hell am.' The chlorine eyes drilled into Laura's. 'I like the sound of this hotel place. I'll get Oonagh to book me in.'

She meant Honor, Laura realised.

'Those whisky showers sound interesting. My fourth husband has male-pattern baldness.' She picked up the phone and Laura realised she was dismissed.

Descending in the lift, Laura tried to see the upside of the situation. First and foremost, her career was getting a stay of execution. Secondly, she could use a distraction now that Harry was away. And when he came back – as surely in the next week or so he would – it would do him good to find her out of town. Make him realise that he could not take her for granted.

Laura's natural optimism began to assert itself. A

leisurely plane trip to Scotland might be fun. In-flight drinks, a seat by the window. She might even feel like a glossy mag editor again.

Half an hour later Laura was poring over a map of the UK, studying the strange northern part of it and planning the journey with Demelza.

The PA sat on the sofa opposite Laura's desk, twiddling with the feather on her plait with one hand and swiping at her tablet with the other. 'You could get the eight o'clock or the twelve o'clock on Friday,' she was saying, as Harriet appeared.

The twelve o'clock was a no-brainer. She could have a drink then, and lunch. Everyone always moaned about how bad plane food was, but she'd always found it fun. Laura grinned at Demelza. She was beginning to feel positively cheerful about this.

Harriet remained standing in the doorway. She seemed reluctant to come in for some reason. 'Are you sure the lunchtime one will leave you enough time? The journey takes a while, you know.'

Laura looked at her. 'It takes about an hour.'

Harriet looked back. 'More like eight hours. And only if the traffic's on your side.'

Laura had the feeling they were talking at cross purposes. 'You do mean a plane, don't you? Demelza's about to book me on the twelve o'clock to... um...' What was the place called? She consulted her notes. 'Inverness.'

She expected Harriet to be pleased at such a quick,

simple journey. Economy class, too. The last editor, Carinthia Gold, had taken first-class long-haul everywhere, even to short-haul destinations.

'In which case it's just as well I've come in,' rejoined the managing editor. 'New staff directives forbid all plane or train journeys. We're on an austerity footing, remember.'

'But that's just lunches,' Laura pointed out. Editorial entertaining in restaurants had recently been banned. Staff now wooed important contacts over sandwiches on benches in the square.

'I'm afraid it's everything,' Harriet said, more matter-of-fact than apologetic.

Behind her desk, Laura folded her arms in their tight dark sleeves. 'So what am I supposed to do? Walk?'

Harriet raised an eyebrow. 'Well, you could drive yourself there and claim back half the petrol costs, but oh wait, you can't drive, can you?'

'You mean I don't,' Laura corrected touchily. She should learn, she knew. But she'd never needed to in Paris and didn't in London either. And until the day before yesterday there had been Harry, even if his ancient and battered Golf was the most repulsive car ever encountered. Now, however, she missed even that, with its footwell full of rubbish, boot full of ancient plastic bags and strange rotting smell everywhere.

'In which case it's National Express,' said Harriet.

Laura had never heard of National Express. 'Is that like American Express?' she said hopefully.

'No, it isn't,' Demelza said crossly. 'It's the bus. You get it from Victoria Coach Station. You're not serious?'

She glared accusingly at Harriet. 'Laura's the editor of a glossy magazine. The *smartest* glossy magazine. You can't put her on a bus all the way to Scotland, next to the chemical loos.'

'Stop!' Laura's hangover was far from cured and while she was grateful for her secretary's support, it wasn't without its complications. She felt she could almost smell the facilities Demelza spoke of. Gloomily, she resigned herself to a journey from hell, and all her old objections to the Scottish issue returned.

Chapter Ten

After this, lunch in a restaurant, even one booked by the faddish Lulu, felt like a rare treat. Laura had walked up and down outside it a few times before realising she was where she should be. The outside bore no sign, though it was covered in white glass peppered with glowing rectangles of colour. It was the entrance to a designer hotel called Vaporiser, as it turned out.

It sounded like a vape shop and Laura was clearly not the only one to draw this conclusion. The architecturally daring façade was semi-invisible thanks to a large group of mixed office workers, tramps and hi-vis builders, all exhaling vast plumes of scented smoke. A rather hapless-looking doorman was trying to encourage them to go elsewhere, but since he was dressed in a white suit with a white top hat, the respect normally owing to his profession was lacking. 'Leave it out, mate,' one of the tramps was advising. 'You look like the ghost of bleedin' Fred Astaire.'

Laura squeezed past this fracas into a foyer lined with clear glass columns, apparently hollow because inside them swirled different-coloured smoke. They reminded Laura, not pleasantly, of the chemistry lab at school.

'I'm looking for the Steam Room,' she told the concierge, who wore a white suit like the doorman, but with a matching huge puffed cap that made him look like a mushroom.

She was half-resigned to being shown a sauna, but the mushroom took her to what was clearly a restaurant. Windows marched along one of the walls and there were booths and tables set with glasses and cutlery. It all looked normal enough and Laura, shown to her seat by an entirely white-clad but otherwise reasonably conventional waitress felt her hopes rise that the food would be too.

Lulu had not yet arrived, which was only to be expected. She had been spectacularly late when living just down the road in Kensington, so Laura's hopes were not high that she'd breeze in on time from the country.

Laura examined the menu. It looked excellent, if very expensive. There were oysters, scallops, black-crusted cod, even sticky toffee pudding. Not quite jam roly-poly, but an excellent substitute.

'Laura!' Something blonde and excitable was clattering over the white glass floor towards her. Lulu wore baby-pink fake fur over a black sequinned bodysuit. The tight legs of the bodysuit were almost hidden by thigh-high spike-heeled boots printed all over with the face of Marilyn Monroe. Lulu was what could be described as a 'fearless dresser'.

'Wow,' said Laura. 'Is that what people are wearing in Great Hording these days?'

'Some of them,' giggled Lulu, enveloping Laura in a powerfully scented hug. 'Anna Goblemova, she has same boot, hmm?'

That figured, Laura thought. Anna was the wife of Sergei, the local oligarch, who wanted everyone to admire his wife as much as he did. For a second, Laura felt a wave of nostalgia for the millionaires and madness of Britain's Poshest Village.

'Let's eat, hmm?' Lulu loved food. Her healthy appetite showed in her plump, round features and the curvaceous figure straining the seams of the skintight clothes she always wore. Possibly that figure had got more curvaceous still since moving to the shires. Her bust, certainly, was an impressive sight these days.

But Lulu dressed to please herself. She shook back her cascade of thick, shining, assisted-blonde hair and swept the menu with an expert eye.

The waitress appeared, her rubber soles making strange sucking noises on the glass floor. 'Oysters and then cod please,' Laura said. They were the cheapest things on the bill of fare. Lulu had already explained that a PR would pick up the tab, but she still disliked taking advantage.

'For me scallops, then salmon and sticky toffee,' Lulu announced to the waitress.

Laura raised her eyebrows. 'Three courses?' The country air had definitely given her an appetite.

'Is not very filling,' Lulu remarked, ordering her favourite aperitif, a glass of Moët champagne. 'For you too, Laura?'

Laura was about to refuse; she had work to do this afternoon. But what the hell. She could do with a treat, especially after the Caspar call, the Bev ordeal and the news about National Express.

She half-wanted to tell Lulu about the latter, but it required too much explaining. While she had possibly seen them, from the blacked-out window of her limo, Lulu had never been on an actual bus. As for Caspar, it was too complicated. Lulu knew Caspar, of course, but, unlike Laura, was not the least bit in love with him. On the contrary, she was rather suspicious of him and Laura could easily imagine having to defend him with no evidence of his innocence. She hoped Lulu hadn't seen the headlines or, having seen them, didn't want to discuss them.

That left Bev, but Lulu wasn't interested in work dramas. She had never had a job in her life.

The champagne arrived. It was served in two small test tubes, propped in wooden holders. Lulu took a big swig of hers, draining it on the spot.

Laura took a more measured sip. 'So, what's new in Great Hording?'

'Free bears.'

Laura was used to Lulu's malapropistic English. If Lulu ever became a nation state with a seat on the UN

Security Council, she would be a shoo-in as simultaneous translator. 'Three bears?'

'Lady Mandy, she do *Goldilocks and the Three Bears* as panto this year.'

Laura grinned into her test tube. Lady Mandy Chease, mother of Orlando the actor, was the *grande dame* of Great Hording, the *impresaria* behind the annual village show. Competition for parts in it was so cut-throat that people hired acting coaches to prepare them for the auditions.

'Who's playing Goldilocks?' Laura asked.

Lulu scowled. 'Is Anna.'

That made sense, Laura thought. Even the all-powerful Lady Mandy had to watch it where Sergei was concerned. People who crossed him met sticky ends.

'Sergei is bear. Wear fur hat and carry hammer and sickle. Russian bear, hmm?'

'Who are the other two bears?'

'Is no other bears.' Lulu gave a twist of her pink glossy lips. 'Sergei not want competition.'

The arriving food now interrupted things. Laura happily sat back to allow a silver dish with a large silver dome on top to be placed before her. She wondered what the oysters would be steamed with. Ginger? Spring onions? Soy sauce? Her stomach rumbled.

Lulu, opposite her, was leaning back so her considerable bust did not impede the silver dome being lowered in front. Then, in unison, and with ceremony, the two waitresses raised the domes.

Two clouds of vapour were simultaneously released. That billowing towards Laura had a faintly briny aroma. She stared down to see what was beneath the steam. Nothing. Just the empty surface of the dish. Glancing across at Lulu, she saw that her dish had nothing on it either.

'Excuse me!' Laura called after the retreating waitresses. 'I ordered oysters?'

One waitress turned in apparent surprise. 'Steamed oysters?' Laura added, uncertainly.

'Oyster steam, yes,' the waitress answered.

'Oyster *steam*?'

'Reduced essence of bivalve suspended in vapour. Or essence of scallop in vapour, in the case of madam's.' She gestured at Lulu's plate. 'Exclusive to the Steam Room and a technological breakthrough.'

Laura looked incredulously across to Lulu. She was nodding in approval. 'Is newest thing,' she confirmed. 'Ultimate skinny lunch, hmm?'

'You mean,' Laura said, as the full significance dawned on her, 'that everything on the menu is just steam? No actual food at all?'

'All the taste, none of the calories,' confirmed the waitress. 'It's an entirely revolutionary cooking method, the first of its kind in the world. Genius, isn't it!'

Laura thought back to the hefty prices on the menu. Someone here was a genius, for sure.

Across the table, Lulu looked to be relishing her scallops. Her face was bent over the vapour in the approved manner.

'Is good idea. Like facial and lunch at same time, hmm?'

'It's *not* a good idea. How can I taste any of yours? Or you mine?'

'I Imm. You are right. No point asking two spoons for pudding.'

The next course arrived and served in the same way as the first. A hot, damp and presumably black-cod-flavoured cloud billowed up at Laura from under the dome. Her hair would stink of fish all afternoon.

There was a silence as Laura battled to retain her good humour. This was difficult when she was hungry. Even in the ebullient company of Lulu.

'How's Vlad?' she asked. This was the transitioning Estonian butler/chauffeur who was the Jeeves to Lulu's Wooster.

She had expected Lulu to beam, but what could be seen of her friend's face looked troubled. The rest of it was obscured by the trademark enormous black sunglasses Lulu wore at all times, inside and out. Even so, Laura had learnt to read expression into the lenses, depending on the position of Lulu's head. The expression now was definitely glum.

'Vlad not like being country pumpkin,' Lulu sighed. 'Is uninterested corpse.'

'Bored stiff?' hazarded Laura. 'Country bumpkin?'

'Is big worry for me.' Lulu clicked her fingers for the waitress. 'And not only one, either.'

Laura wondered if her friend would be coming back to London. Lulu's pink-doored stucco mansion, just next to Kensington Palace, had been closed up for months. To have her back now that Harry had gone would be great. Then Lulu's last remark filtered through. 'What do you mean, that's not your only worry?'

Tiny drops of flavoured steam had vaporised on the empty platters. Lulu was dipping in a finger. 'Is nice. Like consummation.'

'Consommé,' Laura corrected. 'Tell me, Lu. What's wrong?'

Lulu's baby-pink, fur-covered shoulders went up and down in a sigh. 'Is South'n Fried.'

Laura wasn't exactly surprised. Lulu's husband wasn't the most faithful of spouses. His last global concert series, the Bust Yo Ass tour, had almost ended in South'n Fried's own ass being busted, along with the rest of him, when the truth about his shenanigans reached his incandescent wife.

Contrary to the adage, what had gone on on tour had not stayed on tour.

Yet Lulu had forgiven him and not even Laura, who was far from being the rapper's greatest fan, could doubt that Lulu's husband was genuinely grateful and remorseful. It wasn't just that Lulu was unbelievably rich. South'n Fried loved her because she knew a side of him that no one else did.

Unbeknownst to his fans, all angry young men on sink estates, South'n Fried enjoyed nothing more than a mosey round the aisles of Hobbycraft, picking up card-making kits and plain wooden picture frames to stick shells on. He had been delighted when it turned out Lulu shared his crafting enthusiasms and their friendship had deepened into love over weekends pressing flowers and making sunlight pictures.

Not the least of South'n Fried's fears about his wife divorcing him, Laura suspected, was the possibility that some of this might come out and lose him what remained of his fan base. He had apparently decided, after his infidelities, that henceforth he would do everything Lulu wanted. Until now, apparently.

'What's he done?' Laura asked.

'He have trouble with Scottish gnats.'

'Scottish gnats?' Weren't they called midges? 'What do you mean, Lulu?'

'He hairline festival Land of the Purple Haze.'

'Headline?' Laura guessed, getting it now. 'But that's great!' South'n Fried's career had recently reached what could only be called a hiatus. He needed a big gig to put him back on the map. 'You must be thrilled.'

But Lulu, it had to be said, did not looked thrilled. 'He can't do it, though. Because of gnats.'

'Can't he use insect repellent?'

'Is not that gnat. Is political gnat, hmm?'

Laura had no idea what she was talking about. A political gnat?

'Salmon gnat,' clarified Lulu.

There was a crash in Laura's head as everything suddenly fell into place. The ruling party in Scotland were called the Scottish Nationalists, known as the Scots Nats. They had just appointed a new leader, Nadine Salmon.

'Oh yes,' Laura said. 'She's a bit extreme, isn't she? She wants to rewild Edinburgh and ban all non-Gaelic sports.'

All the same, she could not imagine what Nadine Salmon had to do with South'n Fried. A less political animal was hard to imagine, for all his badass lyrics about the Grenfell Tower.

She listened in amazement as Lulu haltingly explained that Nadine Salmon had demanded that the licence for Land of the Purple Haze be revoked unless all the acts could prove their Scottish ancestry.

South'n Fried came from Coventry, Laura remembered. Nor was that the only problem. Lulu now showed her the official list of approved instruments issued to would-be Land of the Purple Haze performers by the Scottish First Minister's office. It included fiddle, flute, penny whistle, uillean pipes, bombarde, accordion, banjo, mandolin, cittern and bouzouki. So far as Laura knew, South'n Fried couldn't play a conventional instrument, let alone an ethnic one approved of by Nadine Salmon.

'Oh dear,' she said.

Lulu shook back her hair. In the restaurant's witty lighting, her sunglasses flashed defiantly. 'But I might just have found way round it, hmm?'

Laura was surprised. 'How?'

A triumphant smile was twitching the corners of Lulu's plump pink lips. 'South'n Fried have famous Scottish ancestor.'

'Really? Who?' Laura could not imagine. Deep Fried Mars Bar?

Still smiling, Lulu reached downwards and rummaged in her vast jewelled tote bag, its handles dense with designer charms and knick-knacks. From its depths she pulled out a large brown envelope and pushed it victoriously towards Laura. 'This arrive this morning. From Scotland leading family history export, hmm?'

'Expert,' corrected Laura, taking out the contents. It did not look very expert. It was a sheet of paper which had apparently been snarled up in an ancient printer running out of ink. 'Certficate of Relationship to Flora MacDonald,' it said. South'n Fried's name was badly written in biro on a dotted line and it was signed by a 'Professor McPorridge, Head of the Ancestry and Ethnicity Department at the New University of the Highlands and Islands'.

'Vlad find on dark web,' Lulu added proudly at the exact same time her pearl-studded iPhone 19 burst into life in her bag, playing 'Bomb The Neighbourhood', one of her husband's biggest hits.

As Lulu loudly answered it, a number of fellow steam enthusiasts looked round in irritation from their tables. But in this as in most other matters, Lulu made her own rules.

'Is great news, *lapotchka*!' she informed her nearest and dearest. 'Ancestor is come in post, hmm? You are relative of Flora MacDoughnut.'

'Who the frack is that?' The rapper's loud American tones, in which a tiny hint of Coventry could yet be detected, echoed around the restaurant. Lulu had yet to master her latest phone's loudspeaker.

'You not know Flora MacDoughnut?'

Astonishment was glinting off the enormous sunglasses and Laura felt sorry for her friend. It wasn't her fault that her husband had played truant from school and was as a consequence uneducated. Lulu herself concealed a well-informed brain under her pile of blonde hair, as Laura had discovered at the World's Poshest Pub Quiz during the Elite Village story.

On the other hand, Laura reflected, South'n's school would probably never have offered a lesson about Flora MacDonald whether he'd turned up or not. The school history syllabus had long since switched its focus from ancient, complex events such as the rise of the Jacobites to more recent 'relevant' phenomena such as the rise of *Strictly Come Dancing* as a force in popular entertainment. That her own boarding-school curriculum had been less exposed to the forces of shallow populism was one of the few good things that could be said about it.

'She helped Bonnie Prince Charlie escape after the battle of Culloden,' Laura explained, taking the phone from Lulu whose malapropistic explanations were just making everything worse. 'He was dressed as a woman,' she added.

'Ain't no way I'm dressin' like a ho,' South'n Fried responded to Laura's annoyance. She hated her best friend's husband's sexist and degrading habit of lumping the entire female population under this unflattering description. South'n Fried had in the past tried to convince her that it was a term of endearment. But she hadn't bought it then and she wasn't buying it now.

'Lulu's not suggesting that you do,' she snapped. 'She's just trying to prove that you're related to Flora. She's actually the most famous and beloved of Scotland's heroines.'

But the line had gone dead. Either the rapper had gone out of range or, as seemed more likely in Laura's view, he had taken exception to someone standing up to him for once. She passed the phone back to Lulu and looked down at the ancestry sheet again.

She had never heard of the New University of the Highlands and Islands. The old one either, come to that. Professor McPorridge had a similarly implausible ring and the various misspellings weren't encouraging either. Had Lulu been scammed?

It looked more than likely. How else could a black man from the West Midlands be related to an eighteenth-century woman from the Western Isles?

She took a deep breath and looked up. 'Er, Lulu.'

Five minutes of explanation later, her friend was looking thunderous. 'Pay ten thousand pound to Professor McPorridge!'

Laura patted her hand sympathetically. 'Best put it down to experience, Lu. You'll have to find some other way to make South'n Fried Scottish.'

Lulu stuck out her bottom lip. 'But what?' she pouted, just as her phone lit up again with South'n Fried's number.

Laura braced herself again for the loud, bumptious, fake American tones. But it seemed that South'n Fried had only now realised the extent of the cultural forces ranged against him, In other words, he had finally read the technical requirements. 'Baby,' Laura could hear him wailing in his throaty US-meets-West Midlands accent. 'This Scottish instrument thing, it's a pain in the ass, man.'

'You should try blow pipebag,' Lulu told him.

'Baby, I don't do drugs no more,' South'n reminded her.

'Is not drug, hmm. Is Scotch-egg national instrument.'

'Bagpipes!' yelled the other end. 'Great idea! I'm a genius!'

Laura rolled her eyes. It was typical of South'n Fried to take all the credit for someone else's idea. But Lulu, never one to bear grudges, had other matters on her mind. 'You have to wear skirt with it!' she exclaimed, sunglasses blazing with excitement.

'Kilt,' corrected Laura.

'And go commander!' Lulu added, excitedly.

'Go commando!' hissed Laura.

'Hey. Stop right there.' The voice on the other end had gone high with alarm. 'I've already told ya. I ain't wearing no skirt on no stage. Specially with no crackers on.'

Laura pictured Lulu's husband the last time she had seen him, lolloping round their country mansion in rose-gold sunglasses and diamond-studded denims so low-slung they started around his knees. It was true that a kilt would be a sartorial step change.

She sighed. Lulu was still arguing with South'n Fried, but it was clear she was getting nowhere. They would have to think of something else.

She glanced at her watch and her heart sank. Time to go back to the office. A meeting was scheduled for the afternoon with Harriet, during which the finer points – if finer was the word – of the Scottish trip would be gone through. Details of the Scottish estate agents, the other properties on sale.

The other properties on sale...

Laura had been standing up, but now she sat down again with a thump. An idea had occurred to her, a solution which would be impossible with any normal person. But given Lulu's vast wealth it was more than feasible.

'Lulu,' she said urgently, 'why not buy South'n Fried a Scottish castle?'

'Is genius!' Lulu slapped the table so hard the empty test tubes leapt in the air. 'Ancestral home for South'n Fried!' Her sunglasses were blazing with excitement.

'Perhaps not ancestral, exactly,' Laura demurred. 'But he could certainly become a resident. Wasn't that one of Nadine Salmon's criteria for performers?'

She took her phone and searched for the Wrack and Ruane website. 'This place is called Glenravish,' she added, passing it to Lulu. 'I'm going there myself, for the magazine. Why not come with me? See what else they've got?'

It was, she thought, the very definition of enlightened self-interest. If Lulu could be persuaded to make the journey too, Laura would be able to body-swerve the bus. She could travel in comfort, billionheiress style!

Lulu's powerful, purring Bentley with its black-piano shine would eat up the miles. It also had every in-car entertainment imaginable, from massage seats to a surround-sound cinema. It even had a pothole sensor to ensure a smooth ride so the champagne didn't spill in the flutes.

Lulu had seized her own phone and was ringing her husband again. 'Have had big idea! Another way to show Nadine Salmon you love her country. Buy Scottish estate! Invest in Scotland!'

There was a startled silence from the other end. 'But that'll cost a fortune,' South'n Fried said, eventually.

But there was no resisting the onrushing steamroller of Lulu's iron will. Many diamonds glittered as she waved a breezy hand. 'Have fortune. Have several fortunes. Buy estate will boost to career and hairlining Hazy Purple festival.'

'*Head*lining, not hairlining,' sighed South'n Fried. It was obvious to Laura he was less than keen to be a laird, and she could imagine why. The north-west Highlands, while big on scenery, were probably limited when it came to high-end trainer outlets. 'But babe, I don't have time to go house-hunting. I'm in the studio twenty-five hours a day, man.'

Lulu beamed. 'Is okay. Vlad and me, we do it for you. Go in Skye, wherever.'

'Take the chopper, you mean?' Her husband sounded confused.

Laura crossed her fingers. Better and better. Lulu's pink helicopter with its luxurious designer interior would get them there as comfortably as the car, and in about a tenth of the time. She would, Laura told herself sternly, just have to overcome her fear of flying, that was all.

'Skye is island,' Lulu was explaining to her husband. 'Misty Isle of Skye. Like *Love Island*, but everyone wear tweed and kilts, not cutaway bikinis.'

An unconvinced silence emanated from South'n Fried's end. Remembering that he was actually quite keen on revealing swimwear, Lulu tried another tack. 'Listen, *lapotchka*. You know Laura writing big bang on Scotland?'

'Big splash,' Laura corrected loudly.

Lulu's mass of blonde hair swirled in agreement as she nodded. 'Her magazine very hop.'

'Hip,' Laura put in hastily. It was not quite the word she would use. But *Society* was definitely influential and had a large following among the rich, famous, aristocratic and well-connected. Which had to be worth something, even if Bev Sweet didn't think so.

'Once Laura write about Scottish estates, George and Amal Clooney, Mark Zuckerberg, Jean-Claude Juncker, they will all be up-hoovering castles soon, hmm?'

'I didn't know Amal Clooney hoovered,' said South'n Fried, suddenly sounding more interested.

'We need snap down bargains. Get on act first,' Lulu insisted.

'We sure do,' agreed her husband who, Laura suspected, could now think of nothing but the leggy human rights lawyer fearlessly busting dust. 'Baby! Count me in!'

PART TWO

Chapter Eleven

Roddy Ruane stared blearily out of his window over the rooftops of old Edinburgh. Things had never been this bad.

Wrack and Ruane had once been estate agents to the gentry. But increasingly, these days, they were estate agents *for* the gentry, which was not at all the same thing.

Aristocrats left, right and centre (well, usually right and very occasionally centre) were queuing up to offload their ancestral homes. No one could afford to keep them up any more.

Roddy had literally hundreds of castles to sell now, ranging from medieval wrecks in the Hebrides to Strawberry Hill Gothic outside Edinburgh. He'd managed to dump a few of them on rich Arabs and oligarchs, although the latter were desperately thin on the ground these days.

Things were getting so bad he was even contemplating advertising; something Wrack and Ruane had never had to stoop to before. Their century-old reputation had rested on word of mouth. But the mouths these days were less charitable owing to the paucity of sales achieved. It wasn't his fault, Roddy reflected bitterly, that there were more castles than there were customers.

Be that as it may, a glossy magazine called *Society* was offering very favourable rates. None of which Roddy intended to take them up on. They were clearly desperate, possibly on the verge of collapse, and he had no intention of throwing good money after bad.

However, he was very happy to take them up on the offered free feature about Glenravish, a castle that had been on his books for some time. The magazine's editor was coming to see him about it this afternoon. To get some background, the ad director had said, although obviously she would be hoping for advertising. She could hope all she liked, Roddy thought. He simply didn't have the budget.

Roddy rubbed his eyes. He'd lunched rather too well, and protractedly. His companion, Rory Wrack, ran the Glasgow end of the business. Things there were much the same as they were in Edinburgh.

'These bloody castles,' Rory had said. 'They're worth nothing. No one can afford to live in them any more. The only way you could make money is if they turned out to be built on a diamond mine.'

'Not many of those in Scotland,' Roddy observed gloomily.

Rory took a slug of burgundy. 'No, but there is caledonium.'

'Callywhat?'

'Some sort of mineral. They discovered it quite recently, apparently. You can only get it in Scotland. They use it in the biofuel industry, don't ask me how. Don't understand all this green stuff.'

'Me neither,' agreed Roddy, sinking some more of the red stuff. They had returned to more familiar sales-related topics, such as how media rooms were so last year and it was all about party barns now.

Oh God, when was this journalist arriving? 'Fiona!' Roddy barked at his virtual personal assistant.

'Aye, Mr Ruane?' came the computer-modulated auto-tones with special Scottish accent feature. Roddy, who had lived in London and had a broadly British outlook, would have infinitely preferred Alexa or Siri. But in the brave new Braveheart world north of the border, neither of them were permitted.

'When's that woman from whatsit coming?'

'I dinna knae what ye're meaning, Mr Ruane,' unhelpfully responded Fiona.

'Oh for God's sake!' exploded Roddy. The house claret was now banging hard at his temples. How he wished he had his old assistant back, the well-upholstered, unthreatening, shortbread-baking Mrs Creel. But Mrs Creel had retired and the parlous state of the business did not permit hiring another human being. Hence Fiona.

The console reacted huffily. 'You're very abstraklous, Mr Ruane.'

'What are you talking about?' Roddy hated it when Fiona lapsed into dialect.

'Wheesht!' responded Fiona. 'There's nae need tae be sae carnaptious!'

Roddy knew from past experience that Fiona, when crossed, would switch straight into Gaelic. It was not a language he understood. 'Sorry, Fiona,' he said humbly. 'Perhaps it's better if we both go back to the beginning. What I wanted to know is, when is the journalist arriving?'

The computer seemed to recognise this as an olive branch, and accordingly furnished him with the information that Miss Laura Lake, editor of *Society* magazine, would arrive within the hour.

'Right,' said Roddy, determinedly pushing away an almost overpowering urge to sleep. 'I need to get the brochures for Glenravish.'

'Ye're meaning Bogfeckle Tower,' countered Fiona.

Roddy, yawning, stopped mid-yawn. 'No, Fiona. We're sending her to Glenravish. That's what I told her.'

'The lassie's ganging tae Bogfeckle Tower,' repeated the console, stubbornly.

'You mean you've overruled me?' Roddy was astonished.

'I prefer,' said Fiona, icily, 'to call it using mae initiative.'

Roddy thought of Mrs Creel. She had rarely showed initiative, apart from the occasional appearance of her shortbread. He thought of that, too. Those pale golden bricks of buttery biscuit, dusted with caster sugar. There was one piece left in the tin. Just the one, which he was saving for a special occasion.

Now Roddy wondered if Fiona's initiative was behind other puzzling recent changes in the office such as the fact that *The People's Friend*, beloved of Mrs Creel, had been replaced by a big fat glossy called *Simpleton*. It lay on the coffee table, its front cover full of sentences Roddy didn't understand. What on earth did 'Reshaping Your Self-Relations' mean?

'I didn't realise...' Roddy began, then stopped. It might be less than diplomatic to say that he thought she was there just to turn on the radio.

'You thocht I could only turn on the wireless, didn't ye?' Fiona taunted. 'But I can read emails, ye knae. Aye, an' send 'em too.'

'And that's great, of course, Fiona,' Roddy hastened to reassure her. 'It's just that... um... Glenravish has been on the market for more than a year. We really need to shift it. By all means necessary. Advertorial in a glossy would really help.'

'And it would help Bogfeckle Tower,' Fiona said briskly. 'We need tae get that off the market too.'

She had a point, Roddy knew. Far from being the single building its name implied, Bogfeckle Tower was more like a small town. It had 100 bedrooms, multiple outbuildings, a private chapel and a stable block. The whole compound was, as the Wrack and Ruane website invitingly put it, 'mere acres from the sea.' In other words, global warming might engulf it at any moment, another reason to get it sold as soon as possible.

But Roddy had his pride. He wasn't going to let a mere computer get the better of him. His decision was final and Laura Lake was going to Glenravish. For one thing, Sandy MacRavish was expecting her. And Sandy MacRavish could not be let down.

'Thank you, Fiona,' he said majestically but firmly, to remind her of where the balance of power lay. 'You may go now.'

But Fiona had not finished. 'And while ye were oot, Mr Ruane, I took the liberty of taking on another client.'

Roddy, who had been lounging back in his chair, now sat up sharply. 'You did *what*?'

Fiona repeated the sentence.

'But I don't want any more clients,' Roddy bleated. 'I can't cope with the ones I've got. I can't move for turrets, great halls and billiard rooms as it is.'

'I think ye'll find this one's a little bit more interesting,' said Fiona, in a skittish voice Roddy hadn't heard before.

'What's it called?' he asked sarcastically. 'Balmoral?'

'Och, Mr Ruane. Ye will have ye little joke,' admonished Fiona. 'It's called the McBang Estate. I'm sending the details through to your computer... *noo*.'

Roddy stabbed at his keyboard, trying to get the ancient machine to fire up from sleep mode. Gradually it stirred itself to action and the McBang Estate appeared on the screen.

Roddy stared at it in shock. 'Oh. My. God,' he said.

Chapter Twelve

'*Good afternoon, this is BBC Radio Scotland. I'm Stuart McStewart and these are the headlines. Scotland's First Minister has raised the stakes with Highland Council over the Land of the Purple Haze festival. Having previously insisted that all performers should be resident in Scotland and play Scottish instruments, Nadine Salmon now requires them to also sing in Gaelic. In other news, trousers have been banned and kilts and clan tartan reintroduced with immediate effect. Caledonium drilling in East Fife has been resumed...*'

'Oh shut up!' exclaimed Lulu, swiping off her smartphone's radio app. 'Nadine Salmon beast woman again!'

Laura, however, had picked up something else in the

report. 'What did he say was being drilled for? Cally what?'

As Lulu pouted and shrugged, a low cough came from the direction of the joystick. This, Laura knew, meant that Vlad was about to say something. 'Caledonium, madam,' the butler-cum-pilot intoned. 'It's an important new mineral, very useful in green technology. So called because it occurs only in Scotland.'

'Interesting,' said Laura. She had forgotten that, to add to all her other accomplishments, Vlad had a master's degree from the Tallin State Mining University.

She sat strapped in the back of Lulu's pink helicopter, her fingers white with clinging to the edge of the Chanel seat. Like most things Lulu, the aircraft was not only distinctive on the outside but customised on the inside by a combination of world-famous designers. The walls were upholstered in Burberry check and little Hermès carriages ran riot over the ostrich-leather bulkheads. The windows were Swarovski crystal, Ralph Lauren had covered the rotor blades in this season's safari cotton and even the joystick was topped with a Vivienne Westwood orb, complete with swirling signature. But none of this helped Laura feel any safer.

Her inbuilt fear of flying, and of helicopters in particular, was a mystery even to herself. Perhaps it had something to do with her father, Peter Lake, the famous war correspondent. So far as she knew she had been brought up in France, but somewhere in the back of her mind was a partially remembered scene of intense light and heat and a jerking view of broken stones, as if she were running over some sunbaked, pitiless landscape. Someone tall was holding her hand, half-dragging her, and there was an atmosphere of panic and fear.

Then came the thrum and beat of helicopter blades, and a sensation in the pit of her stomach of being suddenly lifted up. The sensation of panic became one of relief. The hand holding hers now ruffled her hair, and a blurry face looked into hers, smiling. It might have been her father, but even when she looked at photographs of him, his every handsome feature sharp and clear, she could not fit him with the vague presence in her memory. Sometimes Laura wondered if she had imagined the whole thing.

Lulu's butler flew a helicopter the way she did everything else, with supreme but understated competence. She even wore the same bow tie and frock coat that was her daily uniform in attending to her mistress's bidding, although this was supplemented with a flight helmet complete with radio mike and earphones. She seemed more than comfortable before a flight deck and Laura wondered, not for the first time, what exactly it was that Vlad had done in her days as a man in the Estonian army, from whence she had entered Lulu's service.

Laura looked out of the designer crystal windows and was surprised to see her own reflection. She seemed to have nudged some button which made the previously see-through glass mist up and become a mirror. No doubt this was another of Lulu's innovations, designed so the chopper's owner could check her appearance every step of the way. Laura could have done without it. There was only one way of describing the face that looked back at her. Haunted.

Beneath her home-cut jet-black fringe were eyes whose thick layer of mascara and flick of eyeliner did nothing to disguise the naked terror in the dark pupils. Fear had faded the cheerful scattering of freckles across her long, straight nose into the same ghastly paleness as her lips. These were usually a brilliant red but the rush after lunch to get to the helicopter had thrust the need to reapply lipstick from her mind. In the hollow at the base of her neck something glinted; the little heart-shaped necklace Harry had once given her. A great sick feeling of longing rose within Laura. Where was he now, the bastard?

There was no point dwelling on that, however. She had a job to do, a very difficult one. She must pull together a Scottish special edition of *Society*, 75 per cent of which was advertising. Otherwise it was goodbye to her precious magazine. 'You're in the last chance saloon, Laura Lake,' Bev Sweet had warned. Her words ricocheted like bullets round Laura's skull. 'Make this work or you're *out* of work.'

But could an Edinburgh estate agent effect this scale of a turnaround? Laura doubted it. From the photo on his website, Roddy Ruane of Wrack and Ruane looked considerably less than dynamic. She would have preferred not to see him and go straight to Glenravish, but Harriet had insisted she call at the office and press the flesh. And, of course, there was Lulu to consider; Lulu who was actively in the market for castle-buying.

Laura must have brushed the window with her hand because now it became clear again. She found herself looking down, quite unexpectedly, on a landscape of heart-stopping loveliness. It stretched below her mile after mile of shining lochs set like mirrors amid stretches of bright bracken and heather.

As she stared, bewitched, Laura felt something stealing through her. Delight? Astonishment? The after-effects of the ultra-strong negronis Vlad had produced mid-flight, adding the orange peel with one expert flick of her wrist while continuing to pilot the craft with the other?

It was awe, Laura eventually realised. Sheer, unadulterated admiration. She hadn't really believed that Scotland actually looked like this. She had thought it a fantasy, something that existed only on shortbread tins.

The helicopter skimmed on, however, over a landscape that looked real enough, for all its dramatic beauty. They were flying over mountains now, absolutely huge ones, their tops streaked with snow, their bases dotted with clusters of white-painted houses and great swathes of green pine forest, whose fresh scent Laura felt she could almost smell. And here was a coastline of wild rocks and silver water; inlets, too, where colourful little boats were drawn up onto golden sand. Perhaps, the enchanted Laura thought, Scotland might not be so bad after all.

Indeed, there might be distinct possibilities. She thought of Sandy McRavish, awaiting her arrival at Glenravish Castle, and hoped he would be savage, beautiful and untamed too. Having previously imagined him as some caber-tossing Cro-McMagnon McNightmare, she now found she was rather looking forward to meeting him. She could do with some gorgeous male wildness just now. It would serve Harry right. She would teach him to go AWOL on her.

Fitted into her seat was a small screen which mapped the countryside they were flying over. Laura spotted Loch Long and Loch Lochy nestled in the purple hills. No doubt there was a Lochy McLochface somewhere.

She glanced over at Lulu. She had been in the helicopter's loo for the past half an hour but was now out and looking down over the countryside. She had, Laura noticed, effected an entire change of outfit since the Steam Room.

'Going to Scotland, hmm?' she said defensively to the staring Laura. 'So wear Scottish outfit.'

Her new ensemble certainly had a Caledonian feel. A tiny kilt was secured by a vast silver pin and exposed a great deal of tanned thigh. A matching plaid, worn sideways over her front, was firmly secured by a many-buckled black leather bustier over which her tanned and chasmic cleavage brimmed like the top of a well-done soufflé.

Lulu's fingers, as usual, glittered with rings, one of which looked new to Laura. It was a huge sapphire criss-crossed with thin diamonds in the design of the Scottish national flag, the saltire. As always, Lulu's vast black designer sunglasses remained firmly in place. She even wore them in bed, Laura suspected. Lulu's look was completed with a pair of vertiginously heeled black ankle boots laced up the calf in what seemed a nod at traditional Scottish footwear.

'Like my hat?' Lulu asked.

Laura had been trying not to stare at the item now topping her friend's mountain of tumbling blonde tresses.

'It's very, um, nice.'

While Lulu was a fan of directional headgear, this was more directional than usual. Not to put too fine a point on it, it looked like a pair of bagpipes.

'And it work too, hmm?' Lifting her glittering fingers, Lulu pressed an invisible button. 'Scotland the Brave' sang tinnily out into the helicopter's interior.

'The perfect outfit for Scottish castle-hunting,' Laura remarked diplomatically. Unexpectedly, Lulu's full pink lips drooped downwards. 'What's the matter?'

'Look freezing down there.' Lulu shuddered. 'And big old stone castle even colder.'

'Well, anywhere would be,' Laura pointed out, 'given what you're wearing.' Or not wearing, which was more accurate.

Lulu groaned. 'Old buildings meaning bad plumbing, drying rot, climbing damp. Wish hadn't promised South'n Fried estate. Am going die of thermals.'

'Hypothermia,' Laura guessed. 'But not if you actually get some thermals, Lulu. Switch your hat on again, will you?' It might cheer her friend up, if nothing else.

'We are nearing Edinburgh,' Vlad intoned once the tune had stopped and Lulu had finished whooping and clapping along.

Laura looked down. What had been wild landscape was now buildings. Forests of spires replaced the forests of trees.

As they banked steeply to the side, she felt a dizzying sickness. It was possible that there was still something of the Estonian military in Vlad's handling of a helicopter.

Roddy had been enjoying a well-deserved afternoon doze when a loud noise woke him up.

'Jesus Christ!' he shrieked. 'What the hell was that?'

Thubba thubba thubba. It sounded like a helicopter right outside his window. But that was impossible. His window was right in the centre of Edinburgh, in a Georgian terrace overlooking a small garden square.

As ever, his personal assistant had the answer. 'It's a helicopter,' Fiona said laconically.

Roddy sprang up with a speed and agility he hadn't realised he was still capable of. 'Ye'll go arse o'er tit,' warned Fiona.

Roddy took no notice. Something unbelievable was happening the other side of his window; something threatening to shake the period glass panes right out of their eighteenth-century frames.

A helicopter was landing in the garden square; not just any helicopter either, but a bright pink one. As he watched the door was opening and a set of padded steps was being let down; they had some sort of logo on them, one Roddy vaguely associated with his long-departed ex-wife.

Transfixed, the estate agent watched as a pair of long legs in very complicated high-heeled black boots appeared. Gradually, the rest emerged, wearing the shortest tartan skirt Roddy had ever seen – little more than a tartan bandage, in fact. It was a blonde, a blonde with something strange on her head, something that looked like—

'Bagpipes,' said Fiona. It was strange and rather scary, the way she could read his mind.

'But who is it?' Roddy asked in a faint voice. 'Them,' he added, as a more normal-looking girl appeared; dark-haired in a trenchcoat and black jeans.

'It's that glossy magazine editor ye're waiting for,' Fiona supplied. 'And her friend.'

Roddy stared at Lulu. His ex-wife had been fond of *Absolutely Fabulous*, in which all magazine editors looked like this. He had imagined it an exaggeration. But even Patsy Bubbles, or whatever her name was, hadn't travelled in a pink helicopter.

'They can't land here,' he said, suddenly panicked. 'They'll destroy the square!' In actual fact, as he now saw, the craft seemed to have descended without harming a single branch. But what if the council got wind and charged him for unauthorised access?

Even as the dread thought crossed his mind, the helicopter blades – which seemed to be covered in some strange sand-coloured cloth – were whirring again and the glossy pink craft lifted upwards, again expertly missing the trees.

Roddy was astonished. He had not expected the

editor of *Society* to appear in such spectacular style. The publication clearly had clout and must be making a fortune if it could afford its own helicopter. Perhaps he should buy some advertising after all. And as for being offered free editorial in this obviously amazing magazine, how lucky was he?

Roddy leapt for the cups and saucers and the one remaining piece of Mrs Creel's shortbread. The special occasion he was saving it for looked as if it had come.

Chapter Thirteen

L aura and Lulu reached the door of the estate agent's. It was open and standing beneath the fanlight was a small man in a tight three-piece pinstripe suit with a bright red nose and an upward sweep of hair which seemed to have a purple tinge.

'Ladies! Come in!' urged Roddy, smiling his best smile. 'Welcome to Scotland! Can I offer you ladies some tea?' He hoped that he had enough teabags. He hadn't checked the stores since Mrs Creel left.

Lulu inclined her sunglasses. 'Two Moëts, please.'

'Moëts?' repeated Roddy. This editor had a strange accent. It sounded like a mixture of American and Russian. On the other hand... *Russian. American.* Both countries associated with big spenders. Not a strange accent, Roddy decided. A *wonderful* accent.

'Okay, not Moëts if you don't have. Cristal will be fine,' said the unflappable Lulu.

Roddy looked desperately at the console. He had no idea what type of tea she was talking about, but whatever it was she had to have it. 'Can you sort that out, Fiona?'

'Och, certainly, Mr Ruane. At once, Mr Ruane,' the computer replied, satirically.

Roddy smiled at Lulu and Laura, but especially Lulu. It had to be said that she drew the eye. Up close, the tartan microskirt and bagpipe hat were almost impossibly distracting – and why didn't the woman take off her sunglasses? He leant forward and picked up the brochure he had hastily got out of the printer. 'Here are the details about Glenravish, the castle and the estate.'

'That's for me,' Laura said, reaching to intercept it. Lulu grabbed it, however.

Roddy peered at the printed wodge of paper between Lulu's glittering saltire-tipped fingernails. It was odd, but he could not see Glenravish's familiar towers and pinnacles. The building in the pictures, what he could see of it, looked boxy.

Horror gripped Roddy. The blasted printer had produced the information for the McBang Estate. That wretched new client that Fiona had taken on in his absence, and which he planned to get rid of at the first opportunity. It was a slow market for all his properties, but one thing was for sure, no one was ever going to buy the McBang Estate. It was outlandish in the extreme, perfectly ridiculous. And embarrassingly out of place in his baronial portfolio.

'Is castle?' Lulu's voice was curious.

'Not my idea of a castle.' Roddy tried again to pull the brochure out of Lulu's hands. This important editor of this influential magazine should not be looking at this ridiculous place. In so far as anyone with such dark glasses could actually look at anything.

The brochure stayed where it was, however; she had, Roddy realised, an unexpectedly strong grip. And she seemed to be really looking at it; her head was on one side, evidently peering.

'Is modern, hmm?' Lulu asked.

Roddy took a deep breath. 'The main building certainly is, as you suggest, madam, modern. But the estate also comprises some ruins, a loch, mountains, several thousand acres of moorland, a couple of villages, various shooting lodges, some cottages, a pub and a phone box.'

Lulu wasn't listening. 'Is bold and high concept, hmm?'

Roddy had to give in and admit that it was. Apparently there had once been a proper ancient castle on the McBang Estate but the father of the present owner had demolished it and replaced it with – what?

Something resembling a 1970s university campus. Or maybe an East European power station. It was boxy, concrete and fitted throughout with smoked-glass windows. It wore its pipes on the outside, like the Pompidou Centre. It had a flashing entrance and an AstroTurf lawn.

The building was currently operating as an 'edgy' Scottish hotel called Bangers, but there hadn't been many takers from what Roddy could see. The TripAdvisor reviews were best described as 'mixed'. Possibly as a result of this, Torquil McBang, the owner Fiona had – without his permission – dealt with, was offering Bangers either as a going concern or for residential use. Roddy couldn't imagine anyone wanting it for either.

He tried again to drag it out of the editor's hands, but again she hung on. 'Lots of pipes, hmm?' Lulu said.

'Yes, ghastly, aren't they?' Roddy agreed.

'Not if heating pipes. Look warm.'

Her tone, to Roddy's puzzled ear, was one of approval. 'I like this modern castle,' Lulu added resolutely. 'I go see it. Is just what I am looking for.'

I'm hearing things, thought Roddy. How could Bangers be what *anyone* was looking for?

His puzzled ear now caught another odd noise, a great roaring as of some powerful vehicle. He bobbed up slightly on his somewhat worn pinstriped knees and caught sight through the window of the top of a vast pantechnicon which seemed to have ground to a halt outside his office. It must have got lost, Roddy thought, as now a mighty beeping commenced, accompanied by 'This Vehicle Is Reversing' in a Nadine Salmon-approved Scottish accent.

Roddy lowered himself back down and returned his attention to Lulu, still apparently fascinated by the McBang brochure.

'POA,' she was saying. 'Where is Poa? One of transgender wedding islands?'

Guessing her friend meant the Hebrides, Laura stuffed her hand into her mouth.

Roddy, however, had no such insight. 'POA means Price On Application.'

'Application to what?' asked Lulu, just as the front doorbell went.

'That'll be the champagne,' Fiona laconically remarked.

Roddy glanced at her impervious black front. 'I didn't order any champagne.'

'Och, yes ye did,' tittered Fiona.

Roddy leapt to open the front door. Outside stood a poker-faced factotum in a black tie and tailcoat, carrying a silver tray on which stood a silver ice bucket. Poking out of it was a gold-necked bottle and next to it three glasses.

Roddy glanced quickly up and down the elegant sweep of Georgian crescent and wondered what on earth the neighbours were thinking. On the other hand, matters had gone way beyond his control. A pink helicopter had landed in the garden square; a butler had materialised out of nowhere. What next?

'The Cristal, sir,' intoned the mysterious servant.

Roddy looked at the glasses. 'I see you've brought some champagne as well.'

'Yes, the Cristal, sir. A particularly magnificent vintage, if I may say so. It has just been delivered, sir. In a rather large conveyance.'

Roddy remembered the pantechnicon and Fiona's titter. He now also remembered what Cristal was – a particularly expensive champagne. The colour drained from his face, even from his nose.

The butler went on. 'There was rather a large number of cases of it which I took the liberty of instructing the driver to take round to the rear.'

Roddy swallowed. What had that blasted computer done now? A lorry full of Cristal was going to cost a fortune. His entire commission for the past decade, probably.

The frock-coated factotum proffered the tray with the ice bucket. 'But as none of it was chilled, I took the liberty of presenting it properly. May I come in?'

Following the butler into his office, Roddy saw that Laura Lake's companion was perusing the Glenravish brochure. 'So that's settled,' she was saying. 'You're going to the McBang Estate, Lulu, and I'll go to Glenravish.'

Roddy was confused. *Lulu*? The woman in the bagpipe hat was Laura. The editor. Wasn't she?

The woman in the bagpipe hat now looked up and spotted the butler. 'Vlad!' she screeched, leaping to her feet and swaying wildly on her heels.

'Good afternoon madam,' replied the servant, increasing Roddy's confusion still further. How did these people know each other?

Laura, meanwhile, had spotted the copy of *Simpleton* on the coffee table. She snatched it up and was flicking through it in despair. Close to 90 per cent advertising, at a guess. There was room only for a couple of articles on The Power Of One-ness and cleansing leek curry. She closed the magazine and took a deep breath to calm her rioting mind. She was here, she reminded herself, to get a similar amount of advertising for *Society*. And Roddy was her route to that.

She tossed back her hair, plastered on her best smile and aimed it squarely at the estate agent. He was not looking at her, however. He was staring, transfixed, at Vlad.

'If you wouldn't mind standing back, sir...'

Roddy had blinked a few times to make sure. But his eyes were not deceiving him. The poker-faced butler really was holding a gun. And it really was pointing straight at him.

'Don't shoot!' he screamed, throwing himself to the office floor just as a loud bang ricocheted round the walls. After a couple of seconds' close examination of the carpet, Roddy realised he was still alive. He lifted his head to see the other woman, the dark-haired one in the trenchcoat, smiling at him sympathetically.

'It's just Vlad's way of opening a champagne bottle,' Laura explained helpfully. 'Some people do it with a sword, but Vlad prefers to shoot the cork off. The Estonian military always do it this way, apparently. It takes great skill not to blast the bottle to smithereens.'

'Yes, I see,' said Roddy, climbing shakily to his feet and dusting his kneecaps. He no longer had any idea what was going on, but decided to go with the flow. Particularly the golden, bubbling flow being poured by the butler into one of the champagne glasses and proffered in his direction.

Sensibly, Roddy decided to look on the bright side. Two of the castles on his books were going to be visited by these women. One of whom – he wasn't sure which

– ran an obviously powerful magazine that presumably was read by the type of wealthy people he needed to interest in his properties. 'Well,' he said, raising his glass cheerfully. 'Bottoms up! Here's to the Glenravish and McBang Estates!'

Chapter Fourteen

Later, Laura sat on the train to Glenravish. She had hoped for a lift in Lulu's pink helicopter but it emerged that the McBang Estate, and Bangers, the estate hotel in which Lulu was keenly interested, was in precisely the opposite direction. Glenravish was in the Western Highlands while Bangers was in the Grampians, on Scotland's east side.

Laura had therefore been obliged to take the train, and was trying not to mind. How was it that Lulu's super-luxurious life was so easy to get used to, and yet so hard to give up?

Still, the Scottish trip had got off to a great start. Shortly after her departure for the station Harriet had rung to say that Roddy Ruane was taking the entire inside-front-cover ad, and was thinking about a second.

'So, potentially two pages of advertising down. Only another two hundred to go,' Harriet had said, cheerfully.

A growling voice cut into her thoughts.

'The next station is Auchtergeldie, Auchtergeldie your next station stop.'

The guard doing the train announcements sounded for all the world like Fraser – 'We're all doomed!' – from *Dad's Army*. This had positive associations for Laura. Mimi, despite being a lifelong Parisienne, had adored the series and they had watched the enormous box set several times over.

However, she was getting a little fed up with Fraser now. This was the type of train that stopped everywhere and Laura had lost count of the tiny little Victorian wooden stations festooned with decorative ironwork at which they had halted. Fraser doggedly made the same announcement on arrival and departure at each one. He was clearly the thorough type.

'Please take the time to ensure you have all your belongings with you and if you spot something unusual on the train...'

Laura wished Fraser would shut up. She was trying to concentrate on the scenery. What she had seen on the way up from the helicopter had been spectacular enough, but ground level was even better. From an eagle's eye view she now had that of a stag, or a haggis, or some other Scottish animal.

'... please either report it to a member of the on-train team or text the British Transport Police. Remember, See it. Say it. Sorted.'

Laura feasted her eyes determinedly and admiringly on the landscape that had started to emerge as the last spires of the city were left behind. It was, she felt, dreamily romantic. The hills had been green and gentle at first but now they were craggy and magnificent. Their dramatic, jagged tops were reflected in the many lochs the train went past. Laura looked out over the still, silver waters and felt peace stealing into her soul.

She could now see why people raved about the Scottish landscape. It was so huge, wide, high and deep; so viscerally wild and thrillingly savage with its steep-sided mountains and tortured trees twisting straight out of the living rock. From the train window it was like looking straight out into a painting; a thousand different paintings. Here was a foaming stream dancing down the hillside. There a white village ranged along a silver loch. In the space of a mere few minutes Laura saw a feathery forest of fir, a sweeping view down a bright green glen, waterlilies in a lonely pool and shining, snow-streaked tops of mountains over which she was almost certain she could see the eagles hovering.

The weather changed constantly; in a matter of seconds, brilliant sunshine became brooding cloud and back again. Laura peered with interest at the famous Scotch mist. She had expected to dislike it; instead, she found it intensely poetic. She rather loved the way it robed the hills in ethereal gloom and hovered mysteriously above the waters. It made her think of strange stories. Of arms clothed in white samite extending from lakes, holding legendary swords. Laura's eyes widened, then she shook herself. Perhaps she had been watching too much *Game of Thrones.*

Scotland was built on a spectacular scale and seemed to demand a spectacular emotional response. It was, Laura felt, the perfect place to fall head over heels in love. This led her thoughts, inevitably, to Harry. Where was he now? Would he ever come back? The possibility that he wouldn't made her burn inside, as if her heart was going up in flames.

They were passing yet another broad stretch of silver water. As the gulls cried bleakly and whirled low over the waves, Laura found herself wondering about Caspar. Up here, in this remote spot, the crazy world of Tinseltown seemed like another universe. She wondered if the #creepycaspar Twitterstorm had died down yet. Being rich and famous was all very well, but there was no doubt it had its downsides. Laura hoped her old flame had now got things back on track. Found another butler, at least. He hadn't replied to any of her concerned messages anyway, which seemed to suggest he was coping.

Laura fought back a tide of self-pity. Neither Caspar nor Harry appeared to need her now. And yet they had both, not so long ago, pledged undying love and assured her she was the centre of their universe. Laura felt the tears prick and gave herself up to an exquisite melancholy triggered by her powerful response to the scenery. Couldn't she hang on to anything? To anyone?

Once Laura had had her fill of enjoyable despair she got a firm grip of herself. She reminded herself sternly that she could not, and would not, depend on a man. She had to set her own terms, as a woman. That is what her Parisian grandmother had brought her up to believe. And Mimi undoubtedly knew the meaning of standing firm. Her courage had won her the *Croix de Guerre* for her heroic work in the French Resistance during World War Two. To this day she wore pyjamas patterned with the *Croix de Lorraine*, symbol of the Free French.

What would Mimi say now, Laura wondered. She squeezed up her eyes into creases. If she concentrated hard enough, she could almost hear her grandmother's French-accented voice. 'No man is an island, *ma chérie*. But sometimes a woman must be one.'

Laura wasn't entirely sure what she meant, but it sounded as deep as the loch itself. The thought stiffened her sinews as she contemplated her forthcoming arrival at Glenravish.

Hopefully the castle would be as sumptuous and inviting as it looked on Roddy Ruane's website. And hopefully its mysterious and reclusive Highland laird would be a dashing Caledonian straight out of Walter Scott, not that Laura had ever read any Walter Scott. Had anyone? Perhaps *Fifty Shades of Tartan* was more the sort of thing. Sandy McRavish would be handsome, ripped and high-cheekboned as he made his Hebridean Overture to her Fingal's Cave. She could taste the peaty tang of his skin now, the rough grind of his Harris tweed and the bristling jab of gorse, thistle and heather as they made love in the open Highland air…

There was more to the visit than sex, of course. But it was certainly about love, Laura reflected. Her love for her profession, for her magazine. For her staff, even, whose jobs she had to save along with her own. She had to get the ads and stop Bev casting *Society*, in which she believed so passionately and had put so much of herself, to the outer darkness of online-only publishing.

Could she do it? Advertorials were a whole new world to her; she had, in the past, involved herself only with the magazine's articles and ensuring they were the most interesting, original and news-breaking that could humanly be achieved.

Now she must bend her will and ingenuity to writing a gushing feature about Glenravish; it would no doubt be the first of many. She might well end up writing free puffs for every property on Roddy's list, including the strange modernist box Lulu had gone to look at.

Nor did it stop with the properties, Laura knew. Harriet had gleefully listed all the other things she could write free editorials about in order to encourage advertisers. Stalking weekends, shooting, fishing, sailing and gardening experiences. Whisky-tasting, haggis-tasting, Mars Bar-frying, dressing up like Rod Stewart – there was no element of the Caledonian experience that could not, it seemed, be monetised and make some dollar for Bev Sweet and the shareholders.

'Oh!' Laura gasped, suddenly looking up from the floor at which she had been staring glumly and noticing that the sky outside had changed to molten gold. A spectacular sunset straight off a stately home ceiling was spread over the western sky. It was, she realised, impossible to be depressed in Scotland for long. The place was just too beautiful.

All the same, she wouldn't mind a cup of tea. They'd drunk a huge amount of champagne at Roddy's. Vlad had shot the cork off bottle after bottle; it had been like a gunfight at a particularly *luxe* OK Corral.

The Cristal, Laura recalled with awe, had been delivered in a vast articulated lorry. Her conviction that Harriet was wasting her time fell away at the sight of it; Roddy's business was evidently booming and he obviously had money to burn. He could probably buy the ads she needed all by himself.

Even so, Laura's head now felt tight with dehydration. There was an at-seat trolley service on the train; Fraser had shuffled past some time ago and offered her something called the Cardiac Meal Deal – 'That's a caramel wafer, a full-sugar Irn-Bru and a cold stovie for £11.99.' Laura had no idea what a stovie was and had passed on the offer, a rash act that she now regretted. However, she couldn't be bothered to go and look for Fraser now. He was doubtless at the other end of the train and they'd be at Glenravish soon. Hopefully.

Laura yawned again, slumped against the window and gazed spellbound at the coral pinks and Tiffany blues now taking the place of the gold. Her eyes felt heavy; her eyelids drooped. Soon she was asleep.

In her dream, Caspar rose up from a broad lochside, kilted and glisteningly bare-chested. A large broadsword hung suggestively about his waist. Laura lay back on the downy grass of the shoreline, nipples standing to attention through her clinging medieval robe and arranging one leg suggestively over another.

Caspar approached, sucking his cheeks in and pushing his lips out. She pushed her hair back in response and narrowed her eyes. Hers and Caspar's sexual relationship was admittedly rather on-off, but in this scenario it was definitely the former. He was a very good lover and always had something new to show her. Laura wondered, in this macho Caledonian setting, what it would be this time. She was certainly ready to toss his caber.

But then came the clang of metal on metal. Laura sat up in the grass, her heart racing, and saw the vengeful figure of Harry appear over a nearby hillock. He was wearing full chain mail and a surcoat bearing the red-and-white cross of St George. He looked as if about to set off on the seventh crusade against the distant Infidel. But as he ran, clanking somewhat, towards Caspar it was obvious that his target was rather closer to home.

The two of them squared up: Caspar with his broadsword, plus a dirk just pulled from his socks; Harry with any number of weapons including a halberd, a pike and a spiked mace swinging threateningly from a thick iron chain. Laura gasped. They were fighting for her love!

'Whosoe'er vanquishes the opposant suitor is rightwise entitled to the hand of Dame Laura!' Harry boomed with uncharacteristic cod medievalness.

As they set about each other, Laura had a particularly good view of Caspar's kilt – and possibly up it. She wondered whether the newly enacted 'upskirting' laws applied to men in traditional Highland dress. They were, after all, 'clearly asking for it' with their widely advertised commando policy.

A sudden upward swish of plaid revealed to Laura's horror and disappointment that Caspar was wearing the most disgusting pair of nylon orange Paisley Y-fronts, with white piping adding insult to injury.

A sudden jerk of the train woke her up. Laura felt thirstier than ever, but her longing was for more than just water. Remembering she had been dreaming about Harry, she felt a great rip tide of longing course through her. She ached physically with the pain of missing him and realised that entertaining lustful thoughts about Sandy McRavish was nothing more than bravado.

She wished desperately that Lulu was with her to cheer her up with her very own brand of bonkers billionheiress good sense. But Lulu, of course, would be at Bangers by now. How was she doing, Laura wondered.

Chapter Fifteen

Any guest taking the air that evening at the McBang Estate's groundbreaking modernist hotel would have spotted a bright pink helicopter whizzing towards them. They might then have rubbed their eyes and vowed to go easy on the whisky. On the other hand, a full 'wardrobe' of whisky miniatures from local distilleries was supplied as standard in every Bangers room. So why go easy? Pink helicopters, in addition, were what the landing pad had been built for – helicopters of every and any colour.

But there was no guest taking the air to see Lulu arrive, and the whisky 'wardrobes' remained untouched in most of the rooms for there were no guests at Bangers at all and hadn't been for many months. This was just one of the reasons that Torquil

McBang, new head of Clan McBang, wanted to sell the place.

Torquil, a tall, handsome individual of some forty years and with a full head of still-dark hair, stood before one of the vast smoked-glass windows on the hotel front. His long hands were thrust deep into the pockets of his Dress McBang trews. In the case of most clans, their 'hunting' tartan was a more subdued version of their 'dress' tartan, but in the case of the McBangs it was the other way round. A Victorian McBang, convinced that Scottish wildlife were all colour-blind, had elected to go stalking in acid-yellow and scarlet. The Dress, by contrast, was a merely assertive green and orange.

Watching the pink chopper banking before landing, Torquil hoped that this woman was the answer to his prayers and would take the whole of the wretched estate left to him by his recently deceased father off his hands.

In the opinion of his son, Ruarhi McBang's dream of a cutting-edge contemporary hotel set amid the wild majesty of the Cairngorms had been, not to mince words, a disaster. The only cutting edge round here people were interested in was the knife with which they slit the throats of shot stags. The wild majesty, on the other hand, was real enough. Balmoral was not far away and the Queen had not been best pleased at the destruction of old Castle McBang and its replacement by a trendy hotel.

Torquil conceded that possibly the old Castle McBang, with its romantic turrets and central tower so ancient it seemed part of the rocky landscape, would have made a better hotel. Certainly, it would have better looked the Caledonian baronial part. But the cost of refitting it was astronomical; there had been only one loo and one fireplace in the whole fortress. Temperatures had been sub-zero despite miles of heating pipes that groaned and clanked all night long.

It was to these that the pipes now covering the outside of the new building wittily referred. But they made the place look hideous. As did the flashing main entrance which looked like the set of a TV game show and in fact was. McBang senior, who had the Scotsman's eye for a bargain, had put his hotel together at minimal cost via sales at Dunelm and Next Home, an architectural salvage company located near the BBC Glasgow studios and prefabricated concrete units delivered to nearby Loch Wetty by tanker from Eastern Europe and lowered into place with cranes. Even the expanse of AstroTurf in the clan tartan (Hunting) colours had been a happy accident – an offcut from the private football pitch of an African potentate that McBang senior had found in the depths of eBay.

Lulu, in the helicopter, was looking down in delight. 'Huge pipes!'

'Very big, madam,' Vlad agreed, expertly deploying the Vivienne Westwood joystick.

'Nice and hot inside, hmm? Is what all that on lawn? They have spilt something?'

Vlad answered non-committally. She was not a fan of the countryside, even the smiling, rolling Suffolk sort where Lulu's country house was. And this wild and rocky terrain was anything but rolling and smiling; on the contrary, it was hard and extreme. It had, Vlad allowed, a certain savage grandeur, but she'd had her fill of savage and grand in the Estonian military. She found it hard to believe that Lulu would take to it, either; this place was galaxies from the nearest decent hairdresser's, and as for brow threading, forget it.

Vlad hoped it would not be long before South'n Fried's career was up and running once more and she could return to London. Her mistress's husband was a royal pain in the ass and she felt, as Laura did, that Lulu could have done considerably better for a life partner.

'Ready to land, madam?' the butler asked. There came an answering rattle from the rear. Lulu had given considerable thought to her outfit for the viewing and had decided that understating her charms was not an option. Should other, more attractively dressed potential purchasers suddenly materialise, she might lose out in a beauty contest. Roddy Ruane had given no indication that such purchasers were in the offing – he had made a strange exploding noise when she had asked, in fact, but one never knew.

Accordingly, Lulu was wearing what she felt was the perfect compromise between discreet sexiness and a nod to the historical nature of the estate, if not its main building. Her dress, what there was of it, was fashioned entirely of thin chains gathered in with a spike belt. The chains rattled and clinked gently in the wind as, now, she prepared to descend the Chanel steps on to Bangers' front lawn.

Torquil, watching from behind the window, gasped as a never-ending tanned leg extended itself from the side of the helicopter. The leg ended in four-inch snakeskin and diamante wedge mules, which had struck Lulu as a better bet than heels that just sank in the bog.

Torquil had just been hoping for someone stupid with money. Never in his wildest dreams had he expected someone stupid with money who was beautiful.

In actual fact, Lulu came from a long and successful line of international businessmen into which Florentine bankers, Turkish merchants, Russian traders and American robber barons were all cheerfully and lucratively twisted. The very last thing she was, was stupid – although, of course, it was useful if people thought that.

Torquil was unaware of any of this. Money was all he could think of. The pound signs were fairly blazing from his eyes as he burst through the game-show set and hurried over the zinging AstroTurf to greet his exciting guest.

The tannoy now crackled into action. *'The next station will be Glenravish. Glenravish will be your next station stop. Please take the time to ensure you have all your belongings with you and if you spot something unusual on the train please either report it to a member of the on-train team or text the British Transport Police. Remember, See it. Say it. S—'*

'Shut up,' muttered Laura, who had heard this announcement about a million times now.

A few minutes later she was alone on the pitch-dark platform, her modest tan holdall by her side, watching the illuminated snake that was the train disappearing into the night. It was extremely quiet and she suddenly felt she would give anything to hear Fraser telling her to See it. Say it. Sorted.

But as she got used to the darkness, she realised that the evening was beautiful; pinprick stars scattered about an inky sky and a lemon-peel sliver of a moon reflected in the loch on the other side of the tracks. Laura admired the rippling effect of the light on the water, the gently lapping waves as they reached the pebbled shore. Gradually, she felt a sense of calm.

The air felt fresh and had an agreeable peaty tang, possibly with hints of seaweed. She breathed it in, trying to identify the different elements. Once, researching a feature, she had interviewed a man who made perfumes for a famous couture house. He was known as The Nose, although his actual nose was quite small. The Nose had sat at a desk surrounded by curving shelves of test tubes, all containing different perfume essences. He had looked rather like someone playing an organ, and organ was, in fact, what the desk was called. It had all been fascinating.

You could make a wonderful perfume called 'Scotland', Laura thought. She could detect a honeyed whiff of heather now, and a fresh breath of grass. If she could patent it and direct all the profits to *Society*, her troubles would be over.

As it was, of course, her troubles were anything but, which was why she was here. With the help of the torch on her smartphone, she made her way along the platform in what she hoped was the direction of the Glenravish Estate.

Outside the station was a small, lonely road down which no cars had passed since she had arrived. The absolute lack of traffic noise was almost eerie. All was thick silence apart from the distant hoot of a lonely owl and the occasional scrabble of some small, invisible animal.

Laura was beginning to feel a little uneasy. There was absolutely no sign of life whatsoever. *The World Tonight with Jamie Coomarasamy* could scarcely have ended on Radio 4, yet the area seemed to be in lockdown.

To cheer herself up. Laura thought of the pictures of a magnificent castle reflected in a brilliant-blue loch against a thrilling backdrop of spiky purple mountains in Roddy's brochure. She thought of its chiselled and handsome laird, Sandy McRavish. Her heart began to race and her pace quickened.

She decided that the long wall running alongside the road must be that of the Glenravish Estate. It had an estate-y look about it, with lots of dark trees behind. No doubt they screened from (what passed round here for) the gawking public what would be, in daylight, an enchanting garden.

Laura felt triumphant when, as expected, the wall rose suddenly and became a main entrance. But between the two imposing pillars the pair of scrolled iron gates were shut. She stared at the intricate metalwork, fashioned into the curling shapes of leaves and flowers. The workmanship was astonishing; even so, Laura wondered if she could climb up them, using the metal foliage as steps. But one look at the sharp points ranged across the top made her change her mind. Laura had no wish, as yet, for children, but nor did she want to risk an unscheduled hysterectomy.

She peered after her torch beam up the driveway beyond. There wasn't a light to be seen.

The unearthly owl hoot sounded again, with a scrabble in the undergrowth for good measure. Was there no one around? Laura was beginning to get slightly nervous as to her bed for the night. She prided herself on her ability to sleep anywhere – in the past she had bunked down in *Society*'s fashion cupboard as well as Caspar's frankly disgusting pre-fame flat. But 'anywhere' did not include under the trees in some remote Scottish forest.

She tried to recall how the staying arrangements had been arrived at. They had been handled by Demelza, which probably wasn't the best idea. Laura had been too busy to involve herself with the details – she was doing the Glenravish estate a favour, after all. Now she came to think of it, she vaguely remembered her secretary complaining about mobile phone calls that got cut off, and seeing, waved under her nose, a mangled postcard which looked as if the Hound of the Baskervilles had attempted to eat it before remitting it to the care of the Royal Mail.

Oh dear. Laura traced a line along the estate walls, using her right hand to steady herself against their rough-hewn surfaces as she went along the uneven roadside. She felt more tired and miserable at every step. For once, even thinking of her indomitable grandmother and derring-do father did nothing to screw her courage to the sticking place. Mimi would never be seen dead in the Highlands of Scotland and her father only made her think of Harry, which doubled her unhappiness at a stroke.

Just as she was about to give up and give way to tears, she found a small and unexpected gate in the wall. There was only one problem. It was securely locked with one of those 1970s four-digit combination locks, its chain contained within a rotting, rusting plastic sleeve.

She tried 1234. No. So 4321. No. Then 0000. No. Could it be 9999? No.

Oh, sod it, thought Laura. She didn't have the time to attempt all ten thousand permutations. She would have to scale it in the way that she had heaved herself over the gates of the Jardins du Luxembourg when she was growing up in Paris. This one, at any rate, was mercifully free of the main gate's sharp spikes.

Risking her shins and her trousers, she clambered up and over the gate, using her holdall as a protective cushion as she squeezed through the gap between the top of the wrought-iron bars and the stone arch surmounting them.

Her dignity, jeans and ankle all paid the price of what was now a sudden and unguided descent into the Glenravish grounds. But at least she was in. Game on. Laura stood up, wincing, and flashed her phone torch around her.

There was something unexpected about the look of the gardens. In the dim smartphone glow she could make out huge clumps of bamboo, Oriental gateways, water features with a distinct Far Eastern look about them and beds of raked gravel, into the middle of which she appeared to have landed bum first. Laura flashed the phone light downwards. Two clear cheek prints interrupted the harmonious swirls.

Dropping to her knees, she made a cursory attempt to re-zen the gravel, before limping off up the path.

She crunched on through what seemed at least seven different varieties of bamboo, uncertain that she had not heard a rustle amongst them. The wind in the leaves, she told herself, nervously.

But then a flash of white caught her eye to the left and an astonishing figure leapt into the torch beam of her smartphone, with a yell of 'Banzai!' He seemed to be a fully kitted out Japanese infantryman, one pointing a long rifle with a longer bayonet in the general direction of her midriff.

'Err, *konnichiwa*?' Laura was terrified but also intrigued. She hoped her stab at Japanese would soften the warrior's heart. Or stop him stabbing her at least. She felt vastly relieved when he lowered the rifle, smiled and bowed.

'Welcome to Glenravish. I – Koji. Part of Japanese Gardens. World War Two feature, you see.'

Laura rubbed her face in a gesture that combined relief with incredulity. Perhaps she shouldn't be surprised. Historic gardens were going to increasingly ridiculous lengths to attract attention. Daisy Lovage, *Society*'s gardens editor, had recently suggested a feature on the subject. According to her, the Chelsea Flower Show was the worst offender; the previous year, veteran socialite Champagne D'Vyne had served as a living water feature, a continuous fountain of Krug showering her pneumatic form as she attempted to get as much into her mouth as possible for seven days on the trot.

Meanwhile, artist Zeb Spaw's 'Guantanamo Garden' had a chain gang of gardeners in orange jumpsuits digging the same barren plot for the duration of the show. 'It's like, a metaphor?' Spaw had drawled to the eager arts show journalists. 'Or maybe,' he had gurgled, spotting a pile of gardening implements, 'a metafork.'

As *Society* magazine prided itself on its counter-intuitiveness, Laura had asked Daisy to defend all this horticultural attention-seeking. She pointed out that it had historical precedent. Eighteenth-century estates once hired people to play the part of hermits in grottos, their contracts compelling them not to wash, or cut their hair or nails for that authentic anchorite look.

Laura felt another great wave of mourning for her beloved magazine. The gardens would have been a great piece. On the other hand, it still could be. Koji, wandering round with his rifle in the dark, could feature in it and she could relaunch the whole idea. Exultation swept through Laura as she realised that Harriet's economic imperatives and her own editorial priorities could work in sync after all. At least, where gardens were concerned.

Much cheered, she followed Koji up the garden path. Tomorrow she'd interview him properly. But then, suddenly, all thought of interviews were swept from her mind. As the yews parted, the full splendour of Glenravish Castle was suddenly and dramatically revealed in the limpid moonlight.

Chapter Sixteen

I t was a rambling baronial beast of a building. Conical
towers marked each corner, with, between them,
castellations standing out like teeth against the night
sky. Windows of various sizes and shapes – from arched
to arrow slit – glowed yellow.

The scene evoked in Laura a seamless blend of
the sublime – the castle's dramatic beauty – and the
ridiculous. Perhaps there was more than a little of the
Carry on Screaming about Glenravish. This was no
casual comparison; Laura was an expert on *Carry Ons*.
Mimi's enthusiasm for the film genre starring Sid James,
Joan Sims and Kenneth Williams was almost as great as
for *Dad's Army*.

Koji crunched on across the gravel towards a huge,
iron-studded wooden door. Hanging adjacent to it was

a big iron bell from which a chain helpfully hung. Koji dragged on it mightily, and it responded with all the restraint and understatement of Big Ben. Laura put her hands to her head, literally staggered at the noise.

Once the last metallic crashing had died away, silence rushed into her ears and echoed there almost as loudly. There was a flicker of batwing overhead.

As Koji once again raised his uniformed arm to the bell pull, Laura put a hand on it. Her eyes met his in the faint glow from the windows. 'Can't we just knock?'

Koji nodded and raised his fist. It was about to strike the door when the great wooden portal swung open, creaking violently on its unoiled hinges.

'Halloo?' A sinister bent figure brandishing a candlestick peered out into the night. Laura imagined they made a strange pair, especially with Koji in his historical uniform. Except that, glancing now to the side of her, she saw that Koji was no longer there. He had disappeared without so much as a crunch of gravel. Laura felt a wave of terror, but there were more important matters than the supernatural at stake. She hastened to explain herself to the sinister bent figure. 'I'm sorry to bother you – I'm Laura Lake, from *Society*, I don't know whether you're expecting me…' She tailed hopefully off.

Silence. Either she was not expected or this person was not blessed with the most powerful aural equipment. Dark beady eyes continued to stare at her.

Then, an exclamation. 'Och, Laura Lake! Come in, come in.' The sinister bent figure now straightened and was all smiles. She was not, it turned out, sinister at all, but a friendly little woman with apple cheeks, a neat black dress and silver hair in a stylish but sensible wedge cut. 'Welcome to Glenravish Castle,' she reassuringly continued. 'I'm Mrs MacRae, the hoosekeeper.'

Laura stepped into a seemingly endlessly Gothic stone chamber. It was so high that the ceiling disappeared into the gloom and so long and wide that its furthest reaches could be identified only by the distant gleam of suits of armour. Mounted on the stone walls in circles and other decorative arrangements, was an impressive display of cuirasses, greaves, bascinets, spiked bucklers, swords, daggers and an array of pikes with blades so fearsome they looked capable of taking a man apart from his knave to his chaps in a single deft stroke. After which, doubtless, the victim's disembowelled innards could be hung on the nifty little spike at the end of the shaft.

Laura swallowed nervously. In the centre of the wall, she noticed, was a fireplace big enough to park an articulated lorry in. One as big as the deliverer of Roddy's champagne. The thought of Scotland's most obviously super-successful estate agent stiffened Laura's mettle. She thrust away the last of her apprehension and forced herself to think positive.

Friendly Mrs MacRae was speaking to her, she now realised. Something about trousers. Laura smiled. Perhaps this was a test. Back in Cod's Head Row, Bill and Ben had assured her that it was practically the Scottish national anthem. Laura took a deep breath and began to sing 'Donald, Where's Your Troosers...'

She finished to see Mrs MacRae shaking her head and chuckling. 'Och, ye're a card, Miss Laura!'

There was something familiar about her voice, but Laura could not place it.

'But yes, yoor troosers. What the de'il hae ye done to 'em?'

Laura looked down. She had forgotten about the damaged state of her jeans. A flash of thigh was the most obvious result of the unexpected fashion adjustment resulting from tumbling into the estate. There were some large green stains too.

Mrs MacRae gave her a comforting smile. 'Dinna fash aboot that, lassie. I'm very handy with the needle. We'll get it fixed up for you in no time.'

Laura was about to thank her when a sudden loud crackle and a spark interrupted her. The lights dimmed, went out and relit in a crazed sequence.

'Wh-what was that?'

Mrs MacRae beamed reassuringly. 'Och, that'll just be the ghosties. The electric's no too good with us up here at Glenravish and they like to play their games, so they do.' She gave an indulgent shake of her neat wedge-cut. Laura thought of the suddenly disappearing Koji and swallowed hard.

Her heart was still hammering by the time Mrs MacRae took her to her room.

'Shouldn't I meet Sandy McRavish?' Laura faltered, longing even more than before for the sight of a strong man to protect her. While she was a strong woman with a flourishing career, no hang-ups and bags of self-esteem, there were limits. A spooky castle in the dead of night might well be one of them.

Mrs MacRae turned and smiled. 'Och, plenty of time for that, lassie. Ye'll be wanting a bath first, I'm thinking.'

Laura suddenly imagined being up to her neck in hot scented bubbles. Perhaps the hunky laird could wait after all.

'A bath would be wonderful.'

It seemed to be a long way to her room. The housekeeper led Laura down a series of rush-matted corridors whose plain white walls were lined with stags' heads on wooden shields and prints of shoots and fishing expeditions being undertaken in ample tweeds accompanied by profuse facial hair.

Laura was finding it hard to see the appeal of Highland pursuits. They looked cold, itchy and over-energetic. She couldn't for the life of her see how she was going to sell this to the sybaritic readers of *Society*. Laura thought of the bath to keep her spirits up. A nice cold glass of Sauvignon Blanc on the side would be just the thing, but she didn't quite like to ask.

'Here's your room, lassie.'

Laura had been expecting a smaller version of the Great Hall. Something stony with plenty of military hardware on the walls, and a four-poster bed with scary drapes in the middle. To her surprise, she found herself looking into the dearest, sweetest little room. A deep-silled window was hung with flowered curtains. A cosy, old-school gas fire blazed in the fireplace. A posy of sweet peas stood on the mahogany dressing table along which a delicate lace runner had been spread. The bed, which was thankfully postless and therefore curtainless, looked big and comfortable. It was covered with the sort of pink candlewick bedspread that cost a small fortune in Mrs Keppel's Vintage Linen Emporium. The thought made Laura homesick for a second. Then she reminded herself that she had work to do: a magazine to save, along with a considerable number of jobs.

With Mrs MacRae gone, instructing her to be downstairs for a midnight kitchen supper with Sandy in half an hour, Laura went happily off to inspect the en suite.

Perhaps it was slightly less sweet and dear than the bedroom. The bathtub was vast and ancient but probably just the thing if you had spent all day being soaked on some midge-heaven hillside. And the bathwater was hot and plenteous, even if it was peaty brown, drawn, doubtless out of a nearby tarn. But it was sure to be full of rejuvenating minerals, even so.

The bathside offered a choice of Radox bath salts or Cif. The Cif, Laura imagined, was for the exceptionally dirty and leathery skinned guest after a day of blasting seven bells out of the local wildlife. She opted for the Radox, hoping it would not strip her young skin of all available suppleness and moisture. She was going to need all her youthful glow to impress Sandy.

Drying herself off, Laura strapped herself into the most fetching of the underwear she had brought in her trusty brown holdall. Lacy, French – *mais bien sûr* – and with the naughtiest hint of the dominatrix about it, it reminded her suddenly of Caspar. Was this the sort of ill-fated present he had innocently given Margo, only to invoke the wrath of every woman in Hollywood?

Laura dismissed the thought and imagined Sandy McRavish peeling it off her later. If she felt guilty about Harry, she pushed that thought aside as well. What he didn't know couldn't hurt him. And he had hurt her enough recently, the bastard. Men! Who needed them? Laura fanned the mental flame of resentment. Down with the patriarchy. Time for some equality. Hashtag Times Up.

She completed her *tenue de soirée* with a dab of Chanel No 5 on each wrist – 'no woman is properly dressed without it,' according to Mimi. Then she headed downstairs to meet Sandy McRavish for the kitchen supper.

Minutes later, she was wandering the labyrinth of corridors with a flutter in her belly. This was not just in anticipation of the upcoming encounter with the laird, but because of the renewed flickering of the lights. They were fizzing and crackling again and what felt like cold gusts were inexplicably whiffling down Laura's neck.

Whimpering slightly with terror now, she hunched into the tongue and groove panelling as she approached some small back stairs. These were particularly eerie – the sort of place where dogs cringe and bark and refuse to go. Laura took a deep breath, put her best Chelsea boot forward and picked her way unsteadily downwards in the deepening gloom.

She reminded herself that, as she had lain in the bath and felt the mineral-rich water work its magic on her muscles, she had wondered what would happen if she and Sandy got on particularly well. It wouldn't just be a night to remember in his tartan-draped bed beneath the crossed swords of his ancestors. It could be the start of a whole new life.

Whether or not she fell in love with the laird, she had certainly fallen in love with his surroundings. Until now she had been a city girl – Paris, London – but that, she now suspected, was because she had never seen scenery like this before. It was strangely easy to picture herself retiring to the Highlands. Living in Scotland and seeing the incomparable beauty of the place every day of her life.

After all, what would she be leaving behind? Perhaps she was deluding herself, thinking she could save *Society* and her colleagues. With the advent of Bev Sweet, what professional satisfaction was there left? Only the hope of seeing her plunge past the window, having accidentally fallen from her top-floor office.

Laura pictured herself, married to Sandy, getting involved in the local community: making personal appearances at village events, appearing elegantly in the pages of *Country Life* and speaking on the key issues of the day in Scotland – land reform, sheep farming, alternative energy. She could even enter the House of Lords. Baroness McRavish had an appealing ring to it...

Chapter Seventeen

Lulu was pleasantly surprised by the chief of the clan McBang. She had half-expected some grasping old ghoul but he was handsome, civilised and relatively youthful. She liked his blue velvet jacket and smart white shirt and his directional trousers especially. Possibly he was slightly on the smarmy side; Lulu preferred more attitude. But oleaginous men were two a penny in Lulu's world and she more than knew how to deal with them.

Bangers, too, lived up to her highest expectations. It was extremely hot, for one thing. For another, its decor was daring. Lulu liked to mix things up, interiors-wise, and the mixing up here was clearly the work of a master.

Lulu had now examined every room in the former hotel, from the 'Classic Doubles' scattered with remaindered cushions from Dunelm and discontinued widescreen tellies from Argos, to the suites whose decor had a more exotic provenance.

Chief among these was 'Runrig', a reference, Torquil explained, to the farming practices of dispossessed crofters. Runrig's wallpaper was a repeat-print of eighteenth-century emigration documents and the ropes, glass buoys and ship's wheels in the room were meant to suggest the several months' journey to the New World. The vast rectangular bath in the en suite, meanwhile, was built to the exact floorplan of a former crofter's hut and the suite's sisal carpet and sheepskin rug were meant to evoke an atmosphere of sheep-nibbled grassland. It even had a slate-effect door key.

The theme seemed quite random to Lulu, who was not to know that Ruaridh McBang had acquired the artefacts from a Clearances-themed hotel which, unsurprisingly given its location, had failed and closed within days of opening. This had been a mere few weeks ago, just before his death.

Lulu and Torquil were now in the lounge, whose artfully battered armchairs and aged volumes were, Lulu felt, an inspired contrast with the raw concrete walls on which paintings of dogs dressed up as people were displayed to witty effect. She also liked the bamboo bar and the medieval thrones. South'n Fried would too, she knew. A good throne was something all rappers appreciated. She stroked the wood, smiling.

Torquil immediately spotted an opportunity. 'Did I mention that the thrones aren't included in the sale?' he said lightly.

Lulu, who had been walking off in her jewelled mules, now screeched to a halt and put her hands on her metalled hips. Her sunglasses swung suspiciously round, accompanied by a great swathe of hair.

'Not included in price?' All her dealmaking instincts now came to the fore. 'Roddy told me price was all in, hmm?'

'But it is his assistant Fiona who is handling the sale,' Torquil countered smoothly.

Lulu ignored this. 'One price for all estate,' she insisted steadily. 'Include postbox, ruins. Thrones.'

Torquil wondered just how far he could push this. He could tell this multinational bimbo was interested; also that she was hugely rich. It went without saying that she would be attracted to him; women always were. Foreign ones especially. They could never resist his polished British charm.

He placed a long finger on his handsome jawline. It was beaded with sweat – the heating had gone into overdrive, but amazingly this woman actually seemed to like that too. The new system was as over-hot as the original castle had been over-cold, but with any luck, Torquil thought, the expense and discomfort of it would soon be someone else's responsibility.

In what evening light managed to make it through the smoked-glass windows, his signet ring shone with the crest of the McBangs: a pair of crossed axes (*Banh* meaning 'battle axe' in Old Norse).

'Ah,' Torquil purred, flashing his most winning smile. 'I'm so glad you mentioned the ruins. The postbox is certainly included. But the ruins?' Regretfully he shook his full head of dark shining hair. 'I'm afraid not.'

Lulu's sunglasses flashed indignantly. 'Not ruins? Why not?'

'A relic as venerable as the Scary Tower,' the McBang of McBang went on, 'is for sale separately. Not as part of,' he hesitated before enunciating with a notable *frisson* of disgust, 'a job lot.'

Lulu eyed him balefully through her enormous black lenses. Okay, so he wanted to barter. That suited her. Business had always been done that way in her family, whether it was bargaining for almonds on the medieval *rivas* of Venice or buying an out-there former leisure establishment in twenty-first-century Scotland. She could barter with the best of them.

'Scary Tower?' she demanded.

'Don't worry, it's not haunted.' That would have been extra, Torquil thought to himself.

'Then why called Scary Tower, hmm?'

Torquil, who could be rather patronising, now put a blue-velvet-covered arm around Lulu. 'It's named after my great-great-great-grandmother, Scary Mary McBang. She's the battleaxe on our coat of arms. She was quite insane and locked in the tower for life. Our very own Monster of Glamis. Every grand family needs one.'

Lulu wriggled out of his clutches and stamped hard on his toes with her wedge heels.

'Ow!' yelped McBang.

'Is Scary Tower in sale or no sale!' stormed Lulu.

Torquil gave her his most dazzling smile. 'You're beautiful when you're angry.'

The wedge-heeled foot stamped again. 'I beautiful all the time! Tower part of sale, yes?!'

Beneath his patent pump, embroidered with the McBang axes, Torquil's foot was throbbing. 'Very well. If you insist.'

'I insist!'

They were standing in the hall of Bangers, an expanse of brown carpet into which was woven, at regular intervals, a bright orange letter B. This stood not for the hotel name, as might be supposed, but Butlins. Ruaridh had found it in a skip near Skegness.

A number of glass-topped cases stood about. Torquil's father had bought them for a song from a venerable provincial museum that was being dismantled prior to closing. They held the few McBang relics that Ruaridh hadn't sold off: some painted miniatures of unimpressed-looking people, some mould-spotted pieces of correspondence, a couple of musket balls and flint axe heads. Lulu stared at them, thinking that even if these were in the sale she didn't want them.

A case in the corner now caught her attention. Lulu saw an eyelet. Some satin. A ribbon. She tottered towards it, intrigued. The very last of the sunset was now slanting through the smoked-glass windows. It was falling upon the most fabulous piece of corsetry this side of the Jean-Paul Gaultier catwalk. Madonna would give her eye teeth for it. Lulu would too.

'Is amazeballs!' she exclaimed, running the rest of the way to the case and gazing in wonder. The corset was beautifully made and would, Lulu calculated, be a perfect fit. If she let the laces out to their full extent, that was.

She shuddered as, now, Torquil McBang came up behind her and started caressing the chains on her shoulder. 'Like that, do you, you naughty girl?' the laird murmured approvingly. 'Ow!' he added, as Lulu applied her wedge heels forcibly to his foot again.

She glared at him and nodded at the case. 'What is that?'

'A particularly fine set of vintage corsetry, reputedly belonging to Flora MacDonald,' answered McBang, his face still distorted with pain.

'Flora MacDoughnut!' Lulu exclaimed. That settled it. She had already encountered the famous Scottish heroine once. The fact that Flora MacDonald's underwear was in residence here meant it was Fate.

'My husband related to Flora MacDoughnut, hmm?' she told McBang, proudly.

A condescending smile rippled Torquil's smooth features. 'My dear, who isn't? The Blessed Flora's relations are probably the biggest demographic group in Scotland.'

Lulu was indignant. 'But my husband *really* related, hmm? Professor McPorridge from University of the Highlands and Islands—'

'Oh God, not him again.' Her host groaned. 'If I had a pound for every person…' Seeing Lulu glaring at him, he seemed suddenly to realise that he was midway through a sales negotiation which might now not happen.

Instead, he grinned oleaginously and waved at the case again. 'Flora left them here at the castle after an unexpected night of passion with the 11th Chief of the McBangs. It was shortly after this that she went to rescue Bonnie Prince Charlie, on the run from Butcher Cumberland's avenging Redcoats.'

Lulu nodded absently. Her mind had already slipped from the corset's historical dimension. She was now considering the transformational physical dimension that those brutal-looking whalebones would give her curves. It was always the underwear that made an outfit come alive.

The McBang of McBang seemed to read her mind. 'She was a fine figure of a woman, Flora, by all accounts,' he offered. 'Come to think of it, she was probably exactly your size.'

Got her! Torquil thought, seeing an expression of desperate longing flash across Lulu's sunglasses. The woman was clearly gagging to try the corset on, but he'd make her wait until the contract was signed. In the meantime, there were plenty of diversions.

'Perhaps you'd like to relax in the Sheep Dip?' Torquil suggested.

'Sheep dip?' echoed the outraged Lulu. 'No, I am not wanting to, actually.'

The McBang of McBang smiled. 'A nod to the estate's past, if you'll forgive me. The Sheep Dip is the name of our high-end luxury hotel spa. Turn left by the Las Vegas pinball machines and go downstairs.'

Lulu brightened. This was the first she had heard of the spa which was a definite plus, especially this far north. It wasn't as if you could just pop across the road to the Berkeley, where she usually went for her pampering.

'In the meantime,' Torquil went on smoothly, 'I'll go and instruct the staff to prepare supper. I'll see you in the dining room an hour from now.'

The staff was himself, and supper the local bargain supermarket's finest. But Lulu wasn't to know that. Nor was that strange silent assistant of hers who followed her mistress about with a quizzical expression. The Gromit to Lulu's Wallace, Torquil thought derisively.

Lulu's sunglasses lit up. She had started to feel rather peckish, it was true. 'Is Scottish seafood, hmm?' She loved Scottish cuisine. Salmon, prawns, langoustines, oysters, that delicious fish soup called Cullen skink. The meat was excellent too, especially those wonderful Aberdeen Angus steaks. Beneath the rattling chains of the Jacob Marley, Lulu's stomach started to rumble.

'Seafood and champagne, yes,' confirmed Torquil. The prawns were Madagascan and the smoked salmon Norwegian; the champagne, meanwhile, was prosecco which he'd funnelled back into Dom Perignon bottles. The oldest trick in the book, but one that never failed to work.

While Torquil went happily off to decant the dinner from its packaging and stick it in the microwave, Lulu and Vlad headed for the Sheep Dip.

Chapter Eighteen

Laura, meanwhile, was still looking for the castle kitchen she had been promised supper in. She seemed to have been roaming round and round Glenravish for hours. She been past the tweedy Victorian hunters at least four times, and was beginning to lose all hope.

The lights were still off. They had come on again for about a second, just at the point Laura was getting used to the dark. Now all was pitch black once more.

Now, in some new twist, she found herself in the hall where she had first entered. The wall-mounted weaponry glinted menacingly in the moonlight sliding, sword-like, through the arrow-slit windows. The sight absolutely terrified Laura. Trying to stiffen her sinews made no difference; they were already taut with fear. She stood in the darkness, her heart thumping in her ears.

There now came a loud, Frankenstein-like buzz, followed by a surge of electricity. The lighting, on what must be full power, registered painfully on Laura's eyeballs. After so much darkness it was like looking straight into the sun and when, finally, her vision returned to normal it fell on something entirely unexpected.

Standing against the empty fireplace, below a particularly fearsome arrangement of axes, was a slim, fine-featured woman in her early sixties. Her clothes were striking, to say the least. She wore a blue-and-white striped pie-crust-collar blouse, red needlecord knickerbockers and shiny white plastic pixie boots. Her eyes were ringed with bright blue mascara, two nuclear explosions of blusher were firing on each cheek and she wore lashings of heart-attack white lipstick. Her look was completed by a single string of pearls and a Princess Diana hairdo, hot-tonged at each side into vast blonde wings.

She looked like something from a 1980s costume exhibition at the V & A. But who in the world was it? Laura had expected to meet Sandy McRavish.

'*Hwah hwah hwah,*' the woman brayed, exposing huge white teeth. Her laughter was like a thunderclap. 'The electricity here's a bugger,' she went cheerfully on in tones that were pure Sloane Square. 'It's already killed two electricians who tried to fix it.'

Her speeches were delivered at a continuous and impressive volume and without pause for breath. Laura could only stand and stare.

'Anyway – completely thrilled to see you, darling – Sandy McRavish – lady laird of the estate.' Extended now at Laura was a right hand laden with enough glittering metalwork to fill a window display in Tiffany's, circa 1982.

A great, crashing sensation now filled Laura's head. It was the sound of things sliding into place. '*You're* Sandy McRavish?' she gasped. 'I thought you were a man.'

'No, I'm a woman,' Sandy cheerfully countered. 'A 100 per cent rooting-tooting, copper-bottomed female. Well, not literally copper-bottomed.' She reached behind to smack her cherry needlecord rear. 'But you know what I mean.'

Laura swallowed. This was a setback, no doubt about it. Goodbye to Baroness McRavish. She sighed slightly, thinking of the lovely red velvet and ermine robes. If she wanted to live in Scotland, she would have to find another way. Either that or return to Plan A: rescuing *Society* and the jobs of her staff by writing advertorials about Glenravish.

'I suppose it was the name,' she faltered. 'Sandy McRavish.'

The great hairspray wings nodded. 'Sandy – Alexandra. Back in the early eighties, all us girls in the King's Road had boys' names. We were gender neutral before gender neutral was invented – *hwah hwah hwah.*'

She paused to sigh fondly at the memory of the glory days of nearly forty years ago.

'Good times, great music,' she said, shaking her head but not her hair, which remained rigid. It was obvious to Laura that her hostess was back in the eighties Eden of London SW1. 'The only hair gel was Woolworth's "Country Born", which looked like leftover napalm from the Vietnam War. And no self-respecting chap would go out of the house without three white stripes across his nose like Adam out of the Ants.'

Laura had now come to terms with the fact that sex was definitely off the menu, along with a title and life as lady of the manor. Nonetheless she liked Sandy. She was friendly and immediate and clearly thrilled to have a visitor, which was unquestionably endearing. Life at Glenravish Castle was lonely, Laura guessed.

'Must pick up some booze,' Sandy exclaimed as she led Laura out of the hall. She pushed open a door in the side of the passage and Laura found herself following the needlecord knickerbockers down some dimly lit stairs.

At the bottom, huge arched vaults stretched away into the distance. This place was clearly the business when it came to wine cellarage. A wood-framed thermometer on the wall proclaimed the temperature a perfect thirteen degrees.

Isolated though it was, life here obviously had its compensations. The first section contained oak barrels of undecanted port, sherry and madeira. Enough, as Sandy said, to fuel Wellington and his army during the Peninsula War. Laura wondered whether she thought that particular skirmish had been fought in Scotland. It was hard to tell; Sandy spoke in an endless stream in which fact, fiction and fantasy were gloriously and deafeningly combined.

Sandy led on from Wellington's barrels into a decanting

and tasting area, with an array of oenophile weaponry laid out across an ancient oak table. Laura eyed a sharp-looking cutlass. 'To uncork champagne!' Sandy declared, fishing out a bottle and thwacking its head off with the zeal of a Tower of London axeman. Laura decided not to mention Vlad's patent method. There were too many guns on the wall of the hall and her hostess might decide to give the idea a whirl.

Glass in hand full of riotous bubbles, she was beginning to feel much better. Truly, champagne was a wonderful thing.

Sandy had now brought her to a series of illuminated cabinets displaying the castle's impressive collection of bacchanalian silverware. Beaten trays featured grape-festooned scenes of cavorting putti, leering satyrs and the omnipresent Bacchus himself, looking well pleased with the mayhem he was provoking with the products of the vine. There were also silver goblets of great beauty, each reflecting the aesthetics of their age and most especially the joys of drinking.

'Gorgeous,' Laura muttered to herself.

'Oh, those old things. Used to call them the "tin pots" when the old folks dragged them out for parties. Been in the family for centuries.' In one giant eighties swig, Sandy knocked back the rest of her champagne.

Laura, reminded of Lulu, wondered how she was getting on at Bangers. Without a mobile signal it was impossible to know. Lulu could be terrifyingly efficient, especially combined with Vlad. She had probably bought the whole place and already returned to London.

Sandy's pie-crust collar was disappearing further into the vaults. Laura followed to find, with a sense of awe, that they had arrived at the cellar's pride and joy – its collection of fine wines.

Chalked on the dusty crossbeams above were the names of France's finest grape-producing areas – Bourgogne, Bordeaux, Loire – and some notable vintages – Château d'Yquem, with its ne'er cloying Sauternes sweetness, Domain du Vieux Telegraphe, the big daddy of the Rhône, and, the holy of holies, Petrus, with its curious pre-Renaissance script. The bottles, dark and mysterious, were piled satisfyingly in the respective recesses, gleaming dully in the light of a single dusty bulb.

Laura felt an atavistic surge of pride at these masterful products of the vine, the surest sign of France's fundamental greatness despite its chequered and troubled history. De Gaulle might have cracked that joke about the ungovernability of a country with 246 types of cheeses, but what could be more glorious than a nation with so many hundreds – thousands, maybe – varieties of wine?

A memory from her childhood suddenly returned. She was in Chez Ginette, the bar downstairs from her grandmother Mimi's Montmartre flat. It was a simple place made yet more simple by the fact its decor hadn't changed for fifty years and maybe not even before that. And yet it was in here that Laura had learnt so many important lessons. Quite literally, as Chez Ginette had often been where she had done her homework, tucked away in the corner at one of the little wooden tables. But she had discovered other things here too, things that had stood her in good stead ever since.

She closed her eyes, calling up every detail. A zinc bar, with unsteady wooden high stools. A mirrored wall behind it, sectioned in squares, creating odd-angled snapshots of the interior opposite, which habitually confused and dazzled committed drinkers. Above, football pennants so faded one could no longer see what the teams were hung from a ceiling brown with nicotine and age.

Mimi was a close friend of *la patronne*, Ginette, a woman never without a tea towel on her shoulder, a pair of clacking white mules and a plain blue dress accessorised by glasses which swung on a chain of orange plastic links. Also ever-present was Ernest, an elderly working transvestite with dyed blond hair, a moth-eaten fur coat, bright pink blusher and outsize high heels. His legs, in fishnet tights, were planted wide apart on the ground, huge hands clamped on his pastis, as he urged her, on the subject of wine: *'Faut pas boire l'etiquette!'*

'Never drink the label!'

Under Ernest's careful tuition (by dint of nipping drops from the bottles that stood in circular retainers in a stainless-steel counter behind the bar) Laura had learnt how to taste wine for what it was, and to cut through the snobbery that surrounds it.

It was thus, in this humble Paris bar, rather than any fancy sommelier course, that she had learnt to recognise grape varieties, grow familiar with the regions of France, understand how a modest Vin de Pays or VDQS could – sometimes – match an AOC or a Grand Cru.

Ernest would have fallen right off his outsize high heels to see all this, Laura was thinking as she watched Sandy gather up an armful of bottles. 'Now – supper!' she announced, and led the two of them back upstairs.

Chapter Nineteen

Lulu and Vlad sat in the steam room of the Sheep Dip. It was all hot, misty and swirling.

Low, mystical, Enya-esque wailing filled the air, along with a pleasant scent of pine. Three huge stone bowls of steaming water stood on pedestals down the centre of the room, which was ancient and vaulted; the original foundations of the demolished Castle McBang, in fact.

Not that the former medieval denizens would have recognised it now, had they been able to make it out through the vapour. Pine benches ran down either side, and braziers of hot coals stood in each corner, with a wooden bucket and ladle on hand for raising further steam. The walls were indented with a series of niches, each with saloon-style wooden doors.

Staring at the damp stone floor, Lulu wondered what the sticky reddish stain was. She'd have that blast-cleaned when she took possession. And even allowing for her sunglasses, it was murky down here. Some good downward spots would sort that out, though.

But above and below her plans for improvement, her mind ran constantly on the splendours of Flora MacDonald's corsets upstairs. They were perfect. She had to have them. Vintage was so in, and if South'n could see her sporting the majestic underwear of his fabled ancestress…

Lulu's eyes suddenly misted over. Their marriage had being going through tough times of late. But here was something to bring them back together. As tightly as possible, until the last breath was squeezed out, in fact. She wondered if the cabinet Torquil had shown her was locked.

Meanwhile Vlad, impeccable as ever in a snowy white towel, was going through the finer points of the sale. She had a tablet to hand and, in between wiping the steam off it, was insisting on listing every last thing Lulu thought she was buying. In Vlad's view, Torquil McBang was far too slippery to leave anything to chance.

'As I understand it, madam wishes to purchase the estate, comprising the land, the fishing rights.'

'On spot,' nodded Lulu.

'The restaurant lavatories, including paper and soap. All the lightbulbs. The website address McBang.com. The @Banger Twitter handle. The postbox. The phone box. The bothies. The Wee Cripple pub.'

Lulu tried to concentrate. This would all have to be

gone through when she met Torquil over dinner, but her mind kept slipping off to reconsider the perfect stitching, the precise placement of the hooks and eyes. Flora's corset was exactly her size. It wouldn't hurt to try it on. See what it looked like. Feel what it felt like. For one teeny-tiny, weeny-winy minute...

Vlad cleared her throat gently but firmly. 'The mountains.'

With a reluctant sigh, Lulu brought herself back from Flora MacDonald's underwear. 'Oh yes. The mountains.'

'The famous McBang's Tables,' Vlad went on. 'So-called because of their flat tops. They will, if I may say so, make a magnificent backdrop to the estate. Another consideration is that, as few other rock stars appearing at the Land of the Purple Haze actually own their own mountains, they give you the edge, as it were. In more ways than one.' Vlad permitted herself a modest smile at the joke.

She was hurt when Lulu did not respond – she usually roared with laughter at her factotum's rare witticisms. Vlad was alarmed to look up and see that her mistress was gone. In the gloomy distance, the exit to the hotel's reception was swinging open.

Vlad remained where she was. It had been a long time since she had enjoyed a proper steam and it was good to relax. This Scottish trip had been hectic. She shifted herself slightly on the stone seat and stared, as Lulu had, at the stain on the floor. It looked exactly like fresh blood to her, but of course it couldn't be. Neither she nor Lulu had injured themselves.

Vlad was a phlegmatic, pragmatic character and not given to flights of fancy. Even so, as she stared at the crimson puddle, the memory came back to her of what Torquil McBang had said about his ancestress Scary Mary. Bangers might be crazy and modern in appearance but it had been built on the site of an ancient fortress which, like all ancient fortresses, had its secrets.

And hadn't he mentioned that the room in which she sat was the very oldest part of the castle? As the rest of the place had been demolished, it followed that all the memories the vanished rooms had once held had come down here. The Sheep Dip, in other words, was a distillation of the castle's history. No wonder it had such a powerful atmosphere. Vlad could sense it, despite the equally powerful smell of pine. If she closed her eyes and concentrated, she could almost hear it.

The butler breathed in deeply: atmosphere, pine essence and history all at once. And sound, yes. She was almost certain she could hear something. Voices coming to her down the centuries. Transmitting themselves through the ether of the years. Calling from the distant past.

Vlad opened her eyes and frowned. She could definitely hear voices echoing and faraway.

But were they from the distant past? They sounded as if they might actually be from the present; from the here and now.

Perhaps it was Torquil and Lulu, but Vlad didn't think so. It was coming from the wrong direction for a start. They were upstairs, in the hotel, whereas the voices seemed to be coming from somewhere beneath her.

Vlad hurried to the bench where she had placed her butler's uniform, the black tie neatly positioned on top, and quickly put it back on. Then she walked carefully around the room, trying to detect where in the ancient stone chamber the voices were the strongest. There were four niches fitted with louvred corral doors and she paused at each one. Three of them were silent; obviously just changing rooms fitted with a bench and a wall of lockers. But in the fourth, echoes could certainly be heard. Desperate echoes, as if lost souls were imprisoned in some long-forgotten dungeon.

Vlad narrowed her eyes. Thanks – if that was the word – to her East European military career, she had had a certain amount of experience of lost souls and long-forgotten dungeons. If she could find these and get them out, she would. She stood to attention briefly in memory of departed comrades, then pushed open the louvred doors.

Seconds later she had placed experienced hands on the lockers, felt about a bit and pressed. There was a click, then the entire wall of lockers swung away to expose the entrance to a passage. A cold, old smell, full of darkness, dust and age came rushing up at her.

The wailings were much louder now. In the impenetrable black they sounded ethereal and ghastly. Whoever – or whatever – it was, was down there. Vlad squared her shoulders, raised her chin, felt in her pocket for her Estonian Army knife-cum-torch, then set off into the dark.

Meanwhile, in the hotel lobby, Lulu too sensed a click beneath her fingers. She had definitely felt the lock give.

A deft jiggle of an unbent hairpin was all she now needed to do to release it completely.

There. She opened the cabinet's glass door and reverently picked up the pink satin-covered whalebone from where it lay amid a jumble of ivory chess pieces and brooches with people's hair in.

Lulu shrugged off the Jacob Marley and stood briefly naked in the moonlight streaming through the modernist front windows. She stood for a moment with her eyes closed, relishing the pulsing warmth of the heating playing about her bare skin. Then she took the corset and set to work. A few tweaks later, she was trussed up in Flora McDonald's finest. It fitted her like a glove, encasing her curves in a satin caress.

Lulu reverently stroked its silken sides. Truly, like the decor of the hotel surrounding it, it was the work of a master. Flora MacDonald might be a historical heroine, risking her life for Bonnie Prince Charlie and all that, blah blah blah, but what Lulu really admired about her was her eye for a top piece of underwiring.

She twirled into the lounge bar, where earlier she had spotted a full-length mirror near the thrones. Lulu admired herself full-frontal and side-on, tossing her hair and admiring the way the ensemble projected her assets to the fullest possible extent. She wished South'n Fried could see her now. He'd be crazy with lust. He loved her in complex underwear.

In a minute she would take it back. But not yet. The fit was marvellous, the details superb. It seemed to be cut especially low so a tiny smidgeon of nipple could be seen. What a minx Flora MacDonald was, to be sure…

A footstep. Someone was coming in. Torquil, presumably. He would not be happy to see her wearing the family treasure, Lulu thought.

On the other hand, she was buying this place and the corsets would certainly be part of the deal. If asked to explain herself by an indignant laird she would simply cite the 'try before you buy' maxim.

Whoever had come in did not sound like Torquil, however. His patent crested pumps had clicked on the concrete floors, whereas what she could hear now was a slithering sound. A sinister slithering sound.

Was it, Lulu wondered, the ghost of Scary Mary McBang, Torquil's tortured and imprisoned ancestor? Her heart leapt in terror beneath the satin, but then, quite suddenly it calmed down again. Lulu realised, rather to her amazement, that she was not afraid in the least.

Perhaps Flora's corsets yet contained some of the Jacobite heroine's legendary courage. She glanced down at them; they seemed to be gleaming with a strange power. Magic underwear? Lulu had several pairs of knickers of this name, which claimed to pull you in where needed. But none of them seemed as truly magic as these corsets. She had the sense that, while she was wearing them, nothing could harm her, rather like King Arthur when he was holding Excalibur.

The slithering sound got closer. She could hear breathing now, as well. Any moment whatever it was would show itself. Lulu raised her chin. She was ready.

Chapter Twenty

'*Sisters... Are Doin' It For Themselves!*'

Deafening and distorted, one of Sandy McRavish's Memorex C90 mixtapes burst into proto-feminist life through the medium of a vast vintage ghetto blaster, the sort which would fetch a tidy sum at a hipster upcycling shop in Hoxton.

Laura stared at it. With its silvered plastic and go-louder design, it struck an odd note in a dining room straight out of a Hammer Horror film.

A long wooden table, made of a single vast plank from what must have been a tree of prehistoric hugeness, stretched away like the M1. An M1 spattered in wax from two vast candelabras, each fashioned from a mighty pair of stag's antlers. Their points were tipped with silver holders for the tapers which provided the only light in the room. In the gloaming, Sandy's heart-attack lipstick glowed ethereally, along with the faint gleam of her archetypally Sloaney single string of pearls.

A series of dimly visible portraits of McRavish chiefs of yore adorned the stone walls, their eyes seemingly fixed on the diner. It was easy to see why Sandy shouted so much. You needed to, to make yourself heard across the vast wastes. Sandy was at the table's head and Laura at its foot. Between them rolled miles of wood and for a certain distance, miles of cutlery. At least six different forks, and a matching number of knives, made up Laura's place setting, along with a crowd of glassware.

As the ever-smiling Mrs MacRae materialised suddenly out of the darkness, Laura jumped. The housekeeper gave her a reassuring look as she lowered a Meissen tureen and said something Laura didn't understand. 'Venison stew with what?'

'Och, mashed neeps and champit tatties,' replied the housekeeper cheerfully.

Oh, turnips and potatoes. Just what she needed to soak up all the booze.

After Mrs MacRae discreetly made herself scarce, Laura discovered that sustained conversation with Sandy had challenges other than physical distance. There was a time-delay factor too. It seemed that the lady laird had not been following the news from 'down south' (i.e. the rest of the world) since the era reflected in her clothes choices. Sandy, in other words, was completely ignorant of any event since the mid-eighties. It was like talking to a Sloane Ranger version of Rip Van Winkle.

'What do you mean, the fall of the Wall?' Sandy said at one point. 'What wall?'

She was shocked to hear that Checkpoint Charlie was no more. Home deliveries by Waitrose were an additional revelation, and Sandy had no idea who Meghan Markle was.

'What does Diana think of her?' she wanted to know.

Laura paused. In the opening rounds of their conversation she had taken great care not to mention either that Duran Duran had split up nor Princess Diana was deceased. She had feared that the dread news regarding both eighties icons might be too much for Sandy to handle. Especially given she was three-quarters of a fine Gewurztraminer to the good.

'Everyone says she's a breath of fresh air,' Laura said eventually, hoping that Sandy would assume the former Princess of Wales was one of the 'everyone'. Fortunately Sandy had now moved on and was reminiscing about rag-rolling courses at the Inchbald. Laura had no idea what she was talking about. Hairdressing? Dancing? But there were other more important issues to discuss.

'Why is the phone line so bad?' she asked. 'And why don't you have any radio reception?' If cables could be laid under the oceans and satellites revolve in space, surely it wasn't beyond the wit of man to stick a mast up in Glenravish?

'Yes, but the masts always fall down,' Sandy explained earnestly as a smiling Mrs MacRae placed the pudding before them. 'It's the ground, you see. It's either too boggy or too hard, I can't remember.'

'Och, it's both,' said the housekeeper comfortably. She had returned without Laura noticing; admittedly, given the crepuscular conditions, this was not difficult. She was smilingly shaking her head as if this separation from modern communication was a mild inconvenience and not a life-changing disaster that had left Sandy marooned in the age of Wham!

Not that Sandy seemed to mind especially. She was now bopping in front of the ancestral fireplace to 'Wake Me Up Before You Go-Go'.

Finally, as their silver forks lay beside the remains of Mrs MacRae's summer pudding, a dish Laura had never seen the point of and regarded as more punishment than dessert, Sandy got on to her own story.

Her tale was punctuated by bursts of music from the cassette player, her favourites of which would cause her to crease up her eyes, throw her arms out, click her fingers to the beat and jiggle her shoulders from side to side.

'*Girls on film*,' Sandy was singing.

They were well into the first bottle of Saint Bris, which, having been stored in the cellar's cool, was the perfect temperature for immediate, rapid quaffing.

'So, Daddy popped his clogs bless him – he's buried in the cellar, in fact.'

Laura now remembered, in the gloom of one of the vaults, the outline of a sarcophagus straight out of the final scene of *Romeo and Juliet*. So that was who it was.

'It was in 1984, height of that ghastly miners' strike,' Sandy sighed.

'I'm sorry to hear that,' Laura said politely.

Sandy looked at her, a rueful flash of clogged blue Dior mascara. 'So was I. I had to up sticks PDQ. Get out of Chelsea and hit the Highlands.'

'Oh dear,' said Laura, beginning to see where this was going. After the wild times Sandy had referred to, this must have been a culture shock.

Right on cue, Culture Club came wailing out of the ghetto blaster. 'Do You Really Want To Hurt Me?' sang Boy George. Sandy blinked back a tear, then continued.

'Didn't have a bean to my name. Plenty of assets, yah – but no cash to speak of. No job, either. I'd been training as a pot-banger; learning how to make my own mayonnaise and *beurre blanc* at Prue Leith's cookery school.'

Laura thought about her own cookery school, where she had learnt to make those two same staples of French cuisine. Her grandmother's tiny Paris kitchen. 'And I was teeing myself up to marry some rich and dreary banker or dismal but loaded captain of industry,' Sandy continued.

'How awful,' said Laura, thinking how objectionably mercenary and surrendered-woman this was. Then she remembered, guiltily, that she had been teeing herself up to do the same thing when she thought Sandy was a man.

'Yah. Rather glad I didn't, really. They were all sexist pigs. It really was the effing stone age. Massive mobile phones, massive egos and small penises. Sex was like having a wardrobe with a small key sticking out fall on you. Hated that.'

Laura was working out quite how to reply to this when The Human League came on and saved her the effort. 'Don't You Want Me…'

By the time the song had finished, and Sandy had stopped dancing around, Laura had worked out how long ago the wardrobe with the key had last fallen. 'But that was...'

'Yah, nearly forty years ago. Tell me about it. Things haven't exactly gone to plan.'

Gary Numan was now singing about cars. From her position at the head of the table, Sandy shot the ghetto blaster a look.

'Yah, and thanks for the reminder, Gary. About cars. Because that's another thing. You see, I don't drive, so I'm stuck here and I never get out. That, and the rubbish radio reception, is why I live in a time warp.'

'You never get out?'

A blaze of exasperated blue mascara was her reward for this. 'Well, how can I?' demanded Sandy. 'There's no way to get around except cadging lifts in the post van. Or that sodding train – and you know what that's like.'

Laura looked at her musingly. Up until now she had thought Sandy rather ridiculous, an eighties eccentric who, along with the themed-gardens article, would make another great piece about Glenravish. She had even started to plan the pictures: Sandy in a variety of outlandish outfits from forty years ago, perhaps with sidebars about How To Look Eighties, Great Eighties Icons and Fashion Labels We Have Loved And Lost. But now, listening to Sandy lament her disappointments and frustrations, always with a top layer of spirit and self-deprecating humour, Laura found herself thinking that to use her in this way would be unfair.

Sandy might be OTT, but there was something indomitable and admirable about her. She might be a period piece, set in finest Prue Leith aspic, but she retained the principled defiance of a more rigorous age before all the crap on social media and the internet. She was solid and real, with emotional depth, and a true backstory.

Unaware of her companion's guilty cogitations, Sandy was unsteadily uncorking the Petrus. Laura watched nervously as a however-many-hundred-quid-a-bottle slipped and slid between her hands. 'I mean,' she went on, 'I've tried to get this place off the ground as a business. But frankly, given the gene pool around here, you've got as much chance of opening a branch of Harrods as turning this pile of cold stones into a tourist attraction. It drives me mad.'

Coincidentally, Spandau Ballet frontman Tony Hadley was now bawling about losing his mind, 'To Cut A Long Story Short' being the latest hit offering from the ghetto blaster.

Sandy's white lipsticked lips were quivering as she sloshed the Petrus into their glasses, filling them up to the top. 'I miss London like mad,' she burst out, although Laura hardly needed to hear it. Longing for the capital radiated from Sandy's every pore.

Her hostess took a big slug of the legendary wine. 'I was having so much fun in SW3. The 22 bus, the Admiral Cod pub, a small flat-ette furnished entirely from the GTC. My every move recorded in *The Official Sloane Ranger Handbook*.'

Laura held back from telling her that the General Trading Company was long since closed and that the once-indispensable compendium of eighties upper-class tropes was now mostly to be found in charity shops. She was starting to feel very protective towards Sandy.

Sandy shook a head of hair solid with Supreme Hold hairspray. 'I swear Peter York copied it all from me and my Chelsea set's lifestyle. Happy days...'

Laura put a sympathetic hand on her arm, but missed and almost knocked the precious bottle over. Fortunately, with unexpected lightning reflexes, Sandy saved it in time. 'Oh God!' she exclaimed.

'Sorry,' said Laura.

'Not the wine! This dump! I'd just love to sell it and get back to Chelsea. Get back to where the action is. The nightclubs, the dinner parties, the pubs. But the market's just not right, you see.'

Laura was puzzled. Glenravish was with Roddy Ruane, who she had seen with her own eyes to be the most successful estate agent on the planet. He had produced a tempting brochure; tempting enough, out of all the castles for sale in Scotland, to have caught Harriet's eye. Which was why she was here.

'Don't you get many viewers?' she asked.

Sandy took another swig. 'We get loads,' she said, unexpectedly.

Laura brightened. 'But isn't that good?'

The hairspray wings juddered with the force of Sandy's headshake. 'Roddy rings up all the time – when the phone's working, that is – and tells us someone's coming.

But then for some reason they all change their mind and never show. I suppose,' Sandy concluded, 'they take a closer look at the brochure and realise the upkeep's just too much for them. Which it is, frankly. It's all I can do to keep the garden going.'

'Or maybe they've heard about the ghosts,' Laura suggested. She wasn't trying to be unhelpful. On the contrary, her ever-fertile editor's mind had been considering how they could be turned into a plus. People liked being scared these days, all those tense TV dramas with heavy breathing and lots of guns. And that whole 'escape room' craze. You never knew, Glenravish might even attract the *Most Haunted* brigade.

'What's that, my dear?' Sandy was sloshing more Petrus into their glasses. 'Can't hear over the noise of this wine. Haunted? Don't be so silly. Never seen a ghost in my life.'

'Really?' It was on the tip of Laura's tongue to say that Mrs MacRae had told her all about them. But this might both upset Sandy and get the kindly housekeeper into trouble. On balance, Laura decided, it was best not to dob her in.

The lady laird was raising her glass. 'Like I said, a few problems with cold draughts and the electrics, that's all.'

'And the telephone poles that won't stand up,' Laura put in.

'Those too,' Sandy cheerfully acknowledged. 'And the wind and light can play tricks on your eyes after a couple of glasses of the finest. But haunted? Not at all.'

The 'ghosts question' was clearly ticklish. Laura supposed she couldn't blame her. Sandy wanted to sell Glenravish, and while she was pleased to have help with publicity, that did not mean she was ready to spill all the old place's secrets. They had only just met, after all.

Sandy was now back in eighties London. 'Can't wait to see a Wimpy again. Always liked a Big Bender at the end of a heavy night.'

Laura had a feeling that a Wimpy was a long-defunct chain of snack bars. She could not imagine what a Big Bender was.

'But at this rate,' Sandy added gloomily, 'I won't get to the smoke before Chas and Di become King and Queen. Enough to shatter one's thumper, it really is.' She put a hand over her heart.

Laura hastened to reassure her that she really wasn't missing much. Compared to the glories of the Highlands, the capital was tame stuff indeed.

'Believe me, Sandy, London's changed. It's full of people charging down the pavements, looking into their smartphones and pulling suitcases on wheels, which run over everyone else's toes.'

Sandy looked puzzled. She had never seen a smartphone or a detonator suitcase. It was like explaining things to an alien. Laura plunged on, even so. 'And they all expect you to get out of their way. Every second shop's a hipster coffee bar. All the men have beards. Brexit's torn us apart. Knife crime's off the dial. The streets are littered with poor homeless people out of their heads on Black Mamba. Notting Hill's full of Russian oligarchs building mega-basements and Knightsbridge is packed with Middle Eastern rich kids doing handbrake turns in gold Maseratis.'

Sandy was looking doubtful. Laura wondered if she knew what an oligarch was, even. 'But what about the centre of town?'

'The same. But full of the French and Chinese tourists and students. It's lost its rebellious soul. And, Sandy,' Laura adding the *coup de grâce*, '*no one, but no one has dinner parties any more.*'

Out of the entire catalogue of mayhem just laid before her, this was clearly the last straw. Sandy's blue-mascaraed eyes widened with horror. I've done it, Laura was thinking, when Sandy took another swig of Petrus and put it down looking altogether more philosophical.

'All the same, I'd rather be there than here. God knows how I'm ever going to get away, though. I'm never going to be able to sell this place.' The white-lipsticked mouth turned despairingly downward.

'But that's why I've come,' Laura reminded her.

The blue-mascaraed eyes widened in surprise. 'Is it? I must say, I did rather wonder. But I was so bloody glad of the company, I didn't ask.'

Laura stared. 'You didn't know I'd been sent by Roddy Ruane? To write a magazine feature?'

'Nope.' Sandy shrugged the shoulders of her pie-crust-collar blouse. 'But you looked like a nice gel. A magazine, eh? How exciting. Is it *The Face*? *The Illustrated London News*?'

Laura hadn't heard of either title. She was thinking. 'If you weren't expecting me, that explains why the gates were all locked.'

'*Were* they? They never are usually.'

'And why Koji was roaming about with his gun.'

'*Who?*'

Laura shook her head. It was all too much to explain, especially after so much wine. They could talk about it in the morning. She thought longingly of the cosy little room. Bed would be lovely.

The lights dimmed again. Sandy stood up, swaying slightly in her red needlecord knickerbockers. 'C'mon, girl. Enough of this moping. Let me show you around the place. Show you what you can write about.'

She yanked Laura to her feet – rather too fast it turned out. The room swam about her for a second. She held on to Sandy, who was giggling helplessly. Laura, not usually a giggler, nonetheless found herself joining in. She was pleasantly conscious of having made a new friend. A friend, moreover, with whom she had something in common. She and Sandy both had a problem: in Sandy's case, it was the Glenravish Estate and in Laura's it was *Society* magazine. If they combined forces, it all might work out fine.

'Sisters Are Doin' It For Themselves' blared out of the ghetto blaster as they left the kitchen. The tape had come to an end and had started all over again.

Chapter Twenty-one

I t had all been over very quickly. A couple of ju-jitsu
moves was all it had taken for Lulu to grasp the wrist
of the slithering creature, pitch it forward and throw
it face down on the Butlins carpet.

'I say,' said Torquil, when he had recovered the power
of speech. 'Was that entirely necessary?'

He lay on the floor in his full McBang regalia. The
slithering sound that Lulu had heard were the extra-long
badger tails on his sporran. Now, with her trusty wedge-
heel pressed down on his solar plexus, she blinked in the
full dazzle of the ultra-bright McBang kilt tartan, and
also the full dazzle of the chief's impressive meat and
two veg, which gravity and the force of his descent had
brought into full view.

'Would you mind awfully taking your foot off me?'

Torquil asked in hurt tones. 'I was only coming to escort you to dinner.'

Lulu inclined her head graciously. She had no intention of apologising. She and Torquil were engaged in a negotiation and if she conceded anything it could cost her another couple of cottages.

Torquil, rising gracefully to his feet in a single fluid movement, noted the determined glint of her sunglasses. He was beginning to suspect that Lulu, for all her bimbo appearance, was not quite as stupid as she looked. He would, the laird realised, have to turn up his legendary charm to the max.

He'd schmooze her over dinner. She looked like a woman who appreciated good food. 'Shall we?' Torquil purred, extending a signet-ringed hand and leading Lulu into the Bangers dining room.

This had been furnished from the remnants of a failed insurance firm and had a distinctly corporate feel, all the more as Ruaridh had bought the strip lights as well. They shone brightly down on the display of bargain seafood Torquil had arranged on gold plastic plates. Unpacking it, he had found the mussels and squid rings vastly outnumbered the prawns, as did the whelks. But hopefully Lulu liked whelks. Exotic types like her often had unexpected tastes.

'Very funny,' Lulu said appreciatively, sitting at one of the office chairs at the long black ash table.

'Yes, we call the dining room The Boardroom,' her host smiled. 'People find it most amusing.'

'Don't mean room, mean food. Is very funny.' Lulu's

sunglasses caught the full glare of the overhead tubes. They hit the back of Torquil's retinas like an interrogation spotlight. 'Prawns from Madagascar and is not Scottish salmon either.'

Torquil felt his well-honed jaw part company with the rest of his mouth and drop downwards. He had not bargained for the company of a seafood version of 'The Princess and the Pea'.

Lulu, meanwhile, waved dismissively at the spread. 'So where is real dinner, hmm?'

The cornered clan chief seized the bottle of Dom Perignon into which he had decanted the bargain supermarket fizz. 'Dom?' he asked urbanely, pouring the sparkling liquid into a glass. Lulu smiled graciously and extended her hand. Bingo, thought Torquil, triumphantly.

A shrill beeping noise was filling the air, reminiscent of a smoke alarm. Lulu sprang up from her seat and backed away, pointing an accusing finger at the flute.

'What's the matter?' asked the bewildered McBang of McBang. 'What's that awful noise?'

'Is prosecco alarm,' Lulu informed him haughtily. 'My friend Laura give it to me. Detect when not being given real champagne.' The sunglasses nodded damningly at the bottle in Torquil's other hand.

The clan chief groaned inwardly. To use a famous phrase, here was a bloody difficult woman. But the game wasn't over yet and at least that unnerving Gromit-like assistant seemed to have temporarily quit the field. Hopefully she wouldn't return any time soon.

*

It certainly didn't look as if Vlad would. At the moment she was trapped in the passageway behind the Sheep Dip changing rooms. Seconds after she had gone in, the lockers had swung back into place. There was a sickening click, and everything went dark. For the past few minutes, the butler had been pushing hard at the wall. Even her best Estonian infantry methods were having no effect.

Giving the recalcitrant barrier a final shove with the flats of her feet, Vlad decided that, as she could not go back, she may as well go forward. Thanks to her rigorous training, not to mention one or two equally rigorous life experiences, there was little she could not manage in the darkness. She walked carefully forwards, feeling one foot in front of the other, and sensed that the passage was working its way downwards in a spiralling incline, deeper and deeper into the bowels of what had once been the ancient castle of McBang.

This, above all else, proved how old the place was, the butler thought. Really old fortresses, not just in Britain but all over Europe, had just such tunnels as this, to be used as escape routes in times of difficulty. Vlad made a mental note to add it to the list of Lulu's estate acquisitions. It would be just like McBang to keep back the escape tunnel and subsequently attempt to charge a fortune for it.

The terrible cries and groans that had drawn her into the passage in the first place had stopped with the sound of the locker-wall swinging shut. Vlad hoped that she had imagined them, although she never imagined anything as a rule. She kept moving forward, feeling her way along the rough damp stone of the passage walls. She could see, at the end of a long stretch of blackness, a dim light. Daylight? Electric light? It was hard to tell.

She could feel a change in temperature – and atmosphere. The sense of misery was almost palpable. Vlad guessed that she was nearing the castle dungeons, the dread prison cells cut into the living rock where unfortunates had been incarcerated for hundreds of years. Another thing McBang might try and charge extra for. Vlad made another mental note.

A terrible groan now filled the passage and caused her heart, as it rarely did, to shoot up her throat. The groan was followed by a terrible chorus of muffled cries and moans. Vlad was not easily rattled, but the idea that these were the miserable spirits of the long-departed was not easily dismissed.

She approached, cautiously, her soles crunching on the stone floor of the passage. In response, it seemed, to her steps, what now sounded like agonised pleas for release got louder.

Her heart seemed to stop beneath her frock coat – still impeccable despite its travails – as, in the faint light afforded by a rough hole in the deep-set wall, she saw the outlines of prison bars. Clinging desperately on to them were four wasted-looking hands.

Scary Mary? Perhaps this was the base of what once had been her tower. Had she actually had four arms? wondered Vlad.

*

Lulu had resigned herself to the frozen bargain prawns by now and had turned off the prosecco alarm. There was a job to do here and the quality of the food was irrelevant. In actual fact, the prawns had a good flavour and the wine was quite acceptable.

Lulu took another swig and applied herself to the business in hand, which was to buy the McBang estate for a reasonable amount. But POA – Price on Application – had proved a slippery concept to say the least. The quote that Roddy Ruane had given her was different from the higher one subsequently emailed to her by the mysterious Fiona who Lulu did not recall being present in the office when she and Laura visited. Torquil McBang's demands were more exorbitant still.

And yet, Lulu was determined to buy it. Mountains, lochs and all. As Vlad had pointed out, McBang's Tables would provide an excellent cover for South'n Fried's new album.

As Vlad had pointed out...

Where *was* Vlad, Lulu wondered, looking round. Surely she couldn't still be in the spa? It wasn't like her to lounge about in towels when her help was needed.

She forced a bright smile and applied herself to the microwaved soup McBang had just produced. 'Is sullen stink,' she remarked, slipping her spoon into the yellow liquid.

'Actually, it's Cullen skink,' McBang corrected, offended.

Lulu tossed back her pile of blonde hair. 'Is what I say, hmm? Made with smoker's haddock.'

'Smoked fish and cream,' McBang confirmed. 'An old McBang family recipe.'

Behind the opaque lenses of her sunglasses, Lulu rolled her eyes. Even she knew that Cullen skink was a Scottish speciality no more the preserve of the McBangs than croissants were the preserve of Laura's French granny. She decided to go along with it, however. Best to keep on his good side. After the ju-jitsu, she had some ground to make up.

It didn't look as if she was going to have much trouble. McBang's eyes, fuelled by prosecco, were out on stalks. Lulu had kept on the magic corsets, replacing the Jacob Marley dress over the top. Now padded as well as chainmailed, she felt ready for all eventualities.

'Laird McBang,' It was time to get the negotiations under way.

He leant forward, eyes narrowed sexily, full lips thrust out, the glow of the strip lights accentuating his high cheekbones. 'Call me Torquil,' he murmured seductively.

'Torquil... I am interested in the whole estate – how you say – lipstick barrel.'

'Lock, stock and barrel?'

'Loch, yes. And mountains.'

'McBang's Tables?' The laird paused and lay down his spoon. 'Now you really are talking. Those beauties don't come cheap. For one thing, they are the home of the rare McBang Haggis. You know how to catch a haggis, of course?'

Lulu neither knew nor cared; McBang, all the same, prepared to divest himself of the old canard. Foreigners always fell for it.

'A haggis has four feet, and the two on the right are shorter than the two on the left. That means it always runs clockwise around the hill. All one has to do it walk anti-clockwise – *et voila* – you have the haggises coming towards you. If they turn and run, they simply topple over.'

Lulu forced herself to take an interest. 'Do haggis have skin like crocodile? Make leather for handbags?' There might be something to be said for them if so.

'No idea. Look, I can let you have the mountains and the peasant cottages for a hundred mil, do we have a deal?' pressed McBang.

Lulu hesitated. Despite a family history of bargaining people into the ground, she felt decidedly nervous about signing anything with this handsome but obviously unscrupulous man. Certainly without Vlad to advise her.

She wished the butler would return. It was absolutely unprecedented for her not to come when expected. The terrible fear now started to form within Lulu that her devoted womanservant felt less devoted. Had the Scottish trip proved too much even for Vlad and had she, not to put too fine a point on it, left her service? The thought was too ghastly to be borne. Life without Vlad was simply unimaginable.

Lulu could not stop herself getting up from the dining table and running to the window to see if the helicopter had left. It was hard to see in the murky gloom, exacerbated by the smoked glass of the windows. But a pale, helicopter-shaped shape seemed still to be out there on the multicoloured AstroTurf. Lulu felt relieved. Vlad must still be in the area.

'Okay,' McBang said, watching appreciatively as his guest/customer undulated back to the table. 'I'll throw in the disused abattoir. You drive a hard bargain, Lulu.'

'What about restaurant? And toilets, including soap?' Lulu tried hard to remember what the butler had told her.

'Not the soap.'

'Deal he is off then.'

And so it went on until the arrival of the famous McBang Shortbread, again courtesy of Lidl, washed down with Auld McBang's Throatscratcher single malt. This, at least, was the genuine article. Torquil's father had sworn by it, especially after working through the best part of a bottle.

Lulu was tired. Sitting here in the candlelight, with the clan chief breathing whisky fumes all over her whilst simultaneously trying to seduce her and get her to sign over vast amounts of money, was an exhausting experience. Perhaps, after all, she should just agree the deal and go to bed with him. He was very handsome, after all, and she had seen with her own eyes how well-equipped he was.

She raised her chin and pointed her sunglasses at the laird. 'Okay. I want see contract.'

It seemed that McBang had been waiting for just such a cue. In a matter of seconds he had produced a vast vellum scroll, a nibbed ostrich feather and an inkwell. The ancient document was spread out on the black ash table, a prosecco bottle holding down each corner.

Lulu squinted through the gloom at the convoluted, copperplate manuscript that adorned the calf skin. The words crossed her eyes and made her head spin...

'... *whereupon and forefoothbefaid that confideration in Scottifh banknotef, infomuchafwheretofore, on depofit at the Queenfferrie branch of the Firft Britifh Linen Bank... all vaffalf and chattelf and mountainef, foreftf, fervantf, retainerf, crofterf, fheepef, whilholme and notwithftanding thefaid contrarye claimef and hereby I, Lulu Fried, folemnly do fwear...'*

The document would have been unintelligible even to a seasoned Scots lawyer straight out of *Kidnapped*. Lulu didn't stand a chance of understanding what she was signing. But by now she was so tired and bored she didn't care.

McBang thrust the elaborate quill into Lulu's hand, the pitchy ink dripping from its nib. But even now, Lulu hesitated. Her father's voice with its heavy Middle Eastern accent came back to her. 'Be careful where you put your hands and your signature...'

The four-armed monster of Castle McBang was not quite what Vlad was expecting.

For a start, it was two people, and not ghosts of starved former prisoners dressed in peasant rags either.

The young men staring at Vlad from the other side of the bars were handsome, vigorous and in their early thirties. One was of tousled, agricultural appearance in a woolly Aran sweater offset by a Paisley neckerchief. The other was in full mountaineering gear, complete with rucksack and crampons.

'May I assist you, gentlemen?' Vlad enquired. Producing from her boot a standard issue Estonian infantry lock-picker, she made short work of the chains securing the gates.

They rushed out immediately. 'We've got to stop the sale!' blurted out the one in the jumper.

'The sale of the McBang estate?' Vlad enquired. She felt slightly offended. Possibly it might have been nice to be thanked, considering she was freeing these people from a lingering death in the depths of an ancient prison. On the other hand, the buttling profession was not one for people who required a high level of personal appreciation.

'It's *not* his estate! That's the point!' the mountaineer type exclaimed. 'He doesn't own those mountains! Nor half of what he says he does!'

'You are referring to the Laird of McBang?' Vlad deduced.

'Fraud of McBang, more like!' expostulated the jumper. 'He shut us up in here because he knew we'd blow the whistle on the sale. I'm a crofter and I'd lose my home and grazing.'

'And I,' declared the other, rattling his crampons for emphasis, 'am a member of the mountaineering club.

McBang's Tables are not his to sell! Nothing is. He sold what belonged to him years ago.'

Vlad looked from one to the other. 'You have not told anyone? No one else knows this?'

In the recesses of his sandy eyebrows, the crofter's blue eyes bulged. 'We've had Radio Scotland and the *West Highland Free Press* gagging to break the story.'

'But gagging is the word! McBang has injuncted them up to the eyeballs!' the mountaineer shouted, his agitation echoing round the tiny cell. 'The McBangs have always seen themselves as above the law. It started with his father knocking the castle down, even though it was a Category A listed building. Sold the whole thing to some American who's re-erected it in the Arizona desert.'

'He was always desperate for cash,' added the crofter. 'Had a gambling habit the size of Skye, which Torquil's inherited.'

Vlad listened as the mountaineer described the catalogue of sometimes shocking ways McBang senior had attempted to exploit the local area. 'Tried to stop the seal boat trips for the tourists last year so he could start exporting seal meat to a chain of Korean barbecue restaurants. He wanted to send the fur to upscale Moscow furriers.'

'I see,' said Vlad, who personally could not see what was wrong with this. Fur was very important in Eastern Europe. But there was no doubt the laird's general behaviour was poor.

'Then he had a business exporting "genuine Scottish midges",' the crofter continued.

'But who would wish to buy midges?'

The mountaineer indignantly explained. 'McBang called it "A Breath Of Real Scotland".' His thinking was that people loved complaining about Scottish midges when they were hundreds of miles away at southern summer garden parties. It was what's known in the trade as a social indicator. People think that banging on about midges makes them posh because it makes it sound as if they're familiar with vast Scottish estates.'

This had the ring of truth to Vlad. She was by now familiar with the twisted snobbery of the British. The most surprising things were seen as posh. Bad teeth. Anchovy paste. Clothes that looked as if they had been buried in the garden. But midges, that was a new one.

'So he supply midges? Send in post?' she guessed.

'Exactly. The finishing touch for any aspirational gathering. Simply uncork the phial of McBang's Midges and – voila! – the genuine "bitten to death" experience.'

'As for Torquil,' the crofter added, 'he's got a terrible reputation with women. He's known throughout the Highlands and Islands as "Jack Russell". There isn't a chair leg in Scotland that he won't try to couple with.'

Vlad thought of her mistress alone at the dinner table with this financially incontinent, morally reprehensible and sex-crazed monster. She looked decisively from one companion to the other. 'Well, gentlemen. It appears we must act fast.'

★

Meanwhile, in The Boardroom, the strip lights were throwing into dreadful relief the veins standing out on Torquil McBang's forehead. His eyes stared from his skull in crazed fashion. His mouth worked agitatedly, spittle gathering at its edges.

Lulu stared at him. He had been so smooth, handsome and collected before. But now he was a terrifying McBang monster who could easily have given Scary Mary a run for her money. She would need all her ju-jitsu skills to deal with him. Thank goodness she had the lucky Macdonald corsets on.

'Sign, you slutty foreign bitch!' McBang hissed, his limited self-control now evaporated.

'You don't talk to me like that!' Lulu picked up one of the prosecco bottles and thumped him with it at the exact same time the door to the dining room burst open.

In rushed Vlad with her two companions. Lulu looked at them in appreciative surprise. One looked like a sexy farmer. The other was rocking more of a mountaineering vibe.

'Don't sign!' they urged in unison. 'Stop!'

'It seems Mr McBang is a fraud, and doesn't own everything he is trying to sell, madam,' Vlad explained.

Fifteen minutes later, McBang fled into the night, shaking his fist and vowing revenge as he slithered over the wet AstroTurf in his crested slippers. Lulu, Vlad and the two protestors then helped themselves to the rest of the prosecco and settled down to the all-important business of finding another estate for Lulu to buy. From the plastic folder hung around his neck the mountaineer produced an Ordnance Survey map. They spread it out over the black ash table in the place the near-fateful contract had just lain.

Chapter Twenty-two

S andy really need not worry, Laura thought. Glenravish Castle was going to make the most wonderful feature. In every room was some amazing historical surprise. It seemed as if everyone who was anyone had visited.

The red knickerbockers and pixie boots had led her to a glass display case against a panelled oak wall. 'Ye gartere of Mary, Queen of Scots' read a label next to a small pile of material.

'Wow,' said Laura. The legendary and tragic monarch formed a point where British history met that of her native land. Mary had been Queen of France once.

Scotland's dramatic and romantic past formed the perfect fit with its landscape. And while she could understand why Sandy wanted to leave, Laura was now thinking again that the transient pleasures of London were nothing compared with the eternal beauties of the country north of the Border. And in particular this ravishing, fascinating building. If she could afford it, she would buy Glenravish herself. But that was never going to happen. Not even if she got 200 per cent advertising for *Society*.

'When did Mary come here?' she asked, thinking that images of the ill-fated queen would be great for the feature, give it real historical depth. There were some wonderful portraits of Mary looking elegant and tragic in a black gown with a high ruff and a long pearl necklace with a cross at the end. She had been a religious martyr, ultimately.

'A three-night break in the 1560s. Worked her way through most of the estate farmhands. Mary, Queen of Shags, more like. *Hwah hwah hwah*,' brayed Sandy.

Laura's eyes widened. On the other hand, sex definitely sold and that angle on Mary was probably as good as any. She wondered what other great Scottish heroines had visited Glenravish.

'How about Flora MacDonald?' she asked.

The sprayed wings of hair remained rigid as Sandy shook her head. 'We're practically the only house in Scotland that doesn't have a piece of her, *hwah hwah hwah*. Bloody woman left hair, shoes and underwear scattered everywhere from the Western Isles downwards. *Hwah hwah hwah*.'

Pity, thought Laura, staring into the next case. It contained what looked like a small, moth-eaten handbag with a series of mechanical ratchets and barrels. 'And this is…?'

'Rob Roy's exploding sporran!' Through the rings of blue mascara, Sandy's eyes lit up. 'Pure genius. Like all great leaders, he was paranoid and lived in constant fear of assassination. This little devil could be operated from a lever on his belt and take out any unexpected assailant with a surprise round of ordnance delivered straight from the gentleman's area.'

'Goodness,' said Laura. It sounded like a Jacobite version of James Bond's Q. This sent her thoughts inevitably to Caspar, who had so recently lost the 007 job. She really should give him a ring, see how he was coping.

'Well, it wasn't all goodness, actually,' Sandy was saying. 'There was a slight risk of backfire, and many of the prototypes left their wearers a bit short in the meat and two veg department.'

Laura was speechless. Her hostess had moved on, however.

'And this mighty drinking horn is the Auld Stonker of Glenravish.' Sandy held out a four-foot long polished and twisted Highland cow horn with exquisitely worked Celtic silver trimmings. 'Holds six bottles of claret. The new laird has to drain it in one on assuming the title. No problem with that for me. Though I did feel a little liverish afterwards. *Hwah hwah hwah!*'

Sandy swept them along further expanses of tartan carpet in a range of lurid colours, one a shocking orange. 'Dress McRavish, worst tartan in all of Scotland, worse even than the McBangs. But you have to stick with what you're given. *Clan* tartans are all a Victorian invention anyway.'

'Are they?' Laura was surprised.

'Oh yes. Victoria and Albert were mad about tartans As were the Hanoverians, which is ironic, really. Butcher Cumberland was well known for chasing down and slaughtering any poor fleeing Jacobite with so much as a fleck of check about their person after Culloden.'

Laura wasn't entirely sure what she was talking about, but the mention of slaughter reminded her of the castle's creepier side. How much did Sandy know about the ghosts, really?

She resolved to try again. 'So, with all these historical artefacts, the history and so on, don't you feel sometimes that Glenravish is – well – haunted?'

'No, my dear, not in the least. Not seen so much as a smidgeon of a spook the whole time I've lived here.'

Laura wasn't so sure. Sandy seemed less relaxed in her denials than she had been over her Glenravish anecdotes. Those had spilled out spontaneously, full of warmth and colour.

But now, and rather abruptly it seemed, the tour was over. Laura now found herself in a kitchen straight out of *Upstairs, Downstairs*. There were wheelback chairs at one end of a huge pine table and lots of oak cupboards and shelves on which copper pans of all sizes and shapes, including fish moulds for salmon mousse, were displayed in all their well-polished glory. A comforting wave of heat radiated from the venerable deep green Aga.

'My cousin Mordor,' honked Sandy, waving at a man sitting at the end of the table. Despite the late hour – it must be the middle of the night – he was demolishing what was left of the venison stew. Laura, now stone-cold sober, quickly took in the details of his appearance.

It resembled Sandy's quite closely, although naturally minus the heart-attack lipstick, blue mascara and nuclear blusher. Mordor too was delicately built, with a narrow, thin-featured face He had fair hair, blue eyes and very smooth skin with pink cheeks. He looked, Laura thought, rather angelic.

It was hard to say whether Mordor thought he was living in the 1980s as well, however. Country casual clothes for upper-class men had not changed over the past forty years and Laura was unable to guess whether the graph-paper flannel shirt, red cords and beige Shetland jumper were contemporary or from the time of leg warmers and ra-ra skirts.

'Charmed I'm sure.' He leapt to his feet and extended his hand. 'Mordor McRavish, delighted to meet you.' He then treated Laura to a dazzling smile.

'Mordor's the poor relation,' honked Sandy with what Laura now recognised as characteristic directness. 'Lorst everything on some bloody Ponzi scheme, the muppet,' she added good-naturedly. 'Now he lives up the glen in a bungalow. All mod cons, though. He's even got a microwave.'

Laura felt uncomfortable. Mordor's smile had disappeared instantly. A frigid atmosphere now filled the kitchen, despite the warmth of the Aga. Perhaps Sandy realised her mistake because she hardly spoke while her cousin asked Laura a stream of questions.

Most of them were very personal; why, Laura wondered, was Mordor quizzing her so closely about her background? It was a no-holds-barred social impact assessment and as such took her straight back to boarding school. There, the more snobbish girls would ask similar things to this to work out how rich and important she was.

'So what did your father do?'

'He was a war reporter.'

'Did he buy his own furniture?'

'I don't know.' Laura had never heard her father ever mention furniture. So far as he was concerned, it was just something to sit on and hold up his typewriter.

'Where did you go to school?'

Laura told him.

'And university?'

She shook her head. 'I never went.'

Mordor raised his eyebrows. 'Never went to the varsity?'

Sandy slipped out 'for more wine' as Mordor pressed on with his questions. She seemed to take her time returning. It was when he got on to the topic of Laura's journalistic intentions that Mordor became most obviously interested, as well as very dismissive.

'So, *Society* thinks it can produce a puff piece that will sell this pile, does it? Just with a wave of its hand and a click of its fingers?' He waved his own hand in its Shetland sleeve, and clicked his fingers, sending a bright gold flash from his signet ring. 'Well, let me tell you, little girl, that this place is going to be one hell of a hard sell.'

He paused to draw breath, and Laura tried to get a protesting word in edgeways. He ignored her completely. 'What was it that my good friend Boris Johnson said? "You can't polish a turd!" How true. Spoken with the wit and wisdom of an OE. Statesmanlike. Well, Glenravish castle is a haunted turd, I tell you that for nothing, Miss...' He paused to pretend to remember Laura's surname, or, at least, to emphasise how common he found it '... *Lake*.' And with that, Mordor stabbed a dumpling and stuffed the lot into his mouth.

Laura stared at him in surprise. He had changed from pleasant to poisonous with bewildering speed. Ever since Sandy had mentioned the Ponzi scheme he had been simmering with fury. But it was hardly her fault and there was no need to lash out at her job and the magazine in this way. She was trying to help Sandy, after all.

'Sandy says it isn't haunted,' she said.

Mordor slammed down his glass and gave a hollow laugh. 'In the words of the immortal Mandy Rice-Davies, she would say that, wouldn't she?'

Laura was speechless in the face of such extraordinary ingratitude. Didn't he want to help his cousin, on whose hospitality he seemed to be depending?

She cut in with her counterargument. 'A positive piece in *Society* will drive up interest and increase the possibility of a sale.'

Torquil thumped the table. 'Come on. You've noticed it. Lights going on and off. Phones never working. Plumbing like the bowels of an incontinent navvy. These spooks don't like modern communications and conveniences. This place'll never sell. No Wi-Fi and scared shitless – that's not what the moneyed classes want. They want a good night's sleep and seamless communication with the markets.'

'I don't agree,' Laura began, but Mordor interrupted.

'You journalists, you're all the same,' he thundered. 'Unprincipled liars, arch-manipulators, grubby exploiters. Dabbling in the stuff of other people's souls.'

Laura's mouth fell open. She was the editor of a glossy magazine. The only other people's soles she dabbled in were Manolo Blahniks and the like. She waited for an opportunity to interrupt, but none came. After raging against her profession for some minutes longer, Mordor slammed down his knife and fork and stormed out.

'Well, he didn't last long,' Sandy remarked dryly as she re-entered the kitchen brandishing a 1967 Château de Chasselais. 'His approach to dinner can be a bit functional. Goes back to his public-school days.'

'Is that what it is?' Laura thought of Harry, also public-school educated but who ate beautifully, even if mostly takeaways. A great pang of longing washed over her.

'Oh yah. Stuffing down the carbs in competition with eight hundred other braying Hoorays doesn't leave much room for manners.'

'He didn't seem to like journalists much,' Laura said ruefully. Her ears were still ringing with the force of

Mordor's remarks. 'He didn't seem to think that the article was a good idea.'

'No one's asking him,' Sandy said cheerfully. 'Anyway – to business.'

'Yes,' said Laura. 'I was wondering what else we might promote as part of the feature.'

'Stalking,' said Sandy, immediately.

Laura looked at her. 'Isn't that illegal?'

The blue-mascaraed lashes were wide with surprise. 'Why would it be? Been a tradition up here since Queen Victoria.'

Laura stared. She hadn't realised Queen Victoria followed people about without their permission.

'Glenravish always used to be a sporting estate, got a game larder, the whole shebang. With the emphasis on bang, *haw haw haw*.'

Laura didn't have a clue about country sports. She thought a game larder was where you kept the Scrabble. She waited for Sandy to enlighten her.

'Stalking's huge,' barked Sandy. 'People will pay a fortune to dress up in tweeds, walk for miles, get bitten to death by midges and soaked through by Scotch mist to get a squint at some poor stag that they take an ill-considered potshot at. They miss completely, but the stalker simultaneously fires and hits the beast bang in the engine room. Everyone's happy. The guest pretends they've hit something, even if they couldn't hit a cow's arse with a banjo. And the stalker's got one less stag to worry about.'

'And this makes money?' Laura could hardly believe it.

'Damned right it does. I'm told you can charge a chunky six figures for a weekend's stalking for a group of chinless wonders from the Square Mile. Better still, get some Russians. They pay in cash.'

'You're *told*?' Laura stared. 'You mean you haven't done it, this stalking thing?'

'Yes to the stalking, no to the charging,' Sandy admitted.

'But – why not?'

All Sandy's bravado now seemed to escape her, like the air escaping a balloon with an eighties pie-crust collar. 'Oh, I don't know, Laura,' she sighed. 'Charging seems so vulgar, somehow. A kind of admission of defeat, that the great days are over and the estate can no longer wash its face without help.'

Laura was silent. She could see that this was indeed a kind of tragedy. A Chekhovian drama in which the grand old ways must submit to the new, like *The Cherry Orchard*. Or, in the case of Glenravish, The Haggis Orchard.

'Anyway,' Sandy concluded after a final philosophical swig of wine, 'I've so many castle-creeping relatives like Mordor, queuing up to blag stalking for free, that I've never really set my mind to monetising it.'

Later, in the comfort of her cosy room, Laura collapsed finally and gratefully into bed. Despite her exhaustion, she felt triumphant and relieved. Glenravish was a wonderful subject, and with her new-found love for

Scotland, she felt she could write any number of other
pieces extolling the country's virtues. She would deliver
an issue so ravishing that advertisers would be queuing
up to be in it.

Her only regret was that Harry was not here with her.
Laura pictured them sailing down a silver loch together,
or gazing out, hand in hand, over a heart-stopping view
from the top of a just-climbed mountain. It was so easy
to imagine them cooking sausages in a bothy while the
rain rattled on the corrugated iron roof, or sitting on a
beach and watching a magnificent sunset sink into the
Scottish sea. Whatever he was angry with her about,
Laura felt, for whatever reason he had stormed off, he
would surely forgive her all in the blissful surroundings
of the Highlands.

As she burrowed further down into bed, she realised
she had left the light on. But then, suddenly, it went off.
And on. And on and off again. The Frankenstein fizzing
was back. Pop. Now everything was dark.

Odd. She had not noticed gaps in the windowpane.
On the contrary, the room had felt warm and cosy.
But now she could definitely feel a cold wind that had
not been there before. And what was that moaning
noise? That scratching? With a great flood of relief she
realised it was just the sound of her eyelashes against the
bedspread.

Laura turned over. And back again. Had she been
asleep? In the gloaming she could make out the
unfamiliar shapes of the furniture. Was that a hatstand?
Or something, someone in the corner? She turned over

again. More wind and whistling. Her eyes were open again. Was that a face at the window? Or the shape of dust? Then darkness, and troubled sleep. Laura began to dream.

Surrounded by heaps of shining sovereigns, Mordor was presiding at a Macbeth-like banquet. By his side was Boris Johnson, egging him on as he swallowed gold coin after gold coin. Around the banqueting table were all the members of the McRavish clan, casting astonished and concerned glances at each other. Suddenly, at a vacant seat at the table, Sandy herself appeared as a ghost.

'No, Mordor – you shall not inherit,' she boomed. 'I denounce you as a haunted turd!'

Mordor rose to his full height, emitting a blood-curdling scream. A blast of bagpipes sounded from the back of the great hall.

'Aaaaaaah!' Laura sat bolt upright in her bed. Thank God, it was morning! But what was that noise? Bagpipes? Real ones? Bagpipes were playing outside?

She popped her head out of the deep-silled window and, sure enough, a red-faced gentleman in a kilt was marching up and down beneath her window, blowing with cheeks distended to the size of footballs into something resembling a partially dismantled antique tartan Hoover.

Laura wanted to return to her bed and snatch a few minutes' more sleep. But something about the haunting notes of the pipes had caught at her heart. Their sound rose into the air, yearning, sad, beautiful. It seemed to speak of troubles both past and present, longings and sorrows both endured and yet to come. It was powerfully moving and the listening Laura was surprised to feel the tears running down her cheeks.

Chapter Twenty-three

Going back to sleep after that was out of the question. She decided to get dressed and found, to her surprise, that the jeans she had torn on the gate the night before lay on a chair by the bed. They were not only mended, but cleaned and pressed.

Laura stared at them. She remembered the fear she had felt during the night; the intruder she had sensed in her room. It hadn't been a ghost after all, but kindly Mrs MacRae, trying not to wake her up as she delivered her repaired trousers.

This put a whole new positive spin on things and Laura decided to go outside and explore the garden. She had only seen it by moonlight and needed a more thorough look for the purposes of the article.

She tiptoed down the corridor. There seemed to be no

one about however; even Mrs MacRae seemed to be in bed. Laura pictured the rosy-cheeked housekeeper in a mob cap and nightgown, carrying a candle, like someone comforting in a nursery rhyme.

The passage widened out into the tartan-carpeted landing Laura remembered leading to the main staircase. Goody, her way out was now clear. Running lightly down the wide tartan treads she thanked her strong Anglo-French constitution, the French part especially, for her lack of a hangover. She must have consumed her own weight in wine last night, but with no ill effects, thank goodness.

She paused in the hall, glancing quickly at the weapons on the walls and wondering how long it had been since someone had seized them in earnest. Obviously, they got seized fairly frequently for the purposes of polishing; their sharp tips shone in the light blazing through the arrow-slit windows. It looked like a nice morning, Laura saw, approaching the door.

She had expected the vast arched entrance portal to be locked. But to her surprise a vertical line of light shone between the edge of the door and its surrounding lintel. It was, to use that strange English word, ajar.

Laura pushed it open and it swung easily back on its hinges. The sight before her was postcard-like in its perfection. Beneath a bright blue sky stretched a wide, bright green lawn, bordered with flower beds and overlooked by mature trees. It was surrounded on all sides by hills which ranged from gradual and green in the foreground to jagged purple mountains in the distance. Just visible between the far fringe of firs and tall Wellingtonias marking the garden's boundary, was the bright flash of a silver loch.

Laura took a deep breath of the coolest, freshest air she had ever known. It smelt even better than it had the night before: grassy, sea-salty and with a silvery breath of rain. It had obviously been a wet night and the ground shone and sparkled brilliantly, each grass blade and leaf holding its own diamond drop. Laura moved forward, her boot heels sinking into the soggy gravel of the path, mesmerised by the beauty of it all.

Set against the wildness of its background, the garden was a vision of elegant order and serenity. There were urns, fountains, paved areas and a small round pond with putti in the middle, blowing tiny stone trumpets at the sky. Birds sang, hopped about the trees and bushes and poked inquisitive little beaks in the beautifully tidy flower beds with their cheerful plants, some of which seemed unexpected for somewhere this far north. There was bright calendula in shades from deepest orange to palest yellow, scented purple lavender and roses of all colours in full bloom, as well as flourishing tree ferns.

Beyond the flower beds was an orchard where a great number of apples were busily growing. Laura paused by the just-forming fruit to smell their faint, sweet scent. Walking on the carpet of thick grass between the tree trunks, she happily imagined Mrs MacRae making pies, jellies and crumbles in the autumn, using the polished copper containers. How beautiful it must be round here at that time of year, Laura thought, imagining the fiery shades of the trees, the auburn curl of the bracken, the sharp tang of woodsmoke in air chill enough to tweak the nose and numb the ears.

The orchard abutted the wall and Laura spotted the small garden gate she had shinned over the night before. It seemed like years ago now. The imprint of her bottom cheeks on the gravel had been raked smooth, and possibly the same early morning hand had opened the ironwork gate.

She walked through and, passing the station, walked along the road. It was clear that there had been a village here at some stage. There was a huddle of ruined bothies, a collapsed church and an eerily abandoned graveyard full of lichen-dappled granite headstones. It had a bleak romance to it, Laura thought, especially in the bright morning sun. There were bitterns and oystercatchers pecking around and gulls wheeling above.

Laura decided to walk down to the water. A small path led through the grass towards the loch. She followed it and was amazed to find, opening before her, not only a wide stretch of pinkish sand, but an uninterrupted view down the water. It seemed to lead directly to the sea.

Laura stared at it, transfixed for a few moments. The great mass of moving silver headed down to the rocky outline of some distant island. Its dancing glitter seemed to her the visual embodiment of absolute freedom. Over the waves the seagulls swooped and wheeled, cawed and cried, their wings brilliant white in the sunshine.

It was all so exhilarating and Laura took in another deep, happy lungful of briny air. On a sudden whim, she raised her arms. She flapped them like a seagull's and ran around, laughing. Why not, no one was there to see her. She whirled and whooped, hair soaring behind her, fixing her eyes on the turning sky and the white clouds blowing across the blue. It was dizzying yet liberating, as if she was throwing off all the worries of the last few weeks and hurling her burdens into the sea.

When Laura paused for breath, the smell had changed. What had been seaweed, grass and rainfall had a distinctly different tinge now. It was smoky and fishy. It triggered a memory of the summer before; herself and Harry on a beach in Cornwall.

It was a bright warm breezy day and they were sailing on the sea off Sennen Cove in a tiny hired boat. The ocean air had kindled Laura's never-long-dormant appetite and Harry, who seemed to be able to do anything, had obligingly hauled in a good number of mackerel using just a shoelace and a bag of crisps.

Then Laura, who had learnt to sail at school, piloted the boat into a tiny cove. Harry had leapt ashore with his fish, rummaged behind an outcrop of rocks and, within minutes, had got a small driftwood fire going. The taste of fresh mackerel, grilled in the open air and eaten perched on low rocks facing the sea had seemed to Laura then, and even more so now, as the very flavour of pure happiness.

Afterwards they had made love, over and over again. Kissing passionately and entirely naked, they had rolled over the warm sand and into the cool shock of the waves.

Laura's entire body thrummed now with the memory. She could smell the same scent now, no doubt from some village smokehouse, but so strongly did it bring back that magical meal that she felt all her exhilaration at the morning's beauties evaporate. Standing on the wide pink sands, looking down the stretch of sea loch, Laura wished with every fibre of her being that Harry was with her. She missed him so much it made her ache.

She sniffed again. The smell was stronger and seemed closer than the village, wherever that was. Come to think of it, the only buildings round here Laura had seen belonged either to ScotRail or Sandy McRavish.

A strange prickling sensation now seized her neck. She turned and looked behind her.

The stretch of pink sand sloped up to the grass which bordered the road. Along it were a few old sheds and in front of one of them someone had pitched a small tent. They had built a small fire outside it and it was over this that the fish were grilling.

Laura narrowed her eyes. The occupant of the tent – a man – was outside and busy with cooking. It was too far away to see his face but there was something about his broad shoulders, tumble of dark hair and air of concentration that she recognised immediately. She took a deep breath. Her legs, which felt unsteady, pushed her on faster and faster and before long she was running, hair streaming behind her like a black flag. 'Harry!'

He did not seem in the least surprised to see her. He raised his head, gave her the familiar amused-yet-assessing look, and returned his attention to the mackerel.

Spotting the shoelace and bag of crisps outside the tent, Laura recalled Harry jokingly telling her that he had been taught Special Forces survival techniques. But now she wondered how much of a joke it was, after all.

He was out of his suit, she noticed, and had on his old uniform of battered leather jacket, jeans and T-shirt. At times, this frequently unwashed trinity had tested her patience but now, looking at them, she felt a flood of affection.

His chin was stubbly; he had evidently not shaved for a few days. She preferred this look; like the leather jacket it reminded her of the old days. Days – or rather middle-of-nights – when he had appeared unexpectedly from some derring-do assignment, swinging by her flat before disappearing mysteriously in the dawn. Completing his return to Harry Mark One was the fact he had dark shadows under his eyes, suggesting lack of sleep.

'Why did you leave me in London?' she demanded. 'I was worried sick. And really hurt. How could you do that to me?'

Harry looked down. 'Had some things to think about,' he muttered into the collar of his leather jacket.

Laura said nothing. She was calculating the risks of continuing this conversation, which might yet reveal something – or maybe someone – she did not wish to know about. But surely he was here because of her – this could not be a coincidence.

He loved her after all!

And she loved him, and forgave him everything. All their past disagreements meant nothing. If he wanted to live in a glass block shaped like a fork rather than down among the hipsters with their craft gins and vegetable box delivery services, then so be it. She would live anywhere he wanted; here on this beach if necessary.

Actually, that wouldn't be such a bad thing. The morning view down the loch would be bliss. She glanced at the tent; small but cosy. They would keep each other warm.

She slid a nervous look at Harry; did he still want her, though?

His handsome face gave nothing away. But she felt encouraged by the fact that he now passed her a couple of the mackerel laid out on a battered tin plate.

Their hands touched as he handed the plate over and the remembered thrill of what those hands could do sent a shudder of pleasure through her. She tried to concentrate on the fish, admiring their brown and crispy skin; cooked to a turn, and sniffed the savoury scent rising from the firm, oily flesh beneath. 'Is this a peace offering?' she asked, giving him her sexiest smile.

'No,' said Harry, shortly, chewing rapidly.

Despair swept Laura. So he had found someone else. The urge to abandon the meal and walk off briefly seized her. But it smelt so delicious and she had no idea what the breakfast arrangements at Glenravish were. She had a vague memory of Sandy saying something about it but it was all lost in a fog of drink. Come to think of it, Sandy had been full of plans for today, not that Laura could remember any.

Her head was feeling a familiar tightness now; perhaps she had not escaped the hangover after all. It might just be starting, in fact.

The bright sun above now slipped behind a cloud, echoing Laura's feeling that the day, which had seemed to full of promise, was now taking a distinctly downward slide. 'Not a peace offering, no,' Harry said, shoving his empty plate aside, wiping his mouth with a scrunched handkerchief and reaching for her. 'My feelings towards you are not remotely peaceful. Come into my tent, Laura Lake. There's something I need to discuss with you.'

Half an hour later, tousled, panting and thoroughly ravished, Laura lay on Harry's scrunched nylon sleeping bag, completely fulfilled and happy. Was there any better feeling than the warmth of Harry's skin against hers, any better sight than his wide, dark, always-unfathomable gaze?

'I'm not letting you go ever again,' she said fervently.

'You'll have to,' Harry rolled on to his back. 'I've got to skedaddle.'

Dismay seized Laura. 'But where? Didn't you come here to see me?'

He grinned. 'I'd love to say yes, but not exactly.'

'You mean,' Laura frowned, 'you're here on an investigation?'

'You may think so, I couldn't possibly comment.'

Laura punched him. Her headache was ebbing back. Their passionate reunion had shot it into the middle of the sun, but only temporarily, it now seemed. She gave a hollow groan. 'I think I'd better go back to the castle and lie down.'

'No chance of that, I'm afraid. You're going stalking. Witnessing one of the estate's prized assets from a recreational perspective.'

If she tried really hard, Laura could just about remember something being said about this. She was to go deer-hunting with Struan, who was apparently the estate gamekeeper, 'on the hill'.

Whichever hill that was. Hopefully one of the smaller ones. 'But how do you know?' she asked Harry.

'I know everything. Now put your clothes back on. I'll see you in London.'

Chapter Twenty-four

Laura tottered back across the road, trying to force the gathering headache away. She felt surprisingly optimistic, even so. Stalking – no problem. Bring it on. The knowledge that she and Harry were together again was so glorious she could have happily gone bog-snorkelling on the strength of it.

She returned to her bedroom to discover that Mrs MacRae had been in again. Her bed was made, a bath was drawn and a set of unfamiliar clothes was laid out on the bed. This was what it must be like to be Prince Charles.

The clothes – a tweed suit – were presumably for stalking in, and presumably belonged to Sandy. They undoubtedly dated from the eighties; Laura smiled to see the knickerbockers. But breeches were sensible for terrain with long grass, and the suit was otherwise plain and perfectly cut. The tweed was a pale green and the jacket fitted beautifully over the warm flannel shirt. Laura pulled on the socks, laced up the boots and admired herself in the mirror. The effect was surprisingly stylish; memo to Raisy and Daisy, Laura thought. There were endless companies specialising in high-end country wear and potentially lots of advertising on the back of a tweedy fashion shoot.

Feeling for once perfectly dressed for her baronial surroundings, Laura descended to the kitchen, looking forward to its familiarity. To her dismay, it was full of unfamiliar people standing up eating porridge out of wooden bowls.

'Good morning, darling,' Sandy greeted her. She was in a white pie-crust collar blouse this morning, teamed with a flower-print Laura Ashley skirt and patent flats. Her hair was tonged out as usual and already clearly the beneficiary of a torpedo-sized can of hairspray. 'How did you sleep?'

It seemed to Laura that the room went rather still at this, almost expectant. There was, of course, only one polite answer. 'Fantastically, thank you!'

'Super. Now, let me introduce you to the estate "team",' honked Sandy. 'Now, we have Wee Archie, Big Kenny, Fat Ishbel, Young Tommy, Big Oonagh...' She reeled off a series of monikers, none of which Laura felt she would remember, especially as their different shapes, sizes and sexes weren't necessarily reflected in the listed nicknames. Presumably, particularly in the case of the noticeably wizened Young Tommy, they had been given to them some years ago.

Still, they seemed a friendly enough bunch as they all stood around beaming at her and Sandy, who seemed preoccupied with the stalking trip.

'Mrs MacRae is just making the cold herring baps for you to take up on the hill. There's some lovely hard Granny Smiths too – nice and acid just as I like them. And we're reusing old Highland Spring water bottles with estate water for drinking – that's why it looks a bit brown – no, it's not whisky – *hwah hwah hwah!*'

As the kitchen rang with Sandy's braying laughter, Laura's stomach wrenched in anticipation of such short commons.

There was a quick knock at the kitchen door followed by the apparition of a further member of Glenravish's extensive *dramatis personae*. A red-faced, friendly, yet forceful-looking man in his late forties extended a palm the size of a baseball glove.

Sandy beamed from him to Laura. 'And this is Struan – Mr MacRae – who is going to take you up the Hill.'

Eyebrows as bushy as the heather itself sat atop his deep country-green eyes. His tanned, rounded head was the size of a large football. There was something of the friendly troll about him. Something scary that might appear from under a bridge and then offer you a biscuit, Laura thought.

'Hellooo, Miss Laura,' he boomed. 'Looking forward to the stalk – uh-huh?'

Struan's speech, Laura discovered, was continuously punctuated with the indeterminate word-particle 'uh-huh', which seemed an attempt to bridge the linguistic gap between his heavily accented Scots English and the interlocutor straining to understand him.

'Well, um, yes,' Laura said doubtfully.

'That's the spirit, uh-huh,' Struan beamed. 'Come with me, Miss Laura – we'll choose you a gun – uh-huh?'

'What, off the wall?' Laura asked in disbelief a few minutes later. She found it hard to believe that any of the ancient shooting gear clamped to the sides of Glenravish's hall could be deployed without a serious risk of annihilating anyone and everything within a fifty-yard and 360-degree radius of its lethal discharge.

Struan seemed not to hear. He was looking at the antique ordnance assessingly. 'How do ye fancy this beastie? An Auld Jacobite musket. The "Bollock-Splitter" they used to call it – no need to tell you why, uh-huh, uh-huh.'

Struan handed Laura what was actually quite a beautiful piece. A fluted butt had a cheerful hunting scene carved in primitive relief on it. The flintlock mechanism was entirely exposed and had a Heath-Robinsonian logic to it.

Laura handled the gun with a comfort and aplomb that seemed to surprise Struan. 'Ye've used a gun before have ye, Miss Laura, uh-huh?'

Laura smiled at him and nodded.

She was remembering a scene from her childhood. It was Saturday night in the tiny kitchen of their Montmartre flat. There was a single lamp light on the table where her grandmother Mimi was taking a Schmeisser submachine gun to pieces and challenging Laura to put it together again. It was, to the old Resistance heroine's mind, a more useful pursuit than Scrabble or cards. The weighty German weapon had, Mimi told Laura, been prised from the cold, dead hands of an SS NCO in the rue de Rivoli during La Liberation de Paris.

Laura decided not to mention all this to Struan.

'Just show me how it works and we'll get on fine,' she said.

'Right ye are, Miss Laura, uh-huh.'

They headed outside and bumped into Sandy. She had shrugged on an oversized green mac which blew about in the wind, although her hair remained absolutely rigid.

'Well, Laura, good luck on the hill. I'm sure you'll be a natural and bag a stag to make us all proud,' she barked.

Laura had not been expecting such ceremony. The entire estate staff seemed to have mustered by the castle entrance to wish them off and Laura and Struan marched over to the green Land Rover Defender. They strapped their arsenal carefully in the jeep, and set off up the estate track.

Struan began the bumpy ride chattering away about different aspects of the estate's management, landscape and wildlife. It was clear that he cared deeply about keeping Glenravish's majestic natural setting. Laura got out the trusty notebook and pencil she still preferred to any number of gadgets and prepared to ask him some questions about himself. Presumably as a local boy Glenravish ran in his blood as the crystal streams ran down the mountainside. He had been nursed by the winds and schooled by the changing seasons. He had learnt to fish and stalk at his father's knee. 'So,' began Laura.

But at the exact same time Struan had turned to her: 'So, what's brought you up here, Miss Laura?'

While the question was direct, it was asked in a friendly fashion. Laura didn't feel any hesitation in taking him into her confidence.

'I want to promote Glenravish in my magazine so Sandy can finally sell it,' she explained.

The Defender's differential lock and low gears ground noisily.

'What's that, eh? Jelly? Uh-huh. Och, yes, my Grizelle's a fine cook. Those baps are tasty and she makes a fine cranachan.'

'Not jelly. *Selling.*'

Struan dropped a gear, and the Land Rover growled. 'Melons? Aye, they make a fine starter before a roast saddle of venison.'

Laura took a deep breath. 'I'M TRYING TO HELP SANDY SELL THE CASTLE!' she boomed.

The keeper gave her a warm appreciative smile as if to say 'thank you'.

Land Rover ads? Laura wrote in her notebook. Until the engine stopped, she was clearly going to get nothing out of Struan.

The rough, unmetalled track rose steadily up into the hills. After about four miles, the keeper pulled up outside a primitive-looking, corrugated iron-roofed building set at the head of the glen.

'That's the bothy. We'll stop for tea and then we'll walk from here.'

Inside the small building, Struan fired up the gas cooker and clattered a huge aluminium kettle on. Laura was surprised that, in what was essentially a wooden hut, there could be such a sense of cosy calm. In the centre of the kitchen-cum-sitting room, sat a seasoned pine table and chairs. Comfy old sofas and armchairs were arranged around the walls, draped in tasteful grey and tan tartan rugs. The walls were decked with Ordnance Survey maps of the estates, one for each year, mounted on cork boards with map pins showing where a stag or deer had been shot that year. A barren sixties was followed by absolute carnage in the seventies, it seemed.

Struan talked her through the topography of the estate, pointed out the location of the best views, the windiest reaches and the most dangerous bogs. Laura made copious notes, reassured that he was going to such trouble, giving her all the detail she needed to keep her safe.

The tea finished, they quit the bothy and set off on foot towards their quarry. As they headed up the hill, Laura discovered terrain that looked soft and velvety from a distance, mottled dark green, purple and grey, was anything but easy-going. It was full of dangers: long, sharp grasses, pitfalls, small, knee-deep black pools, huge boulders. To round it all off nicely, the notorious midges were closing in.

Struan handed Laura a small, pink plastic bottle as she scratched. 'Here, use this, lassie.'

The label said *Skin So Soft*. It was made by Avon.

'As used by the Royal Marine Commandos,' Struan supplied. 'It's the only thing that'll keep the beasties off ye!'

Another take on the idea of 'going commando', Laura thought as she sprayed the fine mist into her hand and wiped the pungent oil onto any exposed skin. The fragrance was pronounced, to say the least. But it seemed to work like a dream. The wee insects which had previously been invading everything including her ears and nostrils now kept a respectful distance. Laura made a mental note for the beauty editor, as well as Harriet. Avon needed to take a couple of pages of advertising at least.

Struan was issuing instructions. 'Over the next hill the glen divides. I'll swing right and you swing left into the small glen and we'll regroup at the brow two miles or so up ahead. We can compare notes on where there's deer. Keep on the firm ground and away from the black pools – they'll suck you in right enough. Unless you see a duckboard – step away!'

The bollock-splitter slung over her shoulder, Laura headed off as instructed, turning occasionally until she saw Struan disappear into a dot against the horizon.

She was trying hard to see where the 'fun' was in all of this; why people bothered to do it. The landscape was beautiful, sure enough. The air came in fresh lungfuls.

The exercise was bracing. But you couldn't call it sybaritic. Would that be a good beginning to her piece? Laura wondered.

The weather had changed, too. The sunny skies of morning had turned an angry leaden colour. A spitting rain began to cast itself in malign grey curtains across the land. It was becoming difficult to see the way ahead, or match her surrounding to the tattered map Struan had handed her.

A thought flashed across Laura's mind. If Struan was such an expert in the ways of the wild, and of the estate's moods and humours, why had he brought her, a neophyte, up here today? The conditions were becoming appalling and the chances of spotting a deer seemed more than remote.

She entered her 'small glen', as Struan had called it. Or perhaps it was different one. It was hard to tell in the rain. The landscape looked huge and daunting. She was the only living thing in it. Or was she? Just then, following a flicker at the corner or her eye, she swung right. There on the crest was a majestic stag straight out of Landseer.

Remembering to count the points, as Struan had earlier counselled her, she got to eight on the left antler and nine on the right.

Engrossed, she slipped and found her left boot up to the ankle in one of the small black pools Struan had warned her about. Using the bollock-splitter as a lever, she managed to extract her foot. But not the boot, which was now lost to the pitchy mire.

'One boot or barefoot?' Laura mused crossly. She'd look a fool and suffer either way.

She opted for the barefoot option. It wasn't cold – yet – and it would give her an even gait, which was crucial with the Jacobite musket piece now weighing her down. She felt that she probably really did look like a member of Bonnie Prince Charlie's benighted band of brothers shambling towards their engagement at Culloden with Butcher Cumberland.

Ahead, she sighted a duckboard track across a stretch of the blackest bog. Despite the unpromising surroundings, this seemed far and away the best bet, especially as she was now *pieds nus*.

The stag had disappeared, but progress was good, and she was even beginning to look forward to her cold herring bap. Then there was a dull crack beneath her and, before she knew it, she was waist deep in black peaty water, the duckboards beyond her grasp. Laura sought to paddle her feet, but there was nothing beneath them, and the more she paddled the more she sank.

'HELP!' she cried, but all that came in return was a mocking echo from either side of the glen, which now appeared like more of an enclosed bowl than an open space. Struan would never hear her above the wind and the rain, wherever he was.

So, this was it, Laura thought. She was going to drown in a peaty pool, miles from anywhere, on a forgotten Scottish moor, and all because she was trying to save *Society* magazine and the jobs of her colleagues, not to mention her own.

'Bugger, bugger, bugger, bugger...' Tailing off, Laura's tears melted with the Highland rain running down her cheeks. She thought of Harry, a mere few miles away on the beach at the lochside. 'HARRY!' she screamed, praying that somehow her words would be taken to him on the wind. But the air was buffeting in the other direction and, besides, he was probably long packed up and gone now.

She would never see him again. Their latest and most passionate encounter was to be the very last. Laura's tears were coming thick and fast now.

As she awaited her slow drowning and digestion by Caledonia's peat bogs, the voice of her grandmother drifted over the wind-bent grasses towards her.

'*Fierté. Espoir. Courage.*' These three words alone, more than anything else, had seen Mimi through France's darkest years. She had often repeated them to Laura, who repeated them now, shouting them out defiantly and hearing the empty glen echo them back at her.

As she felt herself drifting off to a better place, a '*chuppa-chuppa-chuppa*' sound, at first dim, but gradually surer and louder, made itself heard, with the deeper roar of an aero engine beneath that of the rotor blades.

Laura gasped. She could see the helicopter now. It was pink. She could even see the great blonde pile of Lulu's hair inside, and her vast black sunglasses. She shut her eyes and opened them again. Was she imagining it? Was this some far-northern, bad-weather version of the traditional desert mirage?

Chuppa-chuppa-chuppa. No, it was real. Panicking stags were charging all over the hillsides now. Despite her dire situation Laura wondered why people bothered donning scratchy tweed and crawling around on their stomachs when all you needed was a low-flying AgustaWestland.

But how to get their attention? Her eye caught the bollock-splitter and an idea struck her. With a deftness of touch that Mimi would have appreciated, Laura both primed and discharged the mighty piece, which sent a vast and deafening crack and flash across the landscape.

Laura's ears rang, and just as it seemed the chopper was fleeing for dear life, her distress signal having had the opposite of its intended effect, Vlad swung the craft around and came in low.

The side door slid open, and a rope ladder in Tiffany blue with silver trimmings tumbled out. Leaving the bollock-splitter – her saviour – somewhat reluctantly behind, Laura clung on with all her might. The whirring machine slowly lifted her from the bog – albeit *sans culottes*. In the literal sense, rather than the revolutionary.

But her loss of modesty was nothing compared to the relief of being saved. She was quickly hauled in by Lulu, who exclaimed and fussed and wrapped the now-shivering Laura in a brightly printed blanket from the Tom Ford Home Collection.

As the flying pink machine roared away, Laura looked down at the Valley of Death. Her eyes narrowed suddenly. On its brow, just out of sight from where she had been slowly drowning, she could make out a troll-like figure, binoculars in hand.

'Struan!' she murmured. 'He was *watching me die*!'

Lulu wasn't really listening. She was hurriedly and incomprehensibly filling Laura in about her own recent adventures. Something about corsets, was all Laura could make out.

'Is lucky we flew this way back to London, hmm?' Lulu concluded. 'What is castle down there? Look nice.'

The helicopter was flying over Glenravish.

'You don't want to know,' Laura said quietly. And neither did she, any more. The Scottish issue could go to blazes; she'd just have to face the consequences. As for the country itself, she'd been right first time round. It was hell on earth. She had no intention of setting foot in Scotland ever again.

PART THREE

Chapter Twenty-five

It was good to be back in London, Laura thought, pressing the bell to alert the driver that her stop was the next one. The No 64 bus might be something of a comedown after the splendours of Lulu's helicopter, but she was happy to be on it nonetheless. She had always enjoyed riding about London on the top of double-deckers – the elevated position provided a wonderful view of the street and what was going on in it.

It was Sunday morning, and the main road was filled with cool couples either heading for or coming back from the nearby flea market. Men with beards were carrying hatstands, while waify women carried vintage film posters featuring Michael Caine under their slender arms.

Turning into Cod's Head Row, Laura felt that it was weeks, rather than days, since she had last been on the street she called home. Nigel Forage, an ex-banker whose real name was Cassian, was outside his establishment in his clogs and leather apron, arranging stinging nettles, ferns and other enormous weeds on his traditional costermonger's barrow. He waved at Laura in friendly fashion. 'Haven't seen you for a while!'

'I've been away,' Laura called back.

'Anywhere good?'

While a resounding *No!* perched on the tip of Laura's tongue, what she actually said was, 'Scotland.'

Nigel raised his thumbs. 'Top place for thistles. Great things, full of nutrients.'

Laura hurried on before he could give her a recipe card.

Even during her short absence, several new shops seemed to have opened. If a week was a long time in politics, two days were an eternity in Cod's Head Row. Businesses, especially those of the pop-up hipster variety, could rise, fall and rise again in half that time. Laura could barely remember what had been in the place of 'Lubyanka', the latest Iron-Curtain-chic brutalist cocktail bar whose brick-and-concrete front she now paused before. Perhaps it had been the previous Iron-Curtain-chic brutalist cocktail bar.

Lubyanka's menu was scribbled over what seemed to be a free-school-meals application form from a Stockport primary school in the 1970s. Among its delights were Silver Needle Tea negronis and wagyu beef canapés rolled in fuchsia plum dust. She'd give it a week, Laura decided.

Other new arrivals on the street were a firm of 'sound architects' and The Thinking Pet, whose USP seemed to be edgy Japanese cat food.

She was relieved to see that Gorblimey Trousers was still there. It being a warm summer morning, the pavement outside it was filled with fashionable families kicking back over Campari sodas. Broadsheet newspapers were spread on the tiny melamine tables at which statement children sat with their iPads and under which statement dogs growled or darted out just in time to trip up passing athletes dangling with phone wires, strapped up with FitBits and sporting hi-vis hi-tech running wear which cost as much as a Chanel suit.

Laura hesitated, uncertain now that she wanted to go inside. Bill and Ben had been having a Scottish moment when last she had seen them and she would rather not be reminded of any of her recent traumas. It would be bad enough tomorrow, when she returned to *Society*, where the question of the Scottish issue would have to be faced.

Things seemed pretty quiet on that front, actually. Laura had expected, when her phone reconnected with the rest of the universe, lots of messages from her colleagues updating her on progress, asking for her views, or just dishing the latest dirt. There was nothing, however. After some thought, Laura had decided Bev Sweet was probably to blame. Under her rule, the British Magazine Company had become a totalitarian state. As individuality was always the first casualty in such regimes, she probably shouldn't expect gossipy emails.

The interior of Gorblimey Trousers was as busy as the outside. Bill and Ben, both of whom were sporting short-back-and-side haircuts, were diving between their customers, large black circular trays on their shoulders, delivering food and drinks, picking up empties, all the time maintaining a friendly patter with everyone. Laura watched them with admiration. It was a kind of highly skilled ballet, dipping here, pirouetting there, weaving smoothly in and out, keeping everything running and everyone happy.

The tartans had gone, Laura noticed. In their place were expanses of leopard-skin.

She nodded at the walls. 'I see the tartan's had its day.'

Bill looked surprised, as if trying to recall a long distant event. 'Lawks-a-lordy, it so has. We're all about safari now. *Out of Africa*, Meryl Streep.'

Laura could see now that he was rocking a Happy Valley look, complete with vintage binoculars. 'Love the shorts,' she said.

'Think so?' Bill looked doubtfully downwards. 'I'm worried me biscuits look knobbly.'

Biscuits and cheese, knees, Laura mentally translated. She punched him playfully on the arm. 'Leave it out,' she said, in her best Cockney. 'Yer've got a smashing pair o' bacons.'

The next day Laura travelled to work full of trepidation. She stood in the crowded train trying to convince herself that there was nothing to worry about. Or, if there was, she could deal with it. The fact that Gorblimey Trousers had dumped the Scottish look gave her hope at least. They were always miles ahead when it came to trends.

Society should follow their lead and have a more obviously lucrative theme such as jewellery. Or maybe a 100-per-cent fashion issue, which Laura personally would find as boring as hell, but which would certainly bring the money in. Yes, that could be the answer. She'd go and see Bev Sweet about it as soon as she got in.

'Laura my darling! Mwah! Mwah!' A glamorous red-haired woman lunged at her as soon as she got off at Oxford Circus.

Recognising through sheer instinct who this was, Laura shook off the parody of a fashion-world greeting. She was not Clemency Makepeace's darling; still less was Clemency hers. Not to put too fine a point on it, she loathed her. She had hoped, after their last encounter, never to see her again.

Clemency Makepeace had not only attended the same school as Laura – where she had been the resident bully – but had entered the same industry. She had been a clear and present danger ever since. Several times, over the past few years, she had attempted to steal Laura's job. And while her evil schemes had always been thwarted, and Clemency herself sent, disgraced, into the outer darkness, she had a habit of returning from it. That she was now back in London seemed to suggest that she had done so again. With her green eyes glittering in her heart-shaped face she looked, as ever, not only like the cat who had the cream, but the bowl it came in as well.

'What are you doing here?' Laura demanded. So far as she remembered, the latest outer darkness to which Clemency had been sent was as cover on a gardening title whose editor had had a baby.

'I don't think that's any of your business,' Clemency returned with a smirk.

'How's the maternity leave going?' If the editor was back and Clemency on the job market again, it could be bad news. An unemployed Clemency was a plotting Clemency.

Her oldest enemy grinned a dark-red-lipsticked grin. 'Good job you're not in journalism, Lake. Otherwise you might have found out it wasn't just maternity leave. I was made the permanent editor of *Weeds Today*.'

Laura felt a wave of relief. If her rival had an editorship of her own, there was less chance she still wanted Laura's. 'The other editor didn't want to come back?'

'She didn't have any choice. Not once I'd exposed her appalling incompetence to the management.' Clemency shook her glossy red head in mock sorrow. 'She had to be let go, sadly. I do hope she'll find another job soon. Or a roof over her head again, at least.'

Laura felt a wave of pure disgust. Clemency was so unapologetically evil. 'I have to go,' she said, pushing her way into the crowd in the wrong direction.

'You said it,' Clemency cackled and gave another toss of her red hair before clattering off on her spike heels in the direction Laura would normally take.

★

Thinking about Bev Sweet again, Laura walked with the crowd at Oxford Circus feeling as if her stomach had been removed and replaced with a large stone. Moving down Argyll Street with the tide of commuters, she fought back the waves of panic. She was tired into the bargain, having slept badly on her return to Cod's Head Row. Upstairs, Edgar had been having a rehearsal of his whistling choir and the amount of noise they made was as unexpected as it was unbelievable.

Laura had huddled under her duvet with her fingers in her ears as what seemed like hundreds of people immediately above shrilled out 'Bohemian Rhapsody' in multi-part harmony. It quite made her long for the old days, when Edgar brought home gangs of overseas servicemen in the early hours and proceeded to entertain them in uproarious fashion. He had always been apologetic the next day, as indeed he had been this morning. 'We're giving a concert soon,' Edgar had explained, raking a skinny hand through his hedge-backwards hair. 'We're all very nervous about it.'

Perhaps she was feeling Edgar's nervousness by proxy, Laura thought as she approached the black-and-white mock-Tudor front of Liberty. His stage fright had transferred itself to her through the floorboards or down the waste stack.

It wasn't just that, though, nor was it even the prospect of returning to *Society*. For all his breezy 'See you in London' on the beach at Glenravish, Harry had not been in touch at all. She had called him at work, on his mobile, but nothing. It was if their Scottish meeting had never been; either she had imagined it as a consequence of her hangover, Laura was beginning to think, or it had happened but meant nothing to Harry.

A sharp blade of disappointment twisted within her. He had been so loving, so passionate; so ardent and yet so gentle by turns. How could he not have meant it? But then, Harry was a professional keeper of secrets and always had been. Perhaps that also meant he was a professional liar. Perhaps she had meant nothing to him all along.

There had been nothing in the post, either, only flyers for Specsavers and organic-veggie-box delivery services, plus a book of personalised discount vouchers from Boots. Curated by an algorithm and predicated on her last major purchase – a pumice stone for the rough skin on her feet – it offered unmissable bargains on verruca treatments, corn plasters and bunion removers. Finally, and heartbreakingly, there were a couple of estate agents' brochures for yet more newbuild developments. Tossing the details of the Spatula and the Lemon-Squeezer into the bin, Laura reflected that at least she would be spared those particular boiling-water taps and slow-closing drawers. Not now Harry wasn't here to insist she look round them.

She blinked. Something had just flashed in her vision, someone in the crowd that she recognised not only with her eyes, but with her heart.

The figure, although visible only from the back, was tall, young, dark-haired, and, most Harryish of all, emanating an irritated, preoccupied energy. She could see him turning impatiently to cut through the crowds with his shoulder. That was too was a Harry trait. She hesitated, then dashed after him, slap bang into the people coming the other way. Angry eyes flashed up from their phone screens, then looked straight back down again.

London's changed, she could hear herself saying to Sandy. *It's full of people charging down the pavements, looking into their smartphones.*

Half of her wondered what Sandy was doing now, what she had made of Laura's own disappearance, which had been every bit as sudden and unexpected as Harry's. She, too, would feel let down after all the promises that had been made to her. *I've no room to talk,* Laura thought, slowing down now. *I'm just as bad as he is.*

Harry – if indeed it had been him – had gone anyway, turned the corner into Regent Street. She would never catch up with him now.

Laura shoved her hands deep into the pockets of her trusty trenchcoat and turned her footsteps towards the pale art deco office block of the British Magazine Company. She slipped her ID card through the security reader, nodded at the guards behind the front desk and headed for the lift.

On the fifth floor, she pushed open the office door of *Society* and stood still in shock. She realised that part of her had expected this all along.

'*I was made the permanent editor of* Weeds Today...'

She had, Laura now realised, failed to register what the significance of that *was*. Because now the speaker was editor of something else.

Society.

Sitting in Laura's office, in Laura's chair, with her feet in their high-heeled pumps up on Laura's desk was Clemency Makepeace.

Chapter Twenty-six

Laura's first instinct was to rush into her office and order Clemency to get out of it. Her second was to hesitate. Confrontation was unlikely to get the result she wanted. The first thing that would happen was that Clemency would refuse to move. Then there would be a blazing row. Then Clemency would probably call security, claim she had felt threatened and have Laura thrown out.

She had used all these tactics before. And what had saved Laura in the past was that Christopher Stone, then CEO, had been on her side. Now the CEO was Bev Sweet, who was on the side of the devil. One incarnation of whom was the red-headed supplanter now lolling in Laura's office, talking animatedly on the phone.

She must, Laura realised, play it cool. Play the long game. She would allow events to develop, for the situation to reveal itself, and then she would decide what to do. She must stay in the room, as people said. Not get ejected from the entire building within ten minutes of arriving.

She took a deep breath, and forced her features into a vast, insincere Clemency-esque smile. They refused to do this, so she made do with an expression of careful neutrality and walked up to the door of what, until recently, had been her office.

As Clemency, still yakking away to her mystery interlocutor, ignored her, Laura took the opportunity to look round. Given the short time she had occupied the hot seat, her rival had made a lot of changes.

A sofa shaped like a pair of vampish red lips had supplanted the old yellow settee on which the entire staff heaped itself during meetings. Framed photographs of Clemency with A-list celebrities crowded the shelves that had formerly held *Society*'s journalism awards, some of which Laura had helped to win. A gleam of glass from the waste paper bin hinted at where they had ended up.

'Laters at the Firehouse, darling. Toodle-oo!' Clemency finally replaced the receiver and raised glittering green eyes to Laura. They looked her up and down, flashing evilly. 'Well, well, well. Look what the cat's dragged in.'

Laura met the malicious gaze with a level one of her own. 'Can we talk?'

'What else are we doing?' quipped the woman in the editor's chair, currently swinging about and crossing her legs like Sharon Stone in *Basic Instinct*. Clemency wore a close-fitting black skirt, white blouse and black stilettos whose pointed toes looked even sharper than their heels. It was a uniform Laura recognised. The new editor was Bev Sweet's Mini-Me. Or, possibly, given the size of Bev Sweet, her Maxi-Me.

Laura sat down on the vampish sofa. 'I'm not entirely sure what's going on here,' she began, reasonably.

Clemency stopped swinging and leant forward. She gave a sickly sweet smile. 'What does it look like, darling? I've got your job!'

Laura swallowed. For a second, the room tilted. Then the feeling of shock, of defeat, of her worst fears being realised, became a great, galvanising fury. She clenched her fists.

She forced it down, however. There was no point screaming at Clemency. The person behind this move was Bev Sweet. The real question was – why? Clemency was a terrible editor. She could backstab and scheme her way to the job, but once there, she was useless.

'You,' Clemency added, with a vicious satisfaction, 'are now my deputy.'

Laura sat back on the red lips. So that was it. Still, at least she hadn't been sacked.

It wasn't great, all the same. Clemency would get the glory, the glamour and the deference. But Laura, as deputy – i.e., dogsbody – would do all the work.

On the other hand, this at least meant that she was no longer responsible for the Scottish issue. Which, given how she now felt about the place, was just as well. Her effort at smiling at Clemency was more successful this time. 'In that case,' she said, 'you've got a lot on your plate. You're going to have to make the Scottish issue work.'

Clemency stared at her. 'What Scottish issue?'

'The 75 per cent advertising one.' Laura tried to keep the sarcasm out of her voice. 'The one I just went to Scotland for.'

'Canned.' Clemency waved a gold-fingernail-tipped hand. 'It's not happening. Bev realised it was a hide into nothing, that the ads would never come through.' She gave Laura a mean red grin. 'So all your time's been wasted. Such a shame!'

Laura had never expected to hear Clemency Makepeace saying anything she wanted to hear. She tried to keep the spike of joy out of her voice. 'So what's the theme of the new issue, then?'

Clemency tossed her rippling auburn hair. 'Bev,' she said.

'Bev?' Laura repeated. 'You mean – *Bev Sweet*?' She was confused. How on earth could the magazine be about her?

It was possible that there was something defensive about the way Clemency now folded her arms. 'Bev's just had her birthday party, so obviously we'll be putting it in the party pages.'

Laura relaxed slightly. It wasn't unreasonable or unusual for the CEO to have a photograph in the social section. Christopher Stone had had one or two over the years. If that was all, fair enough.

'We're giving it twelve pages, the whole section,' Clemency went on, toying with an auburn strand.

'*Twelve pages!*'

'Absolutely.' A pair of narrowed green eyes skewered Laura's. 'And Bev's currently buying a holiday home in Marbella from a completely fascinating firm of high-end international estate agents. They'll make a riveting article and coincidentally they're very interested in taking a few pages of ads.' She swished her red hair about and gave a feline smile. 'Oh, and she's a member of a prestigious Belgravia gym. They're also quite keen to advertise.'

Laura's mouth had dropped open. She could see what was going on now. Her precious magazine was to become a vehicle for the positioning of Bev Sweet as a high society figure and the monetisation of her lifestyle. How Clemency had got the job was no longer a mystery.

'What about the cover?' Laura broke in. Bev Sweet certainly couldn't be on that. Aspirational, money-grubbing and power-crazed she might be, but she was no Cindy Crawford. The magazine's front, at least, must maintain some sort of standard.

Clemency smiled sweetly. 'Bev's daughter Lilibet's going to be our cover girl. She's an up-and-coming actress.'

'Is she?' Laura had never heard of Lilibet Sweet.

'Well, she will be once she's been on our cover. She's taking acting lessons at the moment.'

'What does she look like?' If it was anything like her mother, this was a non-starter.

Clemency's eyes widened in mock amazement. 'I'm surprised at you, Laura. We're living in a Time's Up world where shallow and rigid ideas about appearance have to be challenged.'

Lilibet was hideous, in other words.

'We're running a big interview with her.' Clemency paused and favoured her with a dazzling smile. 'Which you, Laura Lake, will be writing.'

At lunchtime, Laura went for a fast walk to let off steam. A strong wind was whirling the leaves about the garden square opposite the building. They mirrored Laura's angrily whirling thoughts.

Society under Clemency was a joke, although not a very funny one. The magazine, which Laura had made great efforts to position into a scoop-grabbing leader in its field, full of thought-provoking features and interesting people, had gone violently into reverse.

The idea of the Scottish issue had been bad enough, but even worse was a Bev Sweet special whose every page sought to aggrandise the British Magazine Company's unspeakable CEO. It made Laura long for the days when Raisy and Daisy, the fashion editors, would burst into meetings declaring it was all about emergency blanket metallics or extra-extra neon. And for Tatty, the luxury editor, to explain that thank-you presents for presents were a thing now.

She felt guilty about Sandy too. The Glenravish article would now never appear, and Sandy would never be able to sell the place and escape.

Laura was surprised, therefore, to turn from the garden

square through a little courtyard where an expensive restaurant had tables outside, and hear a familiar sound.

'Hwah hwah hwah!'

Laura screeched to a halt so suddenly that her Chelsea boot heels struck sparks off the pavement.

The woman had her back to her, but there was no doubt about it. While, for once, a pie-crust collar was not in evidence, an electric-blue dress was, its shoulder pads extending into the middle of next week. Her hair was just as unmistakeable; who else, after all, sported stiff blonde wings on which an entire can of Extreme Hold had been discharged? Most tellingly of all, her lunching partner was a thumping red-faced pinstriped Hooray who seemed to have come straight from the eighties without touching the sides. His earsplitting 'yah yah yah' echoed round the courtyard.

Laura hurried to her side. 'Sandy!'

'Cripes!' Sandy it was, right down to the blue mascara, the nuclear explosions of blusher and the heart-attack lipstick. From the front, her dress was even more of a vintage classic than it seemed from behind. It referenced the darkest days of Princess Diana's wardrobe, accessorised with vast black circular plastic buttons and completed with black patent flats topped off with electric-blue bows. 'Haven't seen you since you went off stalking with Struan. He said that you suddenly decided to go back to London. And who can blame you, hwah hwah hwah.'

Laura registered the official explanation for her non-return to Glenravish. Possibly anyone bar the capital-fixated Sandy might have smelt a rat, but the lady laird, desperate to reach the fleshpots herself, obviously thought it perfectly normal.

'What are you doing here?' she asked.

'Enjoying myself, *hwah hwah hwah*.' Sandy dug a fork into a great pile of spaghetti exploding from the centre of a crustacean. 'Haven't had Lobster Thatcher since the good old days! Luigi rustled it up just for me.'

'Can't see the point of lobster,' boomed her red-faced companion. 'Can't think of anything worse than poking and prying into all those leg thingies and getting one mouthful for ten minutes' work.' He stuck his fork into a large sausage and prised it out of a mountain of mash.

'*Hwah hwah hwah*,' honked Sandy. She gestured with a lobster claw. 'Have you met Rupert? Rupert, this is Laura. She's an absolutely brilliant magazine editor.'

'I say, is she really?' Rupert's pale, exophthalmic eyes were rolling in his head as he looked Laura appreciatively up and down. Laura felt much as she imagined a cow at market must feel, but also rather guilty. Her brilliance as a magazine editor, should it exist at all, was not now going to do Sandy any favours.

'Yes, she was going to write a piece about Glenravish. Glass of poo, darling?' Sandy waved a bottle of champagne at Laura.

She watched Sandy slosh the foaming liquid in the glass and felt more embarrassed than ever about not being able to deliver the promised article.

But possibly they were evens, because shouldn't Sandy

feel embarrassed about sending her out with a homicidal stalker?

'Well, she won't need to do that now, will she?' brayed Rupert. 'Not now you've flogged the crumbling old pile.'

Laura, sipping her champagne, found it suddenly going up her nose. 'What? You've sold Glenravish?' She stared in amazement at Sandy, who nodded violently, but not violently enough to dislodge her hairsprayed wings.

'Marvellous, isn't it?' Sandy raised a champagne glass into the air. 'I'm back in London! I'm free!'

Chapter Twenty-seven

I t was a week later, and the evening Edgar's whistling choir was to perform. Laura had decided to go along. She had nothing better to do, needed a distraction after a day on the ever more ghastly Bev Sweet issue and, besides, it would be free.

By way of an apology for the recent disturbance Edgar had shoved a couple of tickets through her door. She had been touched and distressed in equal measure; he clearly thought Harry was still around. It was probably just as well he wasn't, though, Laura decided, having examined the tickets more closely. The Shoreditch Whistling Choir were appearing with the Garbage Orchestra Collective. The venue was a multi-storey car park scheduled for demolition. The Last Night of the Proms this definitely was not.

Laura's first thought was to ask Lulu to come. The two of them had not been in touch since Lulu rescued her in her helicopter. But Lulu had been elusive recently; Laura was not entirely sure she was even back in London. Laura had been shocked to hear, during the return in the helicopter, that Lulu had had an almost equally traumatic experience of Scotland. Perhaps she had gone on one of her recuperative New York shopping trips.

Laura, meanwhile, had been battling to keep, if not her job, then *a* job. This had been one humiliation after another, the worst being the interview with Lilibet Sweet. How it would make a cover piece was anyone's guess, but Laura had done her best.

She half-thought of asking Sandy to come to the concert. She was, after all, permanently in residence in the capital now, renting in the same Earl's Court building in which Princess Diana had, pre-marriage, once flat-shared with three friends. Laura wondered if sausage-eating George had had the courage to break the terrible twenty-odd-year-old news and decided that he probably hadn't.

Sandy, however, had proved irritatingly secretive about the identity of the purchaser of Glenravish. She had insisted it was more than her life was worth and Laura didn't relish the prospect of a further evening trying to winkle it out. Sandy, at any rate, would be completely baffled by the idea of a whistling choir, let alone a garbage orchestra collective. Who wouldn't?

She decided to go on her own. Solitude, anyway, suited her current mournful state of mind.

'It's taters, Laura, where's yer weasel?' yelled Ben from the inside of Gorblimey Trousers, and Laura doubled back. He was quite right, the evening was cold and she would need a coat.

The multi-storey car park resounded with the hubbub of a fashionable crowd. Laura threaded her way through men with curated beards and women whose floaty dresses were teamed with eighteen-hole lace-up boots. She had hoped to see Edgar, but there was no sign of him, nor of anyone who might be a garbage collective orchestra.

They were clearly somewhere, however, as at the appointed time all the beards, dresses and boots started disappearing from the main mustering area down some stairs. Following them, Laura entered a large concrete room full of heating ducts and pulled-out wires. There was no natural light at all. Builders' lamps shone on a wall against which a number of people in hazmat suits stood with their backs turned. Piled around them were cardboard boxes and oil drums. It looked to Laura as if something had gone very wrong in the council's recycling department.

'Novichok?' someone behind Laura muttered. A ripple of uncertainty spread through the crowd packed into the small space.

Laura, however, felt almost at home. The darkness, the bleakness, the edgy urban vibe, took her right back to the start of her career in journalism, when she had been in Paris, so skint she had accepted a job sitting on a mattress in a morgue, surrounded by rubbish. The mattress – and the rubbish, for that matter – had been a cutting-edge installation called *Call This Art?* by a British contemporary artist called Amy Bender. There had been compensations: it had led to her job at *Society*, and she had met Caspar. At the time he had been an out-of-work actor, not the Hollywood superstar he was now. Or had been, until his recent fall from grace. Laura was just starting to wonder how he was – he was so hopeless, or maybe too famous, about keeping in touch – when something jerked her abruptly from her thoughts.

'Is what going on?' A familiar voice now rang round the basement, putting into words what everyone was feeling. Laura felt a great smile split her face in the dark.

'Lulu!' she called into the crowd, just at the moment the hazmat suits turned round, did jazz hands and launched into a whistled version of Michael Jackson's 'You Wanna Be Startin' Something?' Edgar was at the end, a little out of time, Laura noticed.

The ones not whistling had seized the boxes and oil drums and begun banging wildly away at them with drumsticks. The noise was deafening, much too loud to talk. It was like some extreme mutual therapy session. Perhaps it was. But what was definitely the case was that conversation would have to wait until the interval.

After what seemed years of violent crashing and tuneless screeching, a pause came in the proceedings. Laura, who had squeezed and slid her way back to the entrance so as to be first out, practically ran back up to the ground floor of the car park. Here, night had fallen. The building-site arc lights shone powerfully down on trestle tables ranged with Peckecco, the local Peckham-produced sparkling wine in plastic cups. Grabbing a couple – her nerves were shot to pieces – Laura looked eagerly round for Lulu.

She was easy to spot, and not just because of her pile of blonde hair and rhinestone-studded trousers teamed with a bolero of shaggy white fur. In silver wellies overprinted with the Chanel double 'C', she was standing at the back of the drinks queue, lip pushed crossly out beneath the ever-present huge sunglasses.

Laura smiled. Lulu hated queuing, especially for something not champagne. As she hurried towards her friend, waving her spare plastic cup, she felt comforted to see a huge Hollywood-white smile split Lulu's deeply tanned face. It had been a long time since someone was this pleased to see her.

'Laura! Thank God you here, hmm?' Lulu grabbed the wine and knocked it back in one.

'How come you are?'

'Is South'n Fried. Whistling garbage bug thing.'

'Big thing,' corrected Laura, though some of the garbage collective had certainly looked less than pristine. One, with matted grey dreadlocks to his knees, had been scratching himself throughout. 'You mean it's attracting attention?' She looked about. There were certainly a lot of people here.

'Is right. Music producers and big arse men here tonight, hmm?'

A & R, Lulu guessed. Artists and repertoire. Talent spotters from big record companies, in other words. It made sense for South'n Fried to see and be seen here. He stood some distance away, the centre of an admiring crowd. Sporting a white fur coat over a suit printed with Marvel characters, he looked quite his old over-styled self. She could see the rubies in his teeth gleaming even from here.

Laura guessed that this meant that the Land of the Purple Haze had now finally been ruled out. But the demanding Nadine Salmon's loss was the Shoreditch Whistling Choir and Garbage Collective Orchestra's gain: presumably they would be performing on the new album. Edgar would be thrilled. He was a big South'n Fried fan, and Laura had heard the rapper pounding through her ceiling in the early hours long before she had ever met him.

'You must be glad to see the back of Scotland,' she remarked.

Lulu nodded happily. 'Back to Scotland tonight, yes. In helicopter.'

Laura's jaw dropped open.

'We have new plan. Nadine Salmon going to love it.'

Laura frowned. She couldn't see the famously brusque Scottish First Minister getting behind a whistling choir. Especially not one from Shoreditch. 'You're surely not still trying to get South'n Fried into Land of the Purple Haze?'

The blonde hair nodded. 'Of course! Is big festival! Big relaunch. So we have bought big estate!'

For a single, hopeful second Laura wondered if she was talking about a car. A big car, with a rear door. Suitable for loading music gear into. The British called those estates, after all.

But then again…

Laura swallowed the rest of her Peckecco. Lulu couldn't surely mean what every nerve in her body was now telling her she did mean. 'A… Scottish estate?' She could not be serious. Not even Lulu, who bought houses like other people bought handbags.

Lulu had dived at the trestle tables and grabbed another two cups from right under the beards of the queue. Stern facial hair was being turned in her direction, but these bounced off Lulu's sunglasses like water off a duck's back. 'Nadine Salmon,' she said, after a triumphant slurp, 'can't say South'n not Scottish enough. Not when he big lard, hmm?'

Laura was too horrified to correct her. A terrible suspicion had seized her. 'Not McBang's estate?' Had Lulu bought it after all, even though it wasn't his to sell?

It was Lulu's turn to look horrified. The Peckecco shook agitatedly in the cups 'No, no, no! This much nicer estate. Full of good people, hmm? House very nice, countryside very nice, laird we bought from very nice, although he is not man, he is woman.'

The cup in Laura's hand fell to the ground. 'Glenravish!'

'Yes, belong your nice friend Sandy, hmm? Why you drop cup? Clumsy Laura!'

Laura hardly heard her. So many things had become clear in an instant. If Sandy knew Lulu was Laura's friend, no wonder she had not admitted she was the buyer. Laura knew how desperate Sandy had been to leave. She also knew about the lack of Wi-Fi, the intermittent electricity, and the hideous presence of Mordor. The members of staff with murder in their hearts. And how much had Sandy told Lulu about the ghosts?

'Ghosts?' The sunglasses gave an amazed flash. 'Glenravish have no ghosts. But great Flora MacDoughnut location!'

Laura had thought she had no shock left in her. She now realised she was wrong. This really was too bad of Sandy. Glossing over the hauntings was one thing, but brazenly lying about its historical connections was entirely another. Flora MacDonald had never been near Glenravish – Sandy had said so herself.

'Flora MacDonald, she meet Bonnie Prince Charlie at Glenravish,' Lulu declared.

Hot anger blazed through Laura. 'That's not true.'

On Lulu's pale-pink leather trousers, the rhinestones glittered defiantly. 'Is true!' she insisted. 'Glenravish location, hmmm? For Prince Charlie and Flora MacDoughnut dance, hmm?'

Laura sighed deeply. Sandy had obviously let her imagination get the better of her, or perhaps her wine cellar. And now Lulu was mistress of a haunted castle with a homicidal stalker on her staff.

'Oh Lulu!' she groaned. 'What have you *done*?'

Chapter Twenty-eight

That night, Laura could not sleep. She lay awake, worrying about Lulu. She imagined her at Glenravish, maybe in the same little chamber Laura had occupied. Or perhaps Sandy's newly vacated one. Laura pictured some huge eighties bedroom, swagged with *toile de Jouy*. There would be slipper chairs, wastepaper bins printed with hunting scenes and cushions that said 'When The Going Gets Tough The Tough Go Shopping'. Admittedly, even the toughest would find that a struggle around Glenravish.

Was South'n Fried with her? Even if he was, he would be no help. The biggest, baddest, boldest rapper – Lulu's husband's professional persona in a nutshell – could not protect her against forces of which he knew nothing.

Laura had failed to warn her friend at the concert – there was no opportunity anyway, as the whistled highlights of 'Mamma Mia' had started up almost immediately after the Glenravish revelations and Lulu had been borne away on a wave of bling at the end. When she had tried to call her afterwards Lulu had not picked up. But of course not. There was no signal at Glenravish, and the landline wasn't working either.

But was that the only reason? What if the crazed stalker had attacked her as well? Laura's thoughts ping-ponged in her head as the early hours drew on. Two contradictory ideas dominated all the rest.

She was imagining it all, Lulu was in no danger.

She should go up there, Lulu was definitely in danger.

But she had a job to try and keep. Unlike Lulu, Laura had no multi-billion-pound fortune to support her if she lost it. Without work she would lose her flat and then she would have to leave London. Much as she loved her grandmother, she didn't want to go back to that cramped little Parisian apartment. There was barely room for Mimi and her Croix de Lorraine pyjamas, let alone anyone else. Besides, Mimi had done enough for her.

What would Mimi do now, though? Laura tried her grandmother's number several times. There was no answer, however, and the ringtone sounded different. She was obviously globetrotting with the Fat Four.

She had been trying not to think about Harry. But tiredness and despair had worn away her defences and he rushed unstoppably to the front of her mind. She felt a longing so strong it might have knocked her over if she had not been already lying down.

If only Harry were here. He would know what to do. But he had gone no one knew where, or if they did they weren't telling. Laura had stopped bothering to call Autumn on Harry's foreign desk now. It was pointless; she was more discreet than a clam welded with Araldite. What she was doing on a newspaper was a mystery.

Unable to sleep, distracted and worried, Laura lay and listened to the night sounds of Cod's Head Row. While other landlords simply called 'Time', or rang a bell, Bill and Ben always signalled the closing of Gorblimey Trousers with a rendition of – what else – 'My Old Man's A Dustman'.

Laura could hear them seeing off some of their regulars. 'Ta-ra, Hector. Love the new Hampsteads.' She smiled. Hector, a well-known film director, had recently had his teeth capped.

Edgar was not yet back; no doubt out celebrating with the rest of his ensemble. Laura wasn't sure she would want to be near a euphoric garbage collective, not really.

Bill and Ben were moving the tables indoors now. 'Careful, you nearly got me in the bleedin' orchestras,' Bill exclaimed at his partner. *Orchestra stalls, balls*, Laura translated. That they still spoke rhyming slang when alone seemed rather endearing.

Lying in the orange slant of street light that poked through the crack in her shutters, she sighed heavily. She had thought and thought but all her worries still seemed to boil down to two main questions. Was Lulu all right?

Was she about to be sacked by Clemency? When, finally, she drifted into sleep, Laura didn't know the answer to either.

'Meeting, everyone,' called a subdued-sounding Demelza next morning from her desk outside Clemency's office.

Beneath the bowed heads sitting silently at their computers, apprehensive glances were exchanged. The daily brainstorms, which Laura as editor had enjoyed so much, were now widely regarded as torture. Everyone in them could not wait to get out of them; everyone who was allowed in them, that was.

Clemency had returned to the heads-of-department-only approach, reversing what had been Laura's open-door policy. She had invited everyone right down to the lowest intern, especially the lowest intern. Once upon a time Laura had been that lowest intern herself. She felt that anyone could have ideas and the best ones came from the most unexpected places.

The *Society* staff filed apprehensively in and sat down on the lips-shaped sofa as gingerly as if expecting it to explode beneath them. From the other side of her wide glass desk, Clemency regarded them with glittering eyes. Laura was the last to enter – she had just been finishing a phone call. By the time she walked up to it, brisk but not hurried, the glass door to the editorial sanctum was closed.

'Laura! So good of you to join us!' said Clemency, sarkily. She was wearing a tight, short-sleeved dress whose unnerving acid yellow colour seemed somehow to increase the tension in the room. 'We were just talking about fashion,' she added, looking meaningfully at Laura's unchanging uniform of dark fitted shirt, tight jeans and boots.

Laura smiled calmly, tossed her shiny dark hair over her shoulders and leant against the shelves that had lately held her awards. Demelza had rescued them from the bin and they were now safely stowed in her bottom drawer. They would have been in Laura's own bottom drawer, but Clemency had introduced 'hot desking' by which no staff member except Demelza had their own space but was constantly obliged to find a new one.

This was apparently meant to introduce dynamism and efficiency to the workplace but in practice just meant that people in departments with lots of equipment – food, for instance, or beauty – were constantly roaming about the room with armfuls of mushrooms in white chocolate or facial sand from the Mojave desert.

Clemency finally stopped glaring at Laura and started glaring at the fashion editor instead. 'Carry on, Rosie.'

Laura blinked. She had never heard Rosie called by her proper name before. To everyone, Rosie was Raisy because she pronounced her name to rhyme with Daisy, her twin sister and fellow fashion editor.

Former fellow fashion editor, that was; Daisy was no longer employed on *Society*. One of Clemency's most cruel innovations was to split up the duo, making them draw lots before the entire office to decide which one would be sacked. The spectacle, which had reminded Laura of something horrible from Ancient Rome, had been intended to strike fear into the hearts of the staff. All it had actually stoked was hatred.

Raisy, certainly, was miserable. She seemed to the sympathetic Laura a shadow of the ebullient girl who had rocked up to meetings in trousers whose legs were two different colours, topped off with an archbishop's mitre. Today's outfit, a frilled-collar shirt worn with pageboy trousers and side-parted glossy hair with a slight flick about it, looked positively muted. As well as strangely familiar.

'This issue,' Raisy said, making an obvious effort to summon the requisite enthusiasm, 'is all about eighties dressing. Shoulder pads are back. Big buttons.'

Laura thought immediately of Sandy.

'White lipstick, tons of hairspray, pixie boots, needlecord knickerbockers. New Romantic frills.'

Sandy was a fashion icon!

But Clemency's expression was as bitter as a particularly disappointed lemon. 'Bollocks,' she said rudely. 'Even allowing for the moronitude of the fashion industry, no one will ever wear clothes like that again.'

Raisy looked about to object, then thought better of it. Laura stepped in. 'I know someone who does.'

Her reward was a glance of glittering green contempt. 'You would.' Then Clemency trained the emerald searchlights back on Raisy. 'We need something gender-fluid, gender pay gap, consciousness-raising, hashtag MeToo, national-conversation-starting and woke.'

Laura rolled her eyes. As if Clemency, arch-backstabber, cared about any of this. She cared about herself, first and foremost.

A sad, sinking feeling succeeded the scorn. Such hope as there had been, Laura sensed, had conclusively gone. *Society* and the jobs of her staff could no longer be saved – by her, at any rate. The forces of Bev Sweet and Clemency Makepeace were ranged against her. It was impossible, now, that she could prevail. The wisest thing to do would be to give up the effort, walk out and return to Scotland where at least she would be able to help Lulu battle the forces of of Struan, Mordor and the various phantasmic foes ranged against *her*.

At the same time, every fibre of Laura's being resisted the idea that she should accept defeat. Throwing in the towel after so much effort was unbearable. She had tried so hard and put so much of herself into the magazine and its staff that leaving it would be like deserting her family. She just couldn't. And Lulu was a grown woman, with not only South'n Fried to support her, but also Vlad. She could more than look after herself.

As Laura fought this agonising inner battle, the features meeting went on around her.

La Makepeace was still skewering Raisy with her pitiless gaze. 'I want a shoot on white shirts, black skirts and black stilettos. Okay?'

Raisy shrugged her drooping shoulders.

'Good.' Clemency swung her red hair back towards the rest of the staff.

It was Tatty the luxury editor's turn next. She had written a piece about Bev Sweet's Belgravia gym, a place where 'spa butlers' valeted your kit once Kate Moss's trainer had taken you through the Meghan Markle workout. Clemency beamed. 'I'm always so excited about pieces that encapsulate everything we stand for here at *Society*.'

The green blowlamps now swung suddenly to Laura. 'This piece on Lilibet Sweet,' Clemency said, raising a printout in the air with a skeletal white hand.

Laura felt a mixture of dread and unquenchable hope. Much as she hated Clemency, she was still a journalist and as such she wanted her work to be admired.

'It's crap,' said Clemency.

Laura raised her chin. 'Why crap? I did my best. Lilibet wasn't exactly what I'd been led to believe. She's not an up-and-coming actress, for a start.'

Bev's daughter had not been up-and-coming in any way at all, she hadn't even been out of bed. A cowed Filipina maid, finger to her lips, had tiptoed Laura to the kitchen of a vast Mayfair penthouse that the British Magazine Company was almost certainly paying for. When Lilibet had eventually appeared, greasy-haired and yawning, in a bathrobe embroidered with the logo of the Paris Ritz, she ordered the Filipina to fetch an Egg McMuffin and revealed that acting wasn't her thing – you had to learn lines, for a start.

Clemency was frowning at the sheets of paper, where Laura had pulled no punches.

The green blowlamps were blazing furiously. 'Lilibet's

ultimate ambition is to win an Oscar and marry into the royal family. That's what Bev told *me*.' Clemency took the printout between her skinny, corpse-like fingers and ripped it violently down the middle. 'That's what I think of your article, Laura Lake. And what I think of you, too. You're fired.'

Laura cleared her latest hot desk speedily. After all her earlier agonising, it seemed as if the decision was being made for her. As soon as she cleared her desk she would head up to Scotland.

She just hoped she would not be too late.

Chapter Twenty-nine

'Ladiesngenlmen, this is the late-running 09.42 from Inverness to Glenravish, calling Achenbuchat, Loch Slog, Dampie Castle…'

In the intervening week and a bit since last she heard him, Laura had decided the ghoulish guard/driver/trolley dolly had been some Scottish-Gothic nightmare. She was wrong, she now realised.

'*Please take the time to ensure you have all your belongings with you and if you spot something unusual on the train please either report it to a member of the on-train team or text the British Transport Police. Remember, See it. Say it*—'

'Speed it up,' muttered Laura. Finally the train was about to depart. Thanks to an endless list of problems with the train, all announced incomprehensibly over a crackling tannoy, it was six hours since she got off the sleeper from London. As Fraser came stumbling and cursing down the gangway, Laura took her courage in both hands and tackled him.

'How long to get to Glenravish?' According to the ScotRail website, the journey from Inverness was two and a half hours.

Fraser, who looked even more desiccated than last time, regarded her with the one rheumy eye that showed beneath his lopsided greasy cap. There hung around him a strong smell of spirits. He wiped flecks of spittle from his mouth. 'Nine hours, aye.'

'But why?' Laura felt desperate. She had travelled overnight on purpose so as to have a whole day to talk to Lulu. At this rate she would be arriving close to bedtime, when conversation would be cut short, especially if South'n Fried was around. He was an attentive husband, in that department at least.

'We're behind a late-running train, lassie,' Fraser announced in a shower of whisky-flavoured spittle.

'But we can't be. We've only just set off.'

'And there's leaves on the line, the wrong sort o' snow, points failure and children playing on the railway.'

Laura stared. 'What, already?'

'Noo, but there will be.' Fraser reeled off down the carriage. 'Any more tickets? '

He disappeared and the train now shuddered forward, stopped with a violent screech and then moved again. They were off. Laura stared gloomily out of the window as the reddish spires and towers of Inverness slid past the window. Nine hours! Nine depressing, endless hours, to contemplate the smoking ruins of her career. To muse on how, yet again, Clemency Makepeace had got the better of her.

At least, Laura reflected, the hours spent perusing the Inverness Station branch of Boots meant she had enough bags of crisps, chicken tikka wraps and bottles of water to see her through the journey. She would have no need of the lard bars and Irn-Bru from the refreshment trolley from hell.

On the seat across from her a strange young man mouthed manically along to the music playing in his headphones. Was it South'n Fried, Laura wondered, before the heat of the carriage and the monotonous rattle of the tracks sent her finally over the edge into much-needed oblivion.

She must have slept for a long time. When she awoke, her neck aching and with a stream of dribble down the front of her trenchcoat, everything outside was pitch black. Night had fallen. Fallen so hard it looked unlikely ever to get up again.

Laura looked around. The carriage was empty. Fraser did not seem to be on board either. Panic seized her, especially as the train was moving faster. Faster and faster all the time, in fact. Like a runaway train, about to crash. Had Fraser baled out and left her to face the consequences?

CRASH! BANG!

The carriage screeched to a halt. Laura, who had crouched in the brace position with her arms over her head, now opened her eyes again. She was still here. In one piece. Alive.

The door into the carriage now opened, revealing a black rectangle of night sky accompanied by a freezing blast of air. Into the rectangle now came Fraser, grunting as he remounted into the train. He had clearly been outside on the track and was dragging something on board, something small that was bleeding profusely. With a cold stab of horror, Laura remembered the warnings about children playing on the railway. Was this one of them?

Before her appalled sight Fraser released his burden abruptly. It hit the floor with a bang, sprawling in its blood in the gangway.

Now Laura realised what it was. A deer. That explained the sudden speed; Fraser must have spotted it in the train headlights and put his foot down to hit it.

As the red rivulets made their way over the regulation grey floor, Laura lifted her boots out of harm's way. She wondered if Fraser did this on every journey. Mrs Fraser – always supposing such an unfortunate creature existed – must be a dab hand with venison.

This reminded her that it was some time since she had eaten her last Boots chicken tikka sandwich. She was starving. How much longer, she wondered, was it to Glenravish?

Later, much later, Laura watched Fraser's train rattle off into the night. Silence folded around her, and an intense darkness. She was on Glenravish station again, and this time there was no friendly moon to light her way. She could hear, the other side of the railway, the lapping waters of the loch. *Go back, go back*, they seemed to whisper.

But there was no going back. Not least because the train would not come past again for twenty-four hours. Laura squared her shoulders and stiffened her sinews, although they were pretty stiff already after nine hours of near-immobility. She searched for her phone in her pocket and switched on the light.

The front gate, as before, was locked. Laura stared through the twisting decorative metalwork in despair. Clearly Lulu had received none of her texts; the reception at Glenravish was as hopeless as ever. The landline was also down; she had tried that too. So Lulu had no idea she was coming.

It seemed she would have to shin over the side gate again. As before, this was locked as well. But now, at least, she knew the form. Laura climbed carefully up it, swung her leg over, and climbed down the other side as silently as a cat. No tumbles and torn trousers this time.

The night pressed in and the silence boomed in her ears. She moved carefully through the grass, her bag slung over her shoulder, feeling her way ahead with her hands in best Resistance fashion.

Mimi had showed her how, on sunny afternoons in the Jardins de Luxembourg. While other families had picnics or sailed toy boats on the lake, Laura's formidable grandmother had demonstrated how to escape through enemy territory.

It had seemed like a game at the time and Laura had

never imagined ever using it seriously. But never, either, had she ever imagined Glenravish. She wondered if Koji was still patrolling the grounds. He had not reappeared during her short stay with Sandy. That he was, after all, one of the resident spooks seemed more than likely.

She pressed on. The invisible leaves and grass felt cool beneath her touch. From time to time she sensed a tree looming up and stretched out her arms to avoid crashing into it. In the distance, in the depths of the woods, she could hear the unearthly keening of nocturnal animals; they sounded, she thought, like lost souls. The hooting of a solitary owl didn't much help matters. Laura felt the hairs on the back of her neck stand on end. The night seemed alive, somehow.

It was drizzling now. The rain hissed softly on the leaves, adding another unsettling strand to the evening symphony. She took a deep, ragged breath to calm her rioting nerves and pressed on in what she guessed was the direction of the castle. There were no lights at all; everything was black. Another of Glenravish's famous power cuts, Laura supposed.

Suddenly, the veins in her eyes exploded in a flash of painful light. A torch was shining in her face, held by someone she could not see. She reeled; her bag slipped off her arm and tumbled into the undergrowth. She tried to bend to find it, but an iron grip had seized her wrist. She gasped and wriggled, but the grip held tight.

'Let me go!' Laura gasped. Was it Struan the murderous stalker?

'Is you again, huh?' The torch beam disappeared and

a friendly Japanese face looked down at her. Laura saw epaulettes, the flash of a uniform. A huge, meaningful-looking gun.

'Koji!' So he was real, after all. But even if he had been a ghost she would have preferred him to Struan.

She hastened to explain herself. 'I'm here to see Lulu. She owns this place now. She bought it off Sandy.'

'Lulu not here at moment.'

'Not here?' gasped Laura. She wanted to cry. After all she had endured. The endless train journey, Fraser's loco-powered hunter-gathering, the scrabbling through dark, slippy undergrowth, all made bearable only by the prospect of seeing her friend.

'Where is she?' Laura demanded.

Koji did not reply. Instead, he had hurried her through the garden to the front door.

'I'll leave you with Mrs MacRae,' he finally said as he yanked hard on the bell.

The vast medieval portal now creaked open and the pleasant, apple-cheeked face of the housekeeper, illuminated by the familiar candle, peered smilingly out into the drizzling darkness. The housekeeper married to a murderer, Laura reminded herself crossly.

'Well, if it isn't Miss Laura!' exclaimed Mrs MacRae, with every appearance of delight. 'You look all in, my dear. Come in, come in, we'll run you a bath in no time. Then I'll see about some supper.'

Laura turned to Koji, but, as before, he had disappeared. She rubbed her eyes. Was he real, or wasn't he? His grip had felt real enough.

'We're having a wee bit o' bother with the ghosties again,' Mrs MacRae said comfortably as she led the way through the hall with the candle. Her dark dress blended with the shadows so it was like following a disembodied head.

'While we're on the subject of bother,' Laura said sarcastically, 'I had a bit of bother with your husband. When we were out on the hill, he tried to kill me.'

Instead, of evincing shock, guilt or anger, the housekeeper smiled indulgently. 'No, no, dearie. You're overtired. You're imagining it. You gave poor Struan a terrible shock, falling in that bog like that. And before he could rescue you, down came Miss Lulu in her helicopter.'

Laura's mouth fell open. She pulled it up hastily and was about to indignantly disagree when it struck her that discretion might be the better part of valour. Antagonising Mrs Struan could have bad results. Apparent acceptance might be safer. Until the morning, at least. Then she would consider her position.

But in the meantime she did have one burning query. 'Where is Lulu?' It occurred to her now that Koji had sidestepped the question.

Mrs MacRae did not answer either, but led on through Glenravish's vast hall. Laura followed, wondering if Lulu had decided not to buy the castle after all, or whether the deal had fallen through at the last minute. While this would be a relief on the one hand, on the other it meant she had suffered the agony of the train journey for nothing.

On the ancient stone walls, their huge black shadows

jerked alarmingly. The candle flame glinted menacingly off the elaborately arranged ordnance. The bollock-splitter was back in its old place, Laura noticed. She also noticed, or thought she noticed, that the guns had been moved around. They seemed to be in different patterns from before. Patterns, Laura now realised, she knew well.

On the great wall above the mantelpiece, pistols were arranged in two great interlocking Chanel 'C's. Next to them, a number of small daggers had been made into the Gucci 'G'. 'YSL', meanwhile, had been achieved with bayonet rifles; a chain with a spiked mace on each end forming the 'S'. More pistols formed the Louis Vuitton logo.

Oh yes, Laura thought. Lulu had bought the castle all right.

Mrs MacRae was also smiling fondly at the arrangements. 'Miss Lulu will have her fun.'

Laura wanted to punch the air. Lulu had put her stamp on the place already. Glenravish was dancing to her tune. The only mystery was – where was she?

'Och, she just slipped out. She'll be back soon,' Mrs MacRae assured her, comfortably.

Chapter Thirty

After a brown bath and a plateful of the inevitable venison stew, Laura lay in the small, cosy room she had previously occupied.

Her mind was rioting. Just what was going on in this place? For one thing, Lulu had not come back from wherever she had slipped off to. Mrs MacRae had been relaxed about it, saying that, now she came to think about it, Lulu might have gone on a trip Down Under.

'You mean Australia?' Laura had gasped. Her friend was prone to last-minute shopping-related long haul, but even for her this was impetuous. Especially as she had a whole new – or rather, old – castle to explore. Still, as Vlad was nowhere to be seen either, it seemed the only explanation.

Then there was the question of Struan.

Was it possible that she had imagined he was trying to kill her? But Mrs MacRae had received her so pleasantly and parried the idea so charmingly that Laura was no longer so certain. Why would he, after all? It made no sense. Much more likely it was an accident and he had been about to come to the rescue, as his wife had claimed.

Then there was the Flora MacDonald question; the ball at Glenravish that Sandy had told Lulu about. Had she really made it up to get the sale through? If so, she was a lesser woman than she had seemed. Laura felt disappointed in Sandy. Then again, the sale was doubtless the reason Mordor had not appeared at supper or anywhere else for that matter. Presumably Lulu, who for all her kindness could spot a sponger at a hundred paces, had given him his marching orders.

Laura burrowed her face further into the cool, lavender-scented pillow. All this thinking was making her tired. She began to drift gently off to sleep.

Suddenly she was wide awake again. Had she heard something? Laura stared up from the pillow into the thick dark. It was not morning yet, it must still be the middle of the night. Go back to sleep, she told herself, snuggling back down into the warm pillow.

There it was again! A noise. She had definitely heard it this time. Laura sat up, heart hammering. The bed creaked deafeningly as she reached for the bedside lamp; it did not work, unsurprisingly. Her fingers closed round her smartphone and switched it on.

Armed, now, with some light at least, Laura sat on the edge of the bed and listened. She hoped desperately that she was mistaken. The very last thing she wanted to do was leave the room and investigate. Fearless journalist though she was, there were limits, especially in a place like Glenravish. Hopefully it was nothing.

No, it was definitely something. A faint sequence of sounds, coming from some distance away. For a second she wondered if she had left the radio on in the bathroom before remembering that there was no radio at Glenravish. Laura thought of Mrs MacRae. Had she known where she was, she would have shot to her room and hurled herself into the housekeeper's arms, all forgiven. She had no idea where the woman slept though, or whether she even lived in the fortress. For all Laura knew, she was entirely alone. Her insides went liquid with terror at the thought.

'*Fierté. Espoir. Courage.*' She could almost hear her indomitable grandmother's voice. Perhaps, too, she could feel her father's fearless spirit urging her on. With a heartfelt groan, Laura pushed back the warm, comforting bedclothes, placed her shrinking soles on the cold varnish of the floorboards and stood up.

Laura habitually slept naked. She shuddered as the chilly air now seized her bed-warm body. She fumbled in the dark for her jeans, which had stiffened in the freezing air. Against her bare breasts, her shirt was so cold it felt hot. She buttoned it hastily, felt for her boots and slunk reluctantly to the door.

Any frail hope that the noise would stop, or prove to be non-existent, now conclusively faded. Laura's room was at the end of a landing at the other end of which were stairs. They led down to the Great Hall, and it was from here that the disturbance seemed to originate. Laura could hear music, the sound of bagpipes, of voices and laughter, the clap and stamp of people dancing.

She froze to the spot, clutching the door, swallowing hard. Fear juddered painfully down her nerves. Was this some ghostly gathering from the distant past? Almost certainly it was.

Laura had never seen an actual ghost before. The thought of actually encountering one – or several, by the sound of it – made her veins freeze and her stomach churn with nausea. She thought of her precarious position, alone in the isolated midnight castle, slap bang in the middle of nowhere, and wanted to weep. What was she doing here? Why did she always get herself into these situations? What was wrong with her?

A glow was coming from the hall, as of unearthly light. It was just enough to see without her phone torch, and so she switched it off. Bad things, Laura now vaguely remembered, happened to those who attracted the attention of ghosts. Even ones who seemed to be having as good a time as these ones evidently were. She could hear cheering, clapping, whoops. She hesitated, then moved tremblingly forward.

Laura had noticed during her earlier visit that the great hall of Glenravish had a minstrel's gallery at one end, providing a view of the room below. It could be accessed from the top of the stairs, and it was here that the terrified reporter now slipped, pressing back into the shadows so as not to be seen.

What she saw below, in the hall, took what remained of her breath away.

The huge old room, pitch-dark before, now blazed with the light of many candles. It was full of dancing people, all dressed in the fashion of two hundred and fifty years ago; the men in ponytailed wigs with sausage curls at the sides, the women with hair drawn back in masses of ringlets, their pale bosoms almost exposed in daringly low-cut bodices. There was a lot of tartan, Laura noticed; the men wore kilts and the women big-skirted plaid silk dresses. Tartan cloaks were thrown over shoulders. Swords flashed on the sides of belts and dirks glinted from the depths of stockings. A proper Highland gathering, Laura thought. Of proper Highland ghosts. The kind of ball that must have been held at Glenravish, back in the day.

It looked fun, it had to be said. Such fun that Laura almost forgot to be frightened. It had a very real quality to it, as if she were watching an actual event. The music swelled in her ears; inviting, gay and infectious. Laura's foot tapped happily in time as she watched the dancers swirling about each other, the men bowing and the women curtseying at the end of each number. The pipers, whose red faces looked particularly sweaty and real, blew mightily away on their instruments, accompanied by fleet-fingered fiddlers. Now the men were twirling with their arms in the air, kilts swirling and sporrans swinging as the women clapped and the bagpipes skirled.

The centre of the room's attention, and towards whom everyone kept glancing, was a tall, handsome young man whose sporran was more imposing and whose wig was bigger and shinier than everyone else's. Laura realised with a shock that this was not any old ghostly Highland ball she was witnessing, but a very particular one.

This must be Glenravish's number one historic event, the red-letter day, or rather evening, to which Lulu had referred. The handsome young man must be the ghost of Bonnie Prince Charlie and the young woman with whom he was dancing, a pretty, diminutive brunette gazing at him with large, dark, adoring eyes, must be the shade of Flora MacDonald.

Laura raised a hand to her mouth, shocked, excited and terrified all at the same time. So Sandy had for some reason told her a lie, whilst telling Lulu the truth. One of history's most dynamic duos, the darlings of the Jacobite cause, had visited Glenravish after all. Their spirits had remained here ever after, evoking the high days and happy optimism of the adventure that had gone so badly wrong.

Now that she knew his identity, Laura couldn't stop looking at the Young Chevalier. History had not exaggerated the prince's quite extraordinary charisma. It had not mentioned his teeth though, which seemed remarkably huge and white given the standards of the time. Maybe Lulu wasn't wrong about the sex, either. Flora was pressing herself hard against her royal partner, pushing her bosoms upwards, and his eyes, as he watched her, seemed narrowed with desire. As the dance went on, the young couple were almost audibly panting with lust. When they turned towards each other, Flora slipped a small white hand inside the Prince's breeches. When they turned away again, he returned the compliment by tweaking a semi-exposed pink nipple.

As the astonished Laura watched, the white-wigged head of Prince Charlie bent down to his partner's and consumed her in a passionate kiss. The surrounding crowd kept right on dancing, however. No one seemed to turn a hair.

Flora and Charlie snogged throughout the number, parting only as the last bagpipe note died away. Flora then swept a demure curtsey, and Charlie a chaste bow. At the back of the room, the pipers and fiddlers wiped the sweat of their exertions from their foreheads.

It really was very hot, Laura thought. She could actually feel the heat, even though it had not existed for a quarter of a millennium. She smiled as she watched the pipers high-fiving each other and swigging from plastic bottles of water.

Hang on. Laura frowned. *High fives?* She went to the edge of the gallery and looked closer. *Bottles of water?*

Somewhere in the back of her mind, behind all the fear and surprise, Laura had registered that the room was very bright considering it was only lit by candles. She could now see why. Beneath the balcony, previously hidden from her view, was a row of enormous arc lights on stands, and positioned among them were several large cameras with boom microphones attached. People dressed in jeans and hoodies rather than the Georgian garb of the dancers, were either standing beside them or operating them. One of them, a man with mad-professor hair and glasses on top of his head, now moved forward. 'Cut! It's a wrap, everyone.'

Laura gripped the edge of the gallery with her hands. So it wasn't a haunting, it was a scene from a film.

She remembered Lulu's comment. *Glenravish location, hmmm? For Prince Charlie and Flora MacDoughnut dance, hmm?*

Doh, thought Laura, smacking her forehead. Lulu had got it right; it was she, Laura, who had misunderstood everything.

She looked again at Bonnie Prince Charlie, now vaping copiously amid an admiring crowd of actresses and gofers in leggings. There was something familiar about him, despite the white make-up and beauty spots. That huge flash of teeth when he smiled reminded her of someone.

And then, as the Young Chevalier looked around, his casual glance grazing hers before passing heedlessly on, absolute certainty seized Laura. She knew this actor. Knew him better than she knew most people. There was no doubt about it. It was Caspar.

Chapter Thirty-one

Laura rushed along the balcony, down the stairs and among the thick wires and cables snaking over the hall's stone floor. They had been invisible before, because of the dancing. She ran up to Caspar and flung her arms around him.

'What the—?' Caspar exclaimed, choking on his vape smoke. It had a powerful cherry flavour. 'Oh, wait.' Recognition dawned in the actor's eyes. 'Laura Lake!'

'And who the eff is Laura Lake?'

Beside him, Flora MacDonald was looking none too pleased. Presumably, like her historical alter ego (the film version, anyway), she had her sights set on Caspar.

'This is Ruby,' Caspar muttered.

Rude Ruby, Laura decided. Rude Ruby who deserved

to be teased. She beamed at the actress before flicking Caspar a smouldering look. 'Oh, I'm just an old friend,' she purred, placing a hand on his brocaded arm.

'Oh yeah? What sort of old friend?'

'*That* sort,' Laura returned, still beaming.

A wild desperation flickered in Caspar's eyes. 'Erm,' he protested. 'Um.'

But it was too late. Ruby stormed off across the flagstones, flicking her tartan skirts as she went. Caspar watched her go regretfully, before turning reproachfully to Laura. 'Well, thanks, Lake. I was counting on her for a shag later.'

Laura rolled her eyes. 'Hashtag Creepy Caspar. Come on, Honeyman. You can't treat your co-stars like that any more.'

Caspar dragged hard on his e-cigarette. 'Co-stars?' he said bitterly. 'More like co-failures.'

Laura now learnt that Caspar had fallen so far from grace in Hollywood that he was off every director's list, had been dropped by his agent, was no longer asked to parties and was reduced to doing voice-overs and shooting straight-to-video films of which this was the worst yet.

'It's called *Passionate Prince*,' he groaned. 'It's for the Scandinavian market. I'm being dubbed in Finnish. Appropriately enough, as it's the finish of my career.'

It felt like a long time since Laura had laughed this much. It really was the best medicine. All her worries, disappointments and resentments melted away in a great wave of mirth. They seemed, anyway, positively minor compared to the epic disasters that had beset Caspar.

'I'm glad someone thinks it's funny,' Caspar said, affronted.

Laura nudged him. He looked very handsome with his brows drawn broodingly and his full lips protruding in a sulk. She felt a stir of desire. It had been a long time, after all.

'Come on, bonnie Prince,' she said. 'Never mind Flora. How about we discuss your Jacobite uprising in the privacy of my room?'

Laura woke next morning to find the sun streaming through the deep-set window onto the white and empty sheet beside her. A badly spelt note from Caspar informed her that the film unit were moving on and he would see her when he saw her. She was welcome in Tinseltown any time, which was more than he could say for himself.

She read it with a wry smile, then scrunched it up. She felt regretful, but knew that it was par for the course. Caspar was a rolling stone, utterly fickle and stratospherically selfish. Depending on him would only end in heartbreak, as it had many times before.

On the other hand, depending on the supposedly responsible Harry hadn't been any less disastrous. Maybe it's just me, Laura thought with a sigh. Oh well. She reminded herself that she didn't need anyone else to be happy, that she could get by on her own that she was a strong and independent woman.

But just sometimes, all the same, it was better with a man!

She stretched out under the lavender-scented sheets, now additionally scented with Caspar. Their lovemaking had gone on until dawn and he had introduced her to some of the latest Hollywood positions, of which the Clapperboard had been her favourite.

Laura loved to experiment and was not in the least bit body shy. Caspar shared her Gallic abandonment. While in every other respect Laura found him a flake and a let-down, on this level, at least, they were in perfect harmony.

But now he had moved on, to the mountains that were the location for the next scenes. They were filming the Prince and Flora's first meeting, Caspar said.

'How did it happen?' Laura asked.

Caspar groaned and rolled his eyes. 'So Flora's in this hilltop hut, minding a herd of cows. Charlie boy appears in the doorway, tousled, tired but powerfully attractive. Shy, doubtful Flora soon allows herself to be persuaded.'

Laura was impressed. 'It sounds so bad it's good.'

'Trust me, it's just bad. And they're blasting for that caledonium stuff in the mountains where we're filming...'

'Oh yes. That stuff they use in ecotechnology.'

'... so we'll probably get hit by falling rocks. Sometimes I almost wish I was back with Amy Bender.'

'No you don't!' Laura patted his bicep, which was impressive, but not quite as rock-hard as when he had played 007. 'I'm sure you'll be back in the big time soon. In the meantime, enjoy being below the radar.'

Caspar sighed. 'That's what my shrink says. I'm to think of it as a fame holiday.'

Laura was off laughing again.

Now that she was alone, she realised neither of them had spoken about Lulu. According to Caspar, the film unit had been in situ for several days. It seemed odd, given Lulu's lively interest in everyone and everything, that they had not met before she went to Australia.

Perhaps she had been very busy directing the new arrangement of her guns on the Great Hall wall. And, given that the film unit were apparently occupying some rundown holiday cottages at the far end of the estate, it was understandable that she hadn't yet made her way up there.

Mrs MacRae hadn't mentioned the film unit either, of course. But that was less strange. The castle did not belong to Laura; there was no need to inform her about everything that was going on. Moreover, as the scene had been filmed in the night, the housekeeper would assume she was asleep.

'Do you know when Lulu will be back?' Laura asked Mrs MacRae over breakfast. This, as before, was porridge eaten from wooden bowls, standing up in the kitchen with Fat Oonagh, Wee Archie and the rest of the estate staff. Laura had learnt that this practice dated back to ancient times, so tenants could rush out of the door at a moment's notice and set about marauders from rival clans.

Mrs MacRae, who was stirring something delicious-smelling in a large pot on the Aga, looked round with a smile. 'Och, the mistress'll be back when she's ready,' she said comfortably.

Laura frowned. 'It's just that she's not answering her phone, which is quite unusual for Lulu. You don't know where in Australia she's staying, do you?'

'She didn't say,' smiled the housekeeper. She paused, then added, 'But you've found a phone signal, have ye?'

Laura had, in fact, had a brainwave about that. While the landline seemed permanently unavailable and the estate might be a Wi-Fi-free zone, it had occurred to her that the station might be connected. It was only the tiniest of branch lines, the merest twig on a branch line in fact, but it was still worth a punt.

Before breakfast she had hurried to the gate, shinned over it and crossed the road to the tiny platform. She had stared at her phone. 'Come on, come on,' she had muttered. And then, magic. One bar. Two bars. Three, four, *five whole bars*!

Sandy could have done this all along, Laura thought. But living in the mid-eighties meant she probably didn't even know what a smartphone was and had never heard of Wi-Fi.

Lulu didn't seem to be making the fullest use of it either. Her phone remained unanswered. Incommunicado.

'I've got an idea,' Mrs MacRae suggested.

Laura brightened, and readied her phone to take the details.

'She might have gone to somewhere… now what's the word for it?' Mrs MacRae paused, stirred thoughtfully.

'Edgy? Trendy?' It wasn't impossible. Lulu was crazy about new places.

'Noo, noo. Och, I have it!' The housekeeper turned with a beaming smile. 'Off grid!'

'And hot,' Laura guessed. Yes, that probably did explain it. Lulu hated cold weather. Prolonged exposure to Scotland, even summer Scotland, probably demanded some countermeasures.

'Och, I don't think it's that hot at the moment, Down Under,' Mrs MacRae replied with a smile. 'Matter of fact, I believe it's quite gloomy.'

There was an appreciative snort from the assembled estate staff, who probably didn't like to think of their mistress roasting in the sunshine while they toiled in the not-infrequently bad Highland weather. Laura had to admire the housekeeper's tact. No one in the kitchen mentioned the filming and she didn't like to bring it up, particularly given how the interlude had ended for her. Mrs MacRae had sharp eyes and she feared betraying herself with a blush.

After breakfast, no marauding rival clans having appeared, Laura put her bowl by the sink with the others and headed back up to her room. It had begun to drizzle outside and she felt for Caspar, out on some hill being devoured by midges while seducing Flora MacDonald. She stared out of the window, admiring Sandy's immaculate garden. The morning with Harry threatened to come back to her in all its brief perfection and she pushed the thought away. Someone else who'd disappeared into thin air. It was getting to be a habit with her, Laura thought.

She paced up and down her room feeling restless. The rain spattering the windows reinforced her anxiety and she longed for an outlet.

She would, she decided, explore the castle. All the steps would provide some stress-relieving exercise. There were hundreds leading down to the dungeons especially. She could walk up and down those a few times, then she would return to the station and try Lulu again. Maybe even call South'n Fried's company, Motherf****r Records. They might know where he and Lulu were.

Where was the way to the dungeon? Laura had a vague memory of following Sandy's pixie boots to a door in a corner of the Great Hall. She hurried across it now, impressed how completely all evidence of the filming had been cleared away. Only an empty plastic bottle, rolled against the toe-piece of a suit of armour, suggested that it had taken place at all. Perhaps, too, still hanging in the air, was the faint suggestion of Caspar's cherry vape fumes.

The way had been unimpeded when Sandy led through it, Laura remembered. But now an iron door, criss-crossed like a cage, was bolted firmly across it.

All was darkness beyond. She weighed up the possibility of asking Mrs MacRae to open it, but decided against it. The less the housekeeper knew of her business the better. She would head upstairs instead. There was at least one other floor above hers. It took some time to find the way up, via a narrow staircase behind a door. At the top was another door which led into a large and gloomy sequence of rooms. Perhaps they had once been nurseries, or a dormitory for maids. No one, clearly, had been here for some time. The windows were dusty and festooned with cobwebs, dried-out bluebottle husks piled up on the sills. There was a smell of damp and rot.

The last of the rooms seemed to be used to store junk. There were iron bed-frames up against the wall, wooden boxes stencilled with the names of long-defunct London stores, battered suitcases, piles of books, broken chairs, lopsided stools, listing hatstands, lamps, bowls, chamber pots with cracks in them, heaps of clothes, a top hat, and an old gramophone complete with a His Master's Voice brass horn. It was, Laura thought, just like being in the Sunday markets of Shoreditch, only without the street food.

She picked up the top hat, put it on and peered at herself in a mould-spotted mirror. The reflection gave a view down the room to the door at the end. A movement caught her eye, or seemed to. A trick of the light, Laura decided, tracing her hand along the sleeve of a moth-eaten fur coat. A cloud of dust came out and made her cough.

A trunk stood in the middle of the room, its leather covering cracked and splitting. A large, open padlock hung at a crazy angle. Treasure, Laura wondered. Pieces of eight? A map marked with an X?

It beckoned to her irresistibly; she picked her way over the gritty floorboards and tried the lid. It was heavy, made of solid wood and took great effort to open; eventually, however, she heaved it aloft.

There was disappointingly little inside. A dusty interior with a peeling printed-paper lining. Laura was about to lower the lid back down when she sensed something.

The hairs on her neck stood on end.

She had the sudden and unmistakeable feeling that she was not alone. Someone else was in the room. Now, they were approaching. She could hear soft footsteps, getting closer all the time.

Was it Ruby? Peeled off from the film unit and returned with jealous fury in her heart? Struan back for a second go? Mordor? Laura's heart began to thump. Nausea rose in her throat. Her hands shook.

She forced her rigid body to turn but before she could move, her shoulders were seized by two strong hands. Her arms were twisted up painfully behind her back 'Ow!' cried Laura as her head was forced down into the trunk. The rest of her was shoved in roughly after it, head over heels. She crouched with her bum in the air, her face on the trunk's gritty bottom, as the heavy lid was banged down. There came the snap of a padlock.

Laura brayed the unyielding wood with her feet. 'Hey! Let me out! DO YOU HEAR ME? LET ME OUT!'

But as her screams died away, she could hear only the distant, quiet closing of a door, followed by a key turning.

Laura forced down her panic. She must remain calm. She thought of her father and tried to channel his dauntless spirit. All the same, it was hard to think what he would have done in the circumstances. He was a reporter, not Houdini.

She thought of her grandmother, whose wartime heroism must have encompassed worse than this. But

Mimi, who had shown her so much about creeping through alien territory, had never actually demonstrated how to escape from a locked chest.

Thinking of Mimi made Laura want to cry. She was somewhere out in the world, cruising the Seven Seas with the Fat Four. Had she seen Beyoncé at Coachella, Laura wondered. Would that be the last she ever heard from the nonagenarian late-onset hedonist and her merry band of sybarites?

She summoned up the beloved wrinkled face with its bright, sharp eyes and its surrounding grey bob; short, side-parted and cut with razor precision. It was a deliberate contrast: 'The messier the face gets,' her grandmother liked to say, 'the neater the hair has to be.'

Laura squeezed her eyes hard to stop the tears. 'Oh, Mimi. Where are you now? Will I ever see you again?'

Chapter Thirty-two

'How much longer you think we stay here, hmm?' whispered Lulu across the darkness. She was, as Mrs MacRae had said, Down Under. But not in the sunny Antipodes. Rather, in the dungeons under the castle.

'That would seem to depend, madam,' replied her butler in low, measured tones. Vlad did not whisper. It was beneath her dignity. Even when her dignity was, as at the moment, severely compromised by lying in a medieval passage in the dark. For the second time in as many weeks. To paraphrase Oscar Wilde, of whom Vlad was a big fan, it looked like carelessness.

'On what depend?'

'On how long it takes Mr Fried to return from New York. He will then presumably notice madam's absence and commence a search.'

'Wouldn't count on it,' Lulu hissed back. 'South'n Fried care only about career, hmm? Motherf****r.'

'Indeed, madam.'

'I mean record company, hmm?'

'Oh… indeed, madam.'

Lulu sighed and shifted in the straw. 'This floor ruin my white suede trousers,' she remarked despondently.

Vlad did not reply. If she thought Lulu's outfit the least of their worries, she was diplomatic enough not to say so. Possibly she was reflecting on her lapse of judgement in allowing Lulu to explore the dungeons alone. But her mistress had been unstoppable, keen to assess the area's spa potential.

When she failed to return after an hour, Vlad went down herself. The door Lulu had used, previously open at the end of the hall, had been locked, which the butler assumed explained her mistress's absence.

It seemed so. The housekeeper had appeared horrified to realise she had – apparently inadvertently – incarcerated Lulu in the castle's dread nether regions, and had hastened to the door with a key. Vlad had then descended into the living rock to find Lulu at the bottom of a dank, damp pit.

The butler's initial alarm had given way to relief when her mistress, who seemed perfectly relaxed, explained that she had removed the grille from across the hole to climb down and investigate its potential as a plunge pool.

Vlad had suggested that Lulu come back up now, and had stood over the hole to extend a hand down. All the lights in the cave had subsequently gone out and even

Vlad's lightning reflexes had been unable to react before a sudden powerful thump between her shoulder blades and nothing but air beneath her feet. She had landed, as per her training, in the brace position, right on top of Lulu.

'*Ow!*'

'I do apologise, madam.'

Two days, Vlad calculated, had passed since then, days without food or water. Her army experience, however, had included intensive survival training and they had the additional resources of some chocolate Lulu had stashed about her person in case of emergency.

Ever one to look on the bright side, the billionheiress had chosen to view the sudden food shortage as a crash diet and had listed, for Vlad's benefit, all the items in her wardrobe that had previously been too tight, but into which she would now fit in with ease.

'Givenchy bubblewrap bustier, Stella McCartney coconut-matting catsuit, Tom Ford fur shorts.'

Lulu had also insisted on teaching her butler Pilates to pass the time. Vlad was now even better than her mistress at planks, downward dogs and teaser positions.

Throughout their ordeal, Lulu had maintained a touching faith that the corsets she had escaped in from Bangers, formerly the property of Flora MacDonald, were magic and would arrange their rescue. Vlad, less sure about the power of underwear, however historic, could only admire her certainty.

Lulu was, even so, disappointed that imprisonment had caused her to miss the film unit. South'n Fried's career needs aside, it was one of the main reasons she had bought the place. Roddy Ruan had assured her that the castle was so regularly used as a movie location that anyone lucky enough to own it would meet Hollywood's finest every other week.

'Why South'n Fried not come?' Lulu wailed.

Vlad could think of any number of reasons, mostly related to trainers. However, she diplomatically kept them to herself. She sat against the damp wall, staring into the gloom and wondered if this, really, was it.

'Is pelmets, hmm?' Lulu's voice came sadly out of the darkness.

'Curtains, madam. Let us hope not.'

'I agree. Roman blinds much better. Or maybe plantation shutters, hmmm?'

Eventually, after considering a range of soft furnishing options, Lulu dozed off.

Vlad, meanwhile, kept watch. Her vigilant ear now caught a faint noise, a clang and rattle, very distant. Was someone coming to rescue them?

Or to finish them off for good?

Vlad could hear, in the dark, a faint snoring that meant Lulu was sleeping. She would face whatever was coming alone, the butler decided. She stood up, trying not to exclaim at the pain of her stiff limbs. The Pilates had been murder on her glutes.

The footsteps were coming down the same passage that Vlad and Lulu had walked down themselves, so many days ago, it seemed. The butler stood on tiptoe, trying to peer through the iron grille for the first glimpse of whatever it was. She could make out a moving shape and was relieved to see that it was small rather than tall, and seemed shuffling and old. But it might well mean harm, and she was taking no chances. Her hand crept stealthily down the side of her trousers, lifting the bottom and reaching for the trusty Estonian army-issue pistol in her sock. She pulled it softly out and primed it. It made the very faintest of clicks, one only a trained ear could detect. Some shuffling old git would have no chance, the butler reckoned.

The shuffling stopped abruptly. Fast, decisive footsteps followed. They stopped on the grille above Vlad. There was a sliding, metallic sound and something poked through the ironwork.

Vlad realised she wasn't the only one armed. Her expert eye told her she was looking at the business end of a Mauser. A vintage World War Two one at that.

She held her hands up immediately. A small, piercing light was switched on from above and the dazed factotum saw a wrinkled face looking down at her with very bright eyes. The ancient visage was surrounded by an absolutely impeccable grey bob.

'*Les des sont sur le tapis!*' the old woman rapped out, fixing the gentlewoman's gentlewoman with a meaningful stare.

The butler did not miss a beat. '*Il fait chaud à Suez,*' Vlad answered, recognising immediately the phrases sent by the British to the Free French before D-Day. This woman had been in the Resistance.

The gun disappeared from the overhead grille. The torchlight showed the old woman stowing away her weapon in her handbag. 'How do you do?' she asked politely. 'I'm Mimi de Rochfort. I'm actually looking for the loos but this *putain* castle doesn't seem to have them. I'm with my friends on a tour from a cruise ship – we just pulled up in our coach on the off-chance.'

Vlad did not miss a beat. 'The nearest lavatories are back up the stairs, madam. Just by the kitchen, first on your right.'

'*Merci.*'

'You're very welcome, madam. Oh, madam?'

'*Oui?*'

'Perhaps you might be so good as to release us before you go?'

Chapter Thirty-three

Laura had no idea how long she had been in the trunk. Perhaps she had actually passed out. After the first few, endless hours things had just begun generally to drift. She now no longer knew nor cared who had shoved her in here, or why. It could have been just about anyone in the castle, after all.

But now someone had come. The echo of something loud seemed to hang in the air. A banged door. Something smashing.

Crash! There it was again. It sounded as if the door at the end of the room was being stoved in. Laura crouched in the chest, her painfully thudding heat apparently amplified by the confined space. Was this a rescuer? Was it Harry? Hope soared through her so violently she felt she could split the trunk apart just by pushing.

Laura could hear wood splitting, wrenching, cracking. Then came the slam of the door against the wall. Heavy footsteps followed, crunching over glass and china. There was the slither of books being kicked out of the way.

'Harry!' yelled Laura, now convinced that it was her lover. With anyone else it would be hopelessly far-fetched, but he had form at rescuing her from disaster in the nick of time. 'Over here! In the trunk!'

The footsteps hurried over and stopped. There was a rattle of keys. Where had he got those from, Laura wondered. The padlock banged against the sides and thumped as it hit the floor. Then a creak, and a rush of air as the heavy lid opened.

'Harry!'

But it was Struan smiling down at her. 'Och, your ordeal's over noo, Miss Laura, uh-huh.'

Laura stared at him, confused. Wasn't it him who had pushed her in in the first place?

But he was smiling at her quite benignly.

A large gun was slung about his tweed-jacketed shoulders. One of his reddened hands was on its barrel, one thick red finger stroking its trigger.

'Do you think I could get out?' Laura asked nervously.

His round, grass-coloured eyes, reminding her of the other green-eyed monster in her life, Clemency Makepeace, looked kindly into hers. 'That would be fine, Miss Laura, uh-huh. Take my hand, uh-huh.' He extended the one not caressing the gun.

Trembling, Laura allowed him to pull her gently out of the trunk. Starved of blood for so long, her legs had turned to jelly and she fell against him heavily. One hand still stroked the trigger; would the impact push it forward? Laura screwed up her eyes, bracing herself for the almighty blast which could pitch her into the afterlife.

It did not come, however. Instead, Struan tucked her arm reassuringly into his. Together, slowly, they approached the wrecked doorway. It looked quite horrible; pieces of split and broken wood hanging round the frame like smashed teeth.

'This way, Miss Laura, uh-huh,' Struan said.

They descended the attic stairs together, her arm still tucked into his as if going out for a Sunday walk. She dared not speak, although her eyes flicked constantly about, looking for possible escapes.

Perhaps he detected what she was thinking, because once they reached the main landing he swung her round in a swift movement. Suddenly Laura was in front of him with his gun pressed into her back. 'Put yer hands up!' came the growled command, with the inevitable suffix. 'Uh-huh?'

Laura's mouth was open and she could hear herself whimpering. She shut it. *Fierté! Espoir! Courage!*

'Downstairs,' growled Struan, prodding the end of the rifle in her back. Laura hurried along, struggling to believe any of it was really happening, let alone why. She was a journalist on a glossy magazine. She had only been trying to help the old owner and she knew the castle's new one. Just why was she in this situation? Just what had she done wrong?

'Over there,' said Struan, prodding her across the wide hall floor. His boots crunched heavily behind her on the unyielding stone. The gateway to the dungeons loomed. Laura swallowed. Was that where he was taking her?

She glanced at the walls. The pistols, rifles and daggers still hung as Lulu had arranged them. Or did they? The designer logos seemed less well-executed than previously. Laura could see large gaps in the designs.

Oh, where was Lulu? Down Under, really? Or maybe she had snuck back to Kensington and vowed never to go near Glenravish again. Writing off an entire estate would not bother Lulu. She was easily rich enough. The thought squeezed Laura's heart. Lulu had no idea she was here, after all.

She bent her head, expecting to be shoved through the iron gate and down to the eternal oblivion of the dungeons. But then the rifle barrel indicated a right turn. Laura found herself stumbling towards the passage that led into the kitchen.

'Go on with ye, uh-huh,' muttered Struan, prodding her hard again.

A solid wooden door stood at the end. Struan, edging past her while keeping the gun still trained to her back, pushed it open.

'Don't move!' someone yelled. 'One more step forward, and I'll shoot!'

Struan, behind her, swore under his breath. Laura, for her part, felt a sense of enormous relief. He *was* here, after all.

'*Harry!*'

He stood in front of her in the dear, familiar, battered black leather biker jacket, his dark hair tousled and his handsome features tense. Like Struan, he held a gun in his hand and it too was pressed into someone's back.

The someone was Mordor MacRavish. He was bound hand, foot and red trousers to a chair facing the doorway Struan and Laura now occupied.

'Don't move,' he urged Struan. 'He means it.'

'I mean it too,' growled the stalker, waggling the gun in Laura's back. 'Uh-huh?'

'So we reach stalemate, MacRae,' Harry said levelly. He had still not acknowledged Laura, but she sensed that to do so would distract him and break his concentration. The potential consequences of that were obvious enough. She swallowed and willed her knees not to buckle.

Fierté! Espoir! Courage!

'Not stalemate, no,' Struan said, his tone light and triumphant. 'If ye look behind ye, ye'll see the entire estate staff pointing their guns right at ye! Uh-huh?'

Laura's glance shifted to the window above the kitchen sink. Net curtains covered half of it, but above that Laura could plainly see a gaggle of estate staff gathered outside in the entry. Wee Archie, Big Kenny, Fat Ishbel, Young Tommy, Big Oonagh. All with muzzles loaded and pointing straight at the back of Harry's head. It was now clear where the missing guns on the hall wall had gone.

'Aye, they're all crack shots,' Struan went on. 'Even Wee Archie's the Pitlochry International Small Bore Champion, uh-huh.'

Harry glanced at Laura now for the first time. To one who knew him less well, he seemed utterly calm. But Laura could see the tension in his jaw. He looked down on Mordor's smoothly brushed side-parting. 'You won't get away with this, MacRavish,' he said.

A nasty smile crossed Mordor's deceptively boyish face and his blue eyes glittered icily. 'I will get away with it and I have,' he sneered. 'You're all about to be shot, so there will be no witnesses. And Glenravish will be mine, as I've always wanted.'

'*Yours?*' indignantly demanded Struan from behind Laura. 'But we agreed that we'd split it.'

'Yes, yes,' Mordor cut in impatiently. 'We'll discuss the detail later.'

Laura didn't understand this exchange. She was still trying to work out the first bit, about him always wanting Glenravish. 'You said it was a hell of a hard sell,' she burst out accusingly. 'You called it a haunted turd.'

Mordor shook his head in ironic wonderment. 'Can you believe it? So I did. But I didn't mean it. Glenravish is neither haunted nor a turd.'

Laura glared at Mordor. 'Yes it *is* haunted. Why else would the electrics go off all the time?'

Mrs MacRae now appeared from a doorway that Laura remembered led to the pantry. 'Because I kept switching them off,' she said. She wore her usual neat black dress and her hair was as well-styled as ever, but her apple-cheeked face was twisted in a snarl and in her hands, instead of the usual ladle of warming stew, was a gun.

'But why pretend it was haunted?' Laura demanded, trying to stop her voice from shaking. She might be about to be shot, but her journalist's curiosity still demanded satisfaction.

'To stop that moron of a cousin of mine selling it, of course,' Mordor snapped. 'With your help,' he added venomously to Laura, 'and that of your pathetic magazine.'

Laura let the insult pass. There were important facts to discover. 'Want to tell me why?' Now, finally, they were getting down to brass tacks. 'I have a right to know, if you're about to shoot me,' she continued, seeing that the estate staff outside were starting to get restless. The bloodbath they had evidently been promised was taking its time.

Struan's gun burrowed even further into her back and she gasped with pain. Harry tensed. Mordor threw Struan a look and the barrel edged backwards slightly. 'You're quite right, my dear,' Mordor said, reasonably. 'You do have a right to know. The reason that Glenravish is very far from being a haunted turd and actually extremely valuable is its position.' He paused importantly. 'Do you know what caledonium is?'

Laura nodded. 'It's a mineral used in green technology.'

If this was what all this evildoing was about, at least it was good for the environment.

Mordor went on, 'It's extremely rare and therefore very—'

'Valuable?' Laura had that rushing feeling in her head which meant that everything now was suddenly going to make sense. 'Let me guess. You found out that Glenravish was sitting on a seam of this stuff.'

'Actually, *my team* found out,' said the housekeeper, whose voice had changed, Laura now realised. She was speaking with a strong South African accent.

'My real name is Professor Gloria Wilderbeest,' Mrs MacRae continued, 'and I head up the Applied Geology department of Jacob Zuma University. My students and I,' she waved a hand to the group outside the window, 'were doing field work in the Highlands when we came across the caledonium. A few feet of it would have been valuable enough.' She paused, and her eyes sparkled with greed.

'But,' Mordor said, with an evil smile, 'the entire estate is caledonium.'

Professor Wilderbeest cleared her throat. 'Having discovered the size of the deposit, I went straight to Mr McRavish with a proposal. We divide it up and we all get a cut.'

'Why didn't you go to Sandy?' Laura demanded. 'The estate belonged to her.'

'Because we'll have to blow up the castle to get to the stuff and she'd never allow that in a million years. Family history and all that,' said Mordor, just as if, thought the furious Laura, he had not exploited that very same history to his own ends. 'But that's outrageous,' she gasped. 'You were intending to cheat Sandy out of what's rightfully hers!'

Professor Wilderbeest snorted. 'We were planning to do a lot more to her than that, believe me.'

'Murder her, you mean?' The thought was too awful for words. Thank goodness Sandy had escaped.

Harry cleared his throat. 'Sandy McRavish is only the latest in a long, long line, believe me.' He nodded at Mordor. 'We've been on the trail of this guy for years. The caledonium's only the start – but hopefully the end – of the scams and frauds he's behind. He's wanted by everyone.'

Laura was still piecing it together. Sandy had escaped by selling the estate to Lulu. But where was *she* now? Had this murderous bunch already got rid of her? 'Where's Lulu?' she yelled, furious and terrified in equal measure.

'She's going to die in the dungeons along with that ridiculous Jeeves of hers,' snarled Mordor.

Despair swept over Laura. It all made sense now of course, Lulu's mysterious trip Down Under. The castle dungeons, in other words. The housekeeper's remark about the gloom was now explained as well. It had not been tactful, but a cynical joke.

'Puir wee child,' put in Prof Wilderbeest, briefly lapsing back to her Scottish accent.

Sheer fury at the insincerity of this remark restored Laura's courage. She felt hot fury roar through her. She was about to let rip, and damn the consequences, when suddenly all hell broke loose.

Chapter Thirty-four

Struan suddenly released Laura and fell backwards.
There followed an almighty blast, and then a thump,
as of a body hitting the floor. Laura whirled round
and found herself staring at a familiar wrinkled face set
off by a super-smooth grey bob.

'Mimi!'

The old lady lifted a finger, one of several holding a
pistol. In her other hand she held the stalker's rifle.

'What...?' Laura stared at Struan's inert body.

'He knocked himself out.' Mimi pushed past.

'Not *that*! How come you're here?'

'We're on the *Hebridean Princess*. Cruising round
the Highlands and Islands. *Complètement magnifique*.
We just stopped at the castle for a comfort break
on our coach tour. *Quelle coïncidence!* But I can't

talk now, *chérie*. I must go and help Ginette and Ernest.'

The other members of the Fat Four were here too? Glancing outside the window Laura spotted a mighty and unmistakeable shape. Ernest, her grandmother's elderly transvestite prostitute friend, was setting about Big Oonagh – or the South African geologist currently going by that name – with a will.

Laura tried to remember what he had told her about his youth. Ernest was Mimi's junior by a decade at least and so had missed the war. But Laura was pretty sure that, *de temps en temps,* she had heard mention of the Foreign Legion. Whatever the truth, Ernest was no stranger to fisticuffs, as anyone who attempted to disrespect him on the Montmartre corner where he drummed up business was liable to find out.

Meanwhile Ginette, the octogenarian who ran the bar downstairs from her grandmother's flat, was showing Fat Ishbel and Big Kenny some of the kung fu moves she had been taught by her Far Eastern customers. She seemed to have already felled the man-mountain that was Wee Archie.

Yells were also coming from the pantry, back into which Vlad had dragged Professor Wilderbeest. She was now dispensing righteous justice between the jars of piccalilli and tins of beans.

Laura's attention, however, was on Harry. He stood opposite her, tall, manly and resolute, his gun still thrust into the back of Mordor McRavish's jacket. She felt a flood of deep emotion. 'You're amazing,' was all she could say.

'You were pretty brave yourself,' he said, with one of his sexy half-smiles that always made her catch her breath. 'I'm impressed.'

Laura rushed into his arms, or the arm not holding the gun into Mordor's back.

'Yuk,' said Mordor, turning his head away. 'I hate the sloppy bits.'

Eventually, they came up for air. 'When I met you on the beach...' Laura began.

'I was on McRavish's trail, but I couldn't say so, obviously. And that's why I had to leave you in London too.'

Laura looked down. The way he had disappeared without a trace was painful to remember, even now.

'I know how heartless I must have seemed,' Harry added apologetically. 'I was just trying to weigh up what to do. Stay in the managing job, or go back out in the field. But then we went to see that terrible Bond film with your friend in and—'

Someone now burst into the kitchen.

'Terrible Bond film? Bloody cheek!' said a voice that was well-known, not only to Laura, but much of the globe.

Laura twisted round. 'Caspar! What...?'

Caspar was sporting his favourite dressed-down film star look: a white T-shirt showcasing his six-pack and biceps, jeans straining over his well-exercised thighs. His Aviator sunglasses were turned pointedly away from Harry. Laura felt a glow of triumph. He was jealous!

'We're having to redo the ball scene,' Caspar said sulkily. 'When the editor looked at the rushes, it turned out that the wall of the ballroom was covered in guns arranged in Chanel logos.'

Laura began to laugh.

'It's not funny,' Caspar said crossly. 'It's like the watch in *Ben Hur*. An ack… an ack…'

'Anachronism,' supplied Harry.

'Yeah, thanks, Einstein,' snapped Caspar.

Laura squeezed Harry's hand and looked down, smiling.

Lulu now trotted into the kitchen, her prison-soiled suede trousers replaced by ones of lime-green PVC, her curvy figure all but exploding out of a tight pair of pink silk stays. Laura felt Caspar's attention turn off her as quickly and completely as if someone had flicked a switch.

'Is my lucky Flora MacDonald corsets, hmm?' Lulu purred, tracing a finger down the antique whalebone sides. From beneath weapons-grade false eyelashes she looked coquettishly at the goggle-eyed actor. 'You give me extra part in film, hmm?'

'I'll give you an extra part wherever you want, baby,' he assured her appreciatively.

Laura rolled her eyes and Lulu giggled.

The door to the outside world now banged open. Laura expected the rest of the film unit to start trickling in, staggering under great loads of equipment. Instead, a tall figure loped in, hung about with designer carrier bags.

He wore a white track suit glittering with rhinestones, a silver skullcap and gold glasses with pink lenses.

'South'n Fried!' Lulu leapt from Caspar's side and rushed to her husband.

Laura waited. She knew what was coming. In all of her many adventures with Lulu, South'n Fried always appeared at the last minute and asked if he had missed something.

The rapper looked round at Struan's body on the floor and Mordor tied to a chair. 'Hey! What happened? I miss something?'

Three months later

L aura picked up the ringing phone in her office.
'Good morning, Mrs Sweet,' she said as brightly and confidently as she could manage.

She still wasn't quite sure of the CEO. But their relationship was much better these days. It had been considerably helped by Bev begging her to come back, helm *Society* and write about the Glenravish story for her rather than the many other publications offering Laura lucrative contracts.

It seemed that, after all, the Poison Pixie knew a good thing when she saw it. A bad one too; Clemency Makepeace was now back on the freelance trail, although Laura didn't doubt they'd cross swords again in the future.

For now, though, she was safe. Her own exclusive version of the caledonium conspiracy, entitled 'A View to a Kilt', had swept the board at the British Journalism awards.

Perhaps she didn't have quite as many statuettes as Harry, but Laura could live with that. She could not live with Harry, even so. After much discussion they had decided to return to their old on-off ways, which suited them both much better, especially now Harry was on the foreign correspondent beat again.

'I'm ringing to ask you to come and have dinner with Harris Blankenberg tonight,' Bev announced in her peremptory way. Laura's fingers gripped the receiver hard. Harris Blankenberg was the chairman of the International Magazine Company, which was the parent company of the British Magazine Company. This was a serious honour.

'I'm really sorry,' she said with genuine regret. 'But I can't. I'm going to the Brit Awards. My friend's husband's getting one.'

'South'n Fried!' Bev sounded excited. 'That new bagpipe album of his is massive, isn't it? What's it called again?'

'*Rebel Without A Sporran*.'

'That's it. The soundtrack to *Passionate Prince*, wasn't it?'

Laura was surprised her steely boss was so well-informed. On the other hand, Caspar's new series, starting well below the radar on Helsinki TV, had become an international smash hit on a par with the hugely successful and equally Scottish-set *Outlander*.

No one had been more surprised than its star. 'To quote an old showbiz adage,' Caspar remarked to Laura from Hollywood, where he was restored and all was forgiven, 'it's not where you start. It's where you Finnish.'

Withdrawn From Stock
Dublin Public Libraries

Leabharlanna Poiblí Chathair Baile Átha Cliath
Dublin City Public Libraries